Mother
Watch

Also by Karma Brown

Come Away with Me
The Choices We Make
In This Moment
The Life Lucy Knew
Recipe for a Perfect Wife
What Wild Women Do
The 4% Fix

Mother Is Watching

A NOVEL

Karma Brown

DUTTON
An imprint of Penguin Random House LLC
1745 Broadway, New York, NY 10019
penguinrandomhouse.com

Book design by Alison Cnockaert

Library of Congress Cataloging-in-Publication Data
has been applied for.

ISBN 9798217045716 (hardcover)
ISBN 9798217045723 (ebook)

Printed in the United States of America
1st Printing

The authorized representative in the EU for product safety and compliance is Penguin Random House Ireland, Morrison Chambers, 32 Nassau Street, Dublin D02 YH68, Ireland, https://eu-contact.penguin.ie.

This one is for the mothers,
who give everything—
their bodies, their hearts,
their dreams, their sleepless nights.
I see you.

All art is at once surface and symbol. Those who go beneath the surface do so at their peril.

—Oscar Wilde, *The Picture of Dorian Gray*

BEFORE

The Painter

The eyes are all wrong.

For one thing, they are not *her* eyes.

Hers are wider set and blue. These golden-chartreuse-color eyes are more realistic than any she has ever painted before.

These are the first thoughts she has when she comes back to herself, soon followed by *What have I done?*

Music plays on a record player in the corner of the room. *Chicago 17.* Newly released, and her current favorite album—easy listening, ideal for painting. She sits on a metal stool in front of the canvas, the gauzy fabric of her paint-spattered bohemian skirt—her artist's uniform—gathered between her legs. She holds her brush in midair, and the tension in her fingers creates a quiver through the wooden handle to the paint-drenched hog bristles. A drop of deep red hovers, falls to the floor, and lands on her bare foot. There are angry scratches on her right forearm, not yet scabbed over. The nails on her left hand are sharp, short but ragged; a few show bloodied crescent moons.

A tickling sensation scurries across her cheek, and she presses a gentle finger against it. Something comes away with her touch—*an insect's wing.* Her gaze snaps to the painting, where she finds more wings—*so beautifully patterned, nature the first artist*—placed carefully, adding texture to the arched eyebrows of the subject's face.

A loud metal screech pierces the silence as she shoves her stool back and stands, trying to get some distance from the painting. Wingless cockroach skeletons fall from her lap as she takes in a deep, urgent breath. Fear thrums through her and her heart races, as though she's run a fast mile.

The goddamn eyes.

She lets out a low moan, shakes her head back and forth until she's dizzy.

But there's no time to be self-indulgent. With a purposeful step forward, she bends and dips her brush into the plastic yogurt container below the easel. She presses her lips into a thin line so the bile breaching her throat doesn't spill out.

Dipping the brush five, six, ten times, soon oversaturates the bristles. She stops, the color streaming thinly back into the container as she pauses, holding still. Then, with a guttural scream, the painter launches herself toward the canvas. Her paint-laden brush connects with enough force to shove the easel back half a foot.

She splashes thick blackish paint across the eyes and cockroach-wing brows with frenzied slashes, covering the subject's entire face. Her mouth hangs open as she sucks in quick, shallow breaths. A moment later she stops and her body stills, except for her heaving chest. The painter watches carefully, wondering if she's done enough.

The answer comes quickly, the newly applied paint shifting. It's subtle at first. Small bubbles, like what form on a barely simmering pot of heated milk. The paint slides away from the subject's face in wide swaths, like someone else is undoing the painter's work. The sudden smell of marigold flowers (*acrid, antiseptic*) fills the air around her, as though she has stepped into a field of the sunrise-orange blooms.

She thinks of her daughter then, and wonders how to explain what she's done. The painter never meant for it to go this far. However, now she needs to finish what she started.

With shaking hands she sets the brush back into the pot, removing a small cardboard box from her skirt's pocket. The wooden matchstick she pulls from the box feels rough in her fingers as she twirls it. Crouching, she slides the match head slowly but firmly along the sandpaper-like strip on the box.

For a moment she stays as she is, holding the now-lit match, inches from the painting.

She drops the match into the linseed-oil-soaked rags, gathered purposefully in a pile under the easel. They catch easily, and she scrabbles backward from the flames, even as she knows she won't leave the room.

The wooden easel catches fire next. As she watches, refusing to blink despite the tears streaming from her eyes, the subject's face comes to life. The mouth opens in surprise, then morphs into a grimace of pain. The eyes lock on her own as the canvas starts to burn. Then the wing-brows rise a half inch and the subject's eyes . . . blink. *Once, twice.*

A piercing shriek that comes from elsewhere fills the room, and the painter presses her hands against her ears. She trips over a tin juice can holding paint when she tries to get farther away. A dark red puddle forms near the tipped-over tin.

As the liquid inches toward her, she knows it will soon reach her bare feet. The quiver starts in her stomach, then spreads all over her body, and she recognizes the sensation as terror. She didn't used to be afraid of blood.

The black-red liquid lazily but thickly fills the crevices between her toes, the space around the painting now a burning inferno. Suddenly, a voice echoes through the fire's roar, and it's childlike. Heartbreakingly familiar.

"Come out, come out, wherever you are . . ."

Tall flames lick the floorboards under her, the fabric of her skirt catching quickly. The thick smoke engulfs her, and she coughs involuntarily and squeezes her eyes shut. But she manages to smile, whispering, “Here I come. . . . Found you, my darling!” before the fire takes her.

NOW

The Conservator

The call comes as I'm halfway between the lab and Clementine's school, walking quickly down the sidewalk. My watch vibrates, flashing orange to let me know it's work, and I slide in my earbud to answer the call. It's hot, and even the inside of my ear is sweating.

"Hi, it's Tilly," I say, not breaking stride. I can't believe I'm late again. It will be the third time this week.

"Hey, Tilly, it's Dale." Dale's my colleague, though he specializes in sculpture conservation while I'm on the painting side of things. "Sorry to call, but a shipment arrived for you and it needs a signature. Request incoming."

I touch my finger to the signature box that pops up on my watch face. "What's the item?"

I hear Dale tell the delivery team to place the package by my station.

"Not sure, though it's climate-crate packed, ten by twelve. Are you expecting a piece?"

Ten by twelve feet? Crate packed? I try to recall what's upcoming on my docket, though I wouldn't forget this sort of shipment. It's rare to receive original artwork at the lab, most of it being housed in climate-controlled warehouses and underground bunkers.

"Nothing I can think of," I reply.

"That's odd. Well, it came with an audio card. I put it on your desk," Dale says.

An audio card? My curiosity is piqued further.

Dale and I work at the Savannah location of the Georgia Institute for Art—nicknamed GIA. I love my job. I'm an art conservator by training, but since most museums went virtual after the fires and then the Great Flood damaged many precious works of art, I've worked as a virtual conservator. We create art experiences: in-person, augmented-reality tours at museums like the Telfair on York Street, and virtual visits from at-home devices, all for a low annual cost. GIA's installations are also free of charge at community hubs and schools, set up to make art accessible to everyone.

My watch vibrates on my wrist again, and I glance down. It's Clementine's school—I'm five minutes late. *Shoot.*

"I better go. Clem's school is buzzing me." My focus immediately shifts from the mysterious delivery to my daughter, who will be displeased with my tardiness. She hates being the last one picked up.

After the end-call pleasantries (*Have a great night! Hope Wyatt spoils you . . .*), we hang up and I remove the earbud, tucking it into my purse.

Speeding up, I navigate a path around two women with a swinging child sandwiched between them, and an elderly man walking a marmalade cat on a crystal-studded harness. He says "Howdy" as I pass, and I offer a quick "hey there," slowing enough to not appear rude. I'll have to tell Clem about the cat. She'll get a kick out of that.

My hair is sweat limp and my thighs stick together under my cotton dress. It's a typical midsummer's day in Savannah—sweltering heat and mugginess, making you dream of ice pops and cool swimming pools. Despite having lived here for years, I've not yet acclimatized to Savannah's weather. In summertime the air is as thick as warmed honey, the humidity record high. Residents stroll sidewalks under the canopy of oaks that drip with moss, no one ever seeming to be in a rush. Racewalking is best saved for less genteel destinations, like New York City, or even my hometown of Toronto.

"The tea is cold and sweet, the people warm and friendly, and the pace of life is best described as 'civilized'" is typically what I'll say when friends back home ask what it's like to live here.

My watch vibrates again. *Seven minutes late.* I walk faster.

The crash and the smell hit my senses at the same time in one startling burst. I gasp, a hand going to my chest (*thump, thump, thump, thump*), the other snapping outward to find Clementine's hand, which is sticky and warm. A whiff of tangy sweetness clings in my nose, and my mouth fills with saliva. My watch releases a series of three short vibrations against my wrist, meant to remind me to breathe, to lower my heart rate. Now I wish I'd opted for drone delivery versus coming to the grocery store myself.

"I'm sorry, Momma," Clementine says, sucking in her bottom lip the way she does when tears are near. At our feet is a smashed jar of preserved sweet cherries, the red syrup a messy puddle dotted with the now-inedible fruit. The syrup is thick, the color of blood. My watch sets off another series of buzzes against my wrist, which I ignore.

Before I can answer my daughter, reassure her that it's fine, an older woman to our right says, "Don't fret, honey." She smiles—pale blue eyes, weathered skin from the too-strong sun—and presses a yellow button on the buggy's handle. "That's what this is for!"

A moment later a cleaner arrives. The hovering white disc chirps out, "Caution, caution, caution," as it approaches the puddle of syrup, a clear tube with silicone feelers releasing from under its belly to suck up the mess. The sounds of suction, interrupted each time a cherry makes its way up the tube, causes my stomach to turn.

"Thank you, ma'am," Clementine says to the woman. Ever polite, ever observant of a stranger's kindness, the way kids here are raised.

We only came to the store to pick up a couple of things, so we have canvas bags and no buggy, which means no cleanup button. Clementine prefers the self-serve kiosks to the buggy, so she can hand-scan the items. I'm partial to the delivery service, but it isn't worth the extra drone cost when you only need a few things.

"Thank you," I say, echoing Clementine. "You didn't have to do that, but thank you."

I know the jar of cherries will be automatically added to this woman's bill, because she hit her buggy's cleanup button. I'm uncomfortable with her generosity, even though it's what I would have done if the situation were reversed.

"Happy to," the woman says, waving my discomfort away. Then to Clementine: "You and your momma have beautiful eyes. I don't think I've ever seen such pretty eyes!"

"Thank you, ma'am." Clementine smiles shyly, pleased by the compliment. "Mine are just green, but my mom's eyes are extra special. They have a funny name . . . What is it, Momma?"

She looks at me, head tilted, her little brow furrowed.

"It's called central heterochromia," I reply. "Two different-colored eyes, or in my case, two colors in the iris." *Green, with a thick gold ring around the pupil.*

"Central he-te-ro-chro-mia," Clementine repeats, taking her time to get it right. Her efforts are rewarded by the woman's generous smile.

"How interesting!" she says, before looking at me, eyebrows raised. "Any others at home?"

I swallow hard. Regret and shame stick in my throat, like a too-big pill I can't get down. I could lie, but I don't. "No."

The woman frowns, giving me a look that could be either pitying or judgmental. "How unfortunate."

She reaches up and tugs on her necklace, which she then presses flat against the knit of her sweater. I see them then, the six silver rings threaded on the thin chain. We lock eyes, and mine drop before hers do.

I think of my own necklace, hiding under the halter neck of my dress. Of the one gold ring it holds, another ring hidden in a small jewelry box at the back of my sock drawer.

"Well, we better get back to it." I grip Clementine's hand firmly and she protests. The woman's frown deepens. "Thanks again for your help."

She smiles tepidly this time and carries on down the aisle. My guilt about her paying for our cherries lessens.

"Well, bless your heart," I say, but she's far enough away that I know she won't hear it.

"Nana says that isn't always as friendly as it sounds," Clementine tells me as I step around the cleaner. It's polishing the floor with soft muslin-cloth fingers to avoid anyone slipping, the robot still chirping out caution warnings at five-second intervals.

"Nana's right, but I meant it *appreciatively*, Clem. Because she paid for our cherries, which was very kind."

I did not mean it appreciatively, and Clementine's dubious look tells me I'm fooling no one.

"Can we get another jar, Momma? You promised." There's a hint of whine in her tone, but her face is wide open and, ah, the power a seven-year-old has over you. Especially when you harbor guilt, as I do.

"You're right, Clem. I did." I release her hand and reach for the cherries from the shelf.

We head to a checkout kiosk, and my watch gives me another set of buzzes. Again, I ignore it.

Clementine presses the "Family Car" button at the train station. I hope it arrives quickly. My stomach is off and I want to get home. I use the hand not holding our groceries to wipe at the back of my neck. It comes away slick with sweat. The air is blow-dryer hot, but at least there's shelter from the oaks that line the train's outdoor platform. A tiny relief.

"Mom, look! Train number one!" Clementine points at the approaching light-rail train, which slows as it gets closer. There's a large white number 1 stenciled onto the front of the first car. Clementine, along with her young peers, believes it's auspicious to ride Train 1. Similar to finding a four-leaf clover or wishing on a shooting star.

"Wow, it's been a while since that happened!" I give her a big smile. Match her enthusiasm. The way we are told to do with our children.

I take a moment to appreciate how such a small thing can feel so big to a child and am grateful for Clementine's easy happiness. The train doors slide open and we step inside the car. The chilly air is scented with a fresh citrus combination—lemon, orange, grapefruit—and I breathe it in, refreshed.

"Welcome to train one, Mathilde Crewson and Clementine Crewson. We hope you enjoy your ride!" The automated voice is pleasant, soothing as it welcomes us aboard, even as it pronounces my name all wrong—*Mat-hildEE* instead of *MAH-tealed*.

I'm used to it, which is why I've gone by "Tilly" since I was ten years old. My mom was the only person who made my name sound beautiful, so I was Mathilde at home and Tilly everywhere else. However, my birth certificate and health records—which the train's automated system draws from—don't acknowledge nicknames, so *Mat-hildEE* it is.

There are a few other parents on the train with us, their children sitting beside them and swinging their legs back and forth, back and forth. Rubber-heeled shoes tap against steel panels under the seats to release the little-kid energy. The rhythm of it is almost meditative, and my shoulders relax.

"Mom, it's Sunny Sam! I haven't seen this one." The screen across from our seats shows an animated sunshine—Sunny Sam—waltzing down a cobblestone path. The sun then picks up an upside-down fluffy gray cloud with a sad face and pops it back into the sky. Clementine tells me the cloud (Clara is her name) keeps flowers and trees healthy with her raindrops and protects us from too much sun.

Another mother catches my eye as Clementine chatters away, and we exchange a smile. I think about what the Adult Car—reserved for those sixteen and older—behind us is playing. News, likely, discussing population numbers, new flood-warning systems, or cost-of-living concerns. Topics better suited for those no longer thrilled by traveling on Train 1.

My watch sets off another set of vibrations, but I'm trying to stay present and so don't look at it. I'm listening to Clementine deliver facts about Sam and Clara when a sudden bloom of wetness fills my underwear, ripping my focus away.

Back at home, I stare at the blood on the toilet paper. Now I understand why my watch was so incessantly trying to alert me. The damn wearable, which is insurance-industry endorsed and worn by everyone over the age of five, knows my cycle better than I do, constantly tracking my basal temperature, my heart rate, my hormone levels, my moods. Sending my biometric information to the cloud, the data ripe for analysis as needed, by either medical professionals or insurance adjusters.

Shaking with the disappointment, I breathe in time to my watch's vibrations. Then I wipe again, and again, until only miniature dots of blood show themselves on the tissue.

Poppy, if born on her due date, would be six today. One year younger than Clementine.

It's particularly cruel that Poppy and I were to share a birthday, with the way everything turned out.

Flushing the toilet, I avoid looking into the bowl at the pink-hued water and open the cabinet under the sink. Straining, I dig through its depths until my fingers find what I'm looking for. The one "just in case" tampon I stashed under here.

In the oval mirror above the sink, my dark hair curls softly to my shoulders, my mother's own face reflecting back at me. It's both a comfort and a curse to be her doppelgänger.

I think about the half-full box of tampons (minus the one under the sink) that I threw out on trash day a week ago, in a particularly hopeful moment. *Maybe if I get them out of the house, the universe will see how serious I am this month?* Wyatt handles the garbage and recycling, so I discarded the box at the lab to avoid a "waste not, want not" conversation.

"If we can't use something, someone else can," he's often reminding Clementine. As a reuse architect, he practices what he preaches both at work and at home. But I didn't want that box in the house, despite knowing I would soon need it. Why would this month be any different from the last twelve, or the twelve before that?

There's a knock at the door and I jump.

"Dinner's ready, Tilly," Wyatt says. His voice is low, deep, full of the southern drawl that still melts my insides. I raced up to our bathroom as soon as Clementine and I got home, Wyatt's train still some minutes behind ours. There hasn't been an opportunity for an in-person greeting yet with my husband, which is good. Even though he never makes me feel broken, somehow always says the right thing, and has the best damn shoulder for crying on, I need a few more minutes to myself.

"Almost done," I reply. Wyatt knows tomorrow is test day—it's in his calendar too. But after all these years, he never asks me outright about any of it. He relies on the information delivered to our joint calendar, telling us when to have intercourse, scheduled like any other appointment. I don't want him to see the tampon on the countertop. To understand what it means—not yet.

"Clem's barely holding it together," he adds, chuckling on the other side of the door. "She's already put the candles on the cake."

Happy birthday, Tilly. Today I turn thirty-nine. Everything is supposed to be different than it is. Poppy and I were supposed to be celebrating together. "Out in a jiffy," I say through the still-closed door, and Wyatt retreats.

I know Clementine will be helping Shelby set the table for my birthday dinner. Maybe pruning sprigs of herbs from our indoor vertical garden for the broiling chicken. Stanley, my mother-in-law Shelby's rescue dog, is likely whining, overexcited about the chicken. Clementine usually sneaks him a bite.

Setting the unopened tampon to the side, I press my palms into the countertop and turn on the tap—which runs for only five seconds to conserve water—and wait for the predictable tears to come. But they don't, which makes me even sadder.

"Why don't you get the tattoo?" Wyatt asks after we've gone to bed, when I confess (as emotionless as possible) that my period arrived. The fiddle-leaf fig tree in the corner of the room glows softly as Wyatt envelops me in a bear hug and I try not to cry, keeping my eyes fixed on the luminescent leaves.

It's one of my birthday gifts, the fig, and something I've been wanting all year. The plant's bioluminescence reminds me of the glow of the blue-green lava lamp I had as a teenager. I wish I still had that lamp, but it was a relic, far too energy hungry for today's regulations. I wonder how it was repurposed, or if it simply ended up in the trash.

"Maybe . . . I'll think about it," is my response to Wyatt's question about the tattoo. In Toronto, where the Canadian regulatory body has yet to approve this technology, it's not even a consideration. But the biomedical tattoos are popular here, especially the fertility trackers that have become commonplace. There's even talk of them being mandated soon.

I've so far avoided the fertility tattoo, made up of three triangular-shaped dots that turn purple during ovulation and seafoam green when the pregnancy hormone is detected. Wyatt has asked about it before, but he's pushier tonight, which both surprises and grates on me. Ultimately, this should be my decision—my husband used to agree. But I suspect he too has grown tired of our monthly routine, of my resistance. Of the disappointment.

"You should try it, babe," he says. "Nick told me it's more precise than your watch, and the latest version ups your chance of pregnancy by twenty-one percent." This last part is delivered with enthusiasm, and I can't help but smile at my husband's golden retriever energy.

Nick Rojas is Wyatt's best friend, but he's also biased, as he heads up Savannah's pro-fertility governmental program, MotherWise. Nick also believes every woman of childbearing age should have the tattoo implanted. Nick can be kind of an asshole.

"Besides, it only lasts for six months," Wyatt says. "Maybe by then we won't need it anymore." I almost cave, acknowledging I'm not alone in my desperation for this to work.

However, I can't bear another thing to pay attention to. Another reminder of my current inability to conceive, despite having done so twice before. Which is what I say a moment later, because I'm not getting the tattoo, and I don't like lying to Wyatt.

He drops it, but I know we'll have this same conversation next month if nothing changes.

The pandemic that led to the alarming US population decline arrived like a whisper. Most people had no clue they'd contracted the virus. At least not until men started showing up at doctor's offices and fertility centers, wondering why they were unable to start, or grow, their families. Soon it was discovered that these young, should-be-virile men had inexplicably low sperm counts. In some cases, no sperm was found in the semen samples. It was then the scope of the problem came to light.

The scientists hadn't learned this yet, but MorA (Mosquito-Borne

Oligospermia-Related Ailment deemed too tedious)—carried by the *Aedes* genus mosquitoes—targeted sperm, altering its DNA integrity. Because there were no physical manifestations of the infection, it went unnoticed.

Sperm banks were decimated after couples failed to have children on their own. Scientists and medical experts argued in circles about the cause. Then a scientist studying mosquito-borne diseases accidentally discovered a new virus. When it came out that this virus was believed to be the cause of the male infertility problem, everyone panicked. Pools, ponds, and fountains were drained, and people spent more time indoors. Eventually, experts figured out how to genetically modify the mosquito species that carried MorA, eradicating the virus, but human live birth rates continued to plummet.

In what felt like a race against time to boost population, the government created aggressive campaigns focused on increasing birth rates. While the men were most affected by the virus itself, it was the women who would bear the burden of everything that came after. Women were expected to become mothers, and mothers were expected to keep having children.

Wyatt was thankfully spared, the two of us not yet living in the United States when MorA took hold. We tested negative for the virus, Wyatt's sperm deemed "excellent, more than up for the task." My advancing age—a pregnancy in one's late thirties deemed "geriatric"—was initially considered a possible issue, but tests revealed a still robust supply of healthy eggs. We simply couldn't get pregnant, and no doctor or fertility expert could explain it. Including the one we visited last month.

Your body knows what to do, it has done this before, the doctor said, patting my knee as she offered a paternalistic smile. *Relax! Have some fun, but try to stick to the schedule.*

Having fun and sticking to the recommended "schedule" were diametrically opposed, but I knew better than to bring that up. The digital prescription note arrived on my watch a moment later (a glass of wine, intercourse every other day, make each other laugh!), and I managed to hold back tears until we were out of the lab.

Shush, Tilly, you are no such thing, Wyatt said, when I apologized again for being barren. We stood there waiting for the elevator, and he wrapped me up in his arms. He murmured maybe we *should* try to relax, have more fun. I nodded, though I didn't understand what that really meant. On the train home we discussed IVF . . . maybe it was time? Fertility treatments are subsidized but come with a plethora of requirements, including the sharing of health records—something I'm unwilling to do, for reasons I've not shared with Wyatt.

Wyatt and I went quiet after that, him watching the news and me staring out the train's window, my lips silently whispering a prayer that Clementine would not be an only child.

Much later I would remember that prayer and wonder what (or who?) had been listening. I could never have imagined the price for getting exactly what I wanted.

"Clem, where's your water thingy?"

I'm crouched at the kitchen island, checking through the drawers, searching for Clementine's HydraPod. She's at a new school this year, and even though it's only the second week, there have been a couple of hiccups—including "us" (me) forgetting the HydraPod twice already. I rummage further and my annoyance ramps up along with my grumbling. I don't need a conversation with the school's administrator over this.

I'm overwhelmed and exhausted, having slept poorly, my cramps forcing me out of bed at three in the morning. Thanks to a pain pill, they're better this morning; only a dull ache remains. I wish to cocoon back into bed and admire my new fig plant. Have another cup of coffee in my pajamas. Allow the aches in my pelvis and solar plexus to dissipate with rest. But life marches on, as they say.

School starts in thirty minutes. We need to catch the train to the city's center, which is a ten-minute trip. It's a short walk to our stop, but I know we're a solid three minutes from getting out the door. Five, if I can't find the water pack and need to come up with an alternate solution. Wyatt is better at the morning routine—all routines, honestly—than I am, but he's already at a jobsite.

"What are you looking for, Tilly?" Shelby asks, coming into the kitchen from her bedroom suite. Wyatt's mother is seventy, but she looks a decade younger. Trim in her white linen pants and sweater set, her hair already out of rollers and settled into its silver-gray bob.

After Wyatt's dad died, Shelby began suffering memory loss. Little things at first—missed appointments or lunch dates with friends—then more concerning things, like when she forgot eggs frying in a pan, starting a small kitchen fire. Luckily, Wyatt had installed an automatic fire extinguisher in the range hood during our prior visit.

Doctors declared it "cognitive decline, likely grief-induced and possibly reversible," and so along with Wyatt getting a fantastic offer from an architectural firm, this diagnosis is why we moved to Savannah. Wyatt converted our town house, a few blocks over from where he grew up, to include an in-law suite so Shelby can live with us. Multigenerational homes are common again. Most everyone I know here, if they're lucky enough to have still-living parents, have in-law suites in their homes.

"My HydraPod," Clementine replies to Shelby.

"Oh, I washed it," Shelby says, opening a cabinet above the sink where a drying rack holds a few drinking glasses and the pack.

I evaluate my mother-in-law for cognitive changes silently, the way I do each morning. Force of habit. She appears energetic today, moving easily about the kitchen without pause to remember why she's there or what she's doing. *Good.* Shelby and Clementine continue chatting while I drink the rest of my coffee as quickly as possible. Clem's mentioning something about an art project involving vegetable-dyed fabrics. This is the first I'm hearing of it, and I feel slightly hurt that Clementine didn't talk to me about it, seeing as I'm the one with art expertise.

"Why don't we work on it after dinner tonight?" Shelby hands Clementine her now-filled HydraPod, then pulls her close for a hug.

"Thanks, Nana." Clementine goes up on her toes to kiss her grandmother's offered cheek. Shelby adores Clementine—the two have a special bond, and for this alone I'm grateful every day that we moved here.

"Let's go, Clem. We don't want to be late."

"*Again*," Clementine adds, rolling her eyes at me. Fair enough. Usually when we're late it's because I'm running behind.

But when did the eye-rolling start? I wonder.

I glance at Shelby and she hides a smile and shrugs. With a sigh I give Stanley a head rub, as he's glued to my leg hoping he's going out for a walk. His furry little white body wriggles in anticipation.

"Careful on the stairs," I say to Clementine, like I always do, a whisper of fear in my voice.

"I know, Momma," she replies, like she always does. Aware this is important to me, but unsure why. I'll tell her one day, maybe. Not anytime soon—it isn't a story for children.

I sling my work bag over my shoulder, bending awkwardly to lace my shoes at the front door, mentally running through my get-out-the-door checklist. The coffee sloshes in my stomach.

Now paces ahead of me, Clementine hopscotches the sidewalk under the large oak outside our home. It's warm already, but the stifling heat is still an hour or so away. Sun speckles through the tree's leaves, the moss hanging long from the branches. As Clementine hops from one foot to the other, she raises a hand to touch the silver-gray tendrils.

"Oh, before I forget," Shelby says, blocking the doorway so Stanley doesn't run out. I'm halfway down the front steps, holding the railing with a tight grip. The stairs are steep; I like to take them slowly. "I have a message for you."

Now on the sidewalk, I turn back toward my mother-in-law. "Oh, from who?"

"Margot. She wanted me to tell you she's sorry. About last night, she said."

I can't catch my breath.

"Momma, please, let's go." Clementine gestures impatiently at me. *Hurry up, hurry up.* The Spanish moss undulates with a sudden gust, tickling her cheek, a section wrapping around her neck. She twists to see what's brushed against her, gently untangling the moss from her neck and the backpack strap where it's snagged. My heart jackhammers inside my chest. I have the irrational urge to shout at her to get away from the tree. *Be more careful near the moss!* But instead I turn back to Shelby.

"What did you say?" I ask. My watch buzzes my wrist. Time for breath work, Tilly? flashes on the screen.

Shelby cocks her head to the side and presses a finger against her chin, frowning. Her nails are mauve, freshly done. I see her bio-tattoo on her wrist. The dots are glossy and uncolored—her sugar and electrolyte levels are fine. But she's not wearing her watch, useful for tracking her other vitals.

"I'm not sure. Oh dear, seems I chose the wrong morning to delay my coffee." She shakes her head, lets out a small laugh. In it I hear her discomfort.

"It's fine," I say, waving my hand about. Still, unease coils in my gut. "Don't forget to put your watch on, Shelby."

Her hand goes to her wrist, and she looks surprised to find it bare. "Thanks, darling."

"Of course," I reply. "Okay, better catch up to Clem."

"Bye-bye, ladies," Shelby says. "Y'all have a great day!" And with a kiss blown into the wind toward us, Shelby shuts the door. I'll send her a note once I get to work, to make sure she put her watch on.

I stand there for a moment longer, staring at the now-closed door.

Margot. She wanted me to tell you she's sorry. About last night, she said.

See, my mother's name was Margot, and she's been dead for nearly twenty years.

"Did you know there are loads of dead people under these sidewalks? Like, maybe right under our feet, right now? And some were *still alive* when they were buried?"

Clementine skips beside me, holding my hand. We're almost at the train platform, and I've resisted asking her to *stop*, to *walk properly*, to *pick up the pace* a half dozen times. At this statement about the dead I abruptly stop. My arm nearly gets pulled out of its socket when she continues her momentum before turning back to me. She never lets go of my hand.

"What made you think of that?" I scan her face for signs of worry, but there are none. It's as though my thoughts of death have somehow telepathically infiltrated Clem's mind.

She tugs my hand. "Mommy, we can't be late."

"Yes, you're right." I step in beside her. The train platform's up ahead; a few others are already waiting. I wave to another mother—Dawn—who has a daughter the same age as Clementine named Briar. Dawn was the one who put me in touch with the administrator of

Clementine's current school, and now I remember I never dropped off a thank-you gift. *Shoot.*

"But who told you that, Clem?"

My instinct is to stop walking so I can get her to focus on the question. But there's no time, so we continue, me walking, Clementine skipping. Evidently not distressed, as though the conversation was about butterflies versus us casually traipsing over the dead under our feet.

"I can't remember. My teacher?" she replies. "But I'm pretty sure it's true."

It is true. Hundreds, maybe thousands, of Civil War–era bodies rest forever under what later became cobblestone streets and town squares. There are ghastly stories of yellow fever victims who were buried alive leaving fingernail marks inside their coffins, as they frantically tried to claw their way out.

Savannah is known as one of the most haunted places in the United States. Ghost tours were commonplace here, as popular with visitors as southern food specialties like Brunswick stew and shrimp and grits. While the ghost tours have dwindled post-pandemic, along with tourism, Savannah's shadowy stories remain—sleeping below the surface, behind ivy-covered brick walls and under sidewalks. I shiver despite the morning's warmth.

"There's a lot of history here. We'll talk more about it later, okay?" is all I say, because the train has arrived and this isn't a discussion to be having with other young ears listening. But I make a mental note to speak with Clementine's teacher. While historically accurate, it seems an unnecessarily traumatic topic to discuss with a second-grade class. I need to be better at staying involved with the school. Dawn apparently volunteers in the classroom three mornings a week.

By the time I drop Clementine at school and make the short walk to the GIA lab, I've moved on from her "dead under the sidewalk" comment to trying to convince myself I heard Shelby wrong. It's a hard sell, which means I'll have to call Wyatt later and tell him what happened. My mother-in-law generally has only good days now, after years of regular neurotherapy, but it falls to us to engage extra support as needed. Wyatt and I share that load, much like we do the parenting one. He's an excellent partner, and I know how lucky I am.

Margot. She wanted me to tell you she's sorry.

Tears prick my eyes, and I hastily wipe them away. I miss my mom desperately, even all these years later. The last time I saw her I was nineteen, home from university for Christmas break and oblivious to the imminent tragedy that would change my life forever. A too-long skirt. A missed step. *So much blood.* So many questions, too, the answers buried along with my mother. No child—even one deemed an adult by society's standards—should see her mother the way I found mine that day. I shudder through the gag at the back of my throat, before pushing the memory down again where it hurts me less.

I wish she could have known the adult me. Met Wyatt and Clementine, both of whom she would have adored. The longing for her whip-smart wisdom, her ability to know what to say in every situation, intensifies around this time every month. I wonder what advice she'd offer about my inability to get pregnant again. While she was a wonderful mother, she was not the sort to snuggle your sadness away.

If I was melancholic or upset and brought my mood to her for help, my mom would turn from her studio's easel, where she often was when not at the museum, and say, *Mathilde—non tutti le ciambelle riescono col buco*, a favorite saying she picked up in Venice during an apprenticeship, which translates to "not all doughnuts come out with a hole." I never understood how this saying was meant to help, but I pretended I did.

I once offered the same line to Clementine, when she came home in tears after a school project didn't go her way.

"That doesn't make any sense, Momma," she said, after I translated it for her. I had to admit she was right, but I explained it was something my mother used to say to me. And even if it didn't make sense, for some reason I felt better after she said it.

"Maybe it doesn't have to make sense?" Clementine mused, upon further consideration. "Because doughnuts are delicious, and no hole means there's more doughnut to eat, and that's a happy thought." My mom would have loved that response.

My mother's career was her first child, relegating me to second in line, though she made it clear I was planned and very much wanted. The sperm donor was a Parisian-born art aficionado and collector who agreed to a no-strings-attached arrangement with his dear friend my mother. I never met him, and she never referred to him as my "father"—only as "Bernie" (pronounced *Bear-nee*).

I received a condolence card in the mail after her death, from a "C. Bernard," sent from Paris on gorgeous stationery. *Bernie?* I wondered. My mother had plenty of acquaintances around the world, but I was curious enough to do a Paris name search. It returned thousands of "C. Bernard" results. I left it at that. If my mother wanted me to know more, she would have told me.

I'm relieved to arrive at the GIA building, knowing once I get inside I'll be deliciously distracted with work. Shifting my focus to the package waiting for me, I run through ideas about what it might be. I step into the elevator, and as the doors close they turn into a large screen. A news banner runs across the screen's bottom (*. . . bee and pollinator population has seen an increase of 38% since the banning of pesticides and decorative lawns two years ago . . . Know Your Neighbor community social networks are now available in all 50 states . . .*). The remainder of the door-screen is a giant breath ball. It's a glowing sphere that shrinks and expands, changing color as it does, meant to help riders relax before stepping into work. I focus on the sphere, timing my breath to its pattern, but am soon distracted again by the news.

> *. . . President Vasquez is said to be "bolstered and encouraged" that both the House and Senate have passed the MotherWise bill, bringing it one step closer to being signed into law.*

MotherWise's pilot program has been running for six years in a handful of states, including Georgia, New York, and California. President Vasquez added that once the law is passed, all women across the US will become eligible—

There's a ping and the doors open. I'm mid-breath, and the remaining air I've taken in leaves me with a whoosh. My watch releases a staccato vibration, as though clapping. Recognition for my efforts, a gold star flashing across the watch face. I'm happy about the star, then feel silly and turn off my notifications.

As I walk into the lab, I can't know that these are the last few moments of normalcy I'll have. If I could have seen what was coming . . . well, I never would have signed for the delivery. I most certainly would never have unwrapped it.

"Tilly, I hope you and the family are doing well." The voice on the audio file crackles with warmth and age. It belongs to my mentor, Cecil Danby, a world-renowned art conservator. Among his many accolades is his conservation of Johannes Vermeer's *The Concert*, recovered years after it was stolen from the Isabella Stewart Gardner Museum in Boston. Cecil is pushing eighty and has mostly retired, though he still dabbles in the occasional project. It's nice to hear his voice.

"A collector reached out to me about this piece and asked for you by name. It's a complicated project, but one you're uniquely skilled to tackle—you'll understand when you open it. I've spoken to Raoul already"—Raoul Grady, the head of GIA and my boss—"and because this collector agreed to have this piece, and the entirety of the collection, included in the upcoming modern art exhibit, he said you can be a hundred percent on this project."

I'm surprised to hear this, because Raoul rarely lets anyone be "a hundred percent" on any project. He believes that creates a stagnant conservator and prefers that his teams work more fluidly. Whatever is in the package must be of some value, or have historical significance, for it to be worthy of an exhibit. This makes me even more curious, beyond the collector asking for me specifically. I have plenty of experience but am not well-known like Cecil is or my mother was.

"You'll need an air-lock room, as the fire damage is severe," Cecil continues. "It's going to require a high level of skill. I would have loved to take a crack at it, but you have much younger hands and eyes than I do." As he laughs I picture him—a full head of white hair, knees nearly to his chest as he sits (he's tall, six foot six). Gray slacks riding up his ankles, showcasing a pair of the brightly colored socks he wears, a bow tie at the neck of his button-up shirt. I smile, nostalgic for my younger self, when I worked with Cecil. Before Wyatt, before Clementine, before half my brain was constantly running a program trying to replicate her.

I glance at the shipment, now out of its crate and secured on a dolly. The packaging surrounding the piece is puffy, telling me the interior is filled with air to help protect the art. Fire damage is some of the hardest and most painstaking work.

"Another thing, Tilly." Cecil pauses now, and I hear him take a breath. "This is highly sensitive, so please keep it between us."

I immediately press stop on the recording. I slide earbuds in and then hit play again. "We believe this is a Charlotte Leclerc. Her final piece."

I'm gobsmacked. *Charlotte Leclerc?* My heart rate increases enough that my watch—knowing I'm at rest and therefore shouldn't have such a high rate—lets out a series of vibrations against my wrist. Shivers run through me, the hairs on my arms rising.

Charlotte Leclerc was an obscure American surgeon turned artist from the 1980s whose only child choked to death at the age of five. The details of this tragedy are scant, but it's apparently what prompted her to leave medicine and turn to art. Leclerc was known for using natural materials, like fingernails, hair, insect parts, and even human blood, in her work. Her macabre methods remain mysterious to this day, as she never spoke publicly of them, or of her art in general. Famed in art circles, she was otherwise unknown. At least until her death, which caught the attention of the general public for a short time, giving Charlotte Leclerc and her art a name in mainstream media until the next news cycle took over.

There are three known Charlotte Leclerc paintings, owned by one anonymous collector. But a fourth? It's only rumored to exist. There's lore she was working on a fourth piece when she died tragically at the age of forty-one, in a fire. A neighbor, who was a shift worker and kept odd hours, told a reporter she saw Charlotte Leclerc through her attic's studio window at five a.m. *She had something in her hand, a paintbrush I'm guessing? I could see the easel through the window but couldn't say if she was painting anything*, the neighbor said when questioned. *It was early . . . I was tired, coming home from my shift.*

What was she like? As a neighbor? the reporter asked the middle-aged woman in the purple nursing scrubs, the burned-out top half of Charlotte Leclerc's suburban house behind her.

Quiet. Keeps her lawn tidy, the woman replied, glancing down presumably at the grass. *She's a private person, and I respect that. No one likes a busybody.*

The fire broke out around six a.m., fire marshals determined. Most everything in the studio was burned, Charlotte Leclerc's charred bone fragments all that were left of the artist. No work in progress was found in the debris, however, and it was presumed Leclerc's legacy consisted of only the three paintings.

Until now.

However, my increased heart rate and goose bumps have less to do with Cecil's revelation, exciting as it is, and more with my personal connection to Charlotte Leclerc. It explains why a collector might ask for me by name, why I'm "uniquely skilled" to conserve such a project.

My mother worked on the third Charlotte Leclerc piece, *The Child*, surmised to be painted in remembrance of her dead daughter. Mom always said *The Child* conservation was the highlight of her career, but the experience changed her. I was sixteen and self-absorbed, so while

I noticed these changes in my mother, I didn't really contemplate what they meant.

She became more withdrawn, muttering as she padded about our house, using conservator lingo I didn't yet understand. Eyes glassy and red from lack of sleep, she spent so much time with the painting sometimes she didn't get home from the museum until dawn. During those six months I often ate dinner alone. Sometimes I'd catch her staring at me across the room, and when I'd ask, "What?" in the way egotistic teens do, there was a lag before she'd blink, responding, "Nothing . . . just thinking."

Then, there were the strange occurrences, the "bumps in the night" never explained, and, toward the end of the project, the nightmares. The panicked shouts from my mother's room that woke me out of my own slumber. I never told her I too had nightmares around that time—dark, gauzy, hard to remember once I woke up. Eventually they stopped, Mom's moxie returned, and after I left for university we never spoke about Charlotte Leclerc again. A year and a half later she was gone.

"It was found in a long-ignored storage locker when the police precinct was being refurbished," Cecil continues, bringing me back. "Oddly, the piece isn't mentioned in the evidence log. Likely overlooked because of the damage, no one realizing what it was. You'll understand when you see it. It's both intact and burned beyond recognition."

I take shallow breaths as I listen, my watch buzzing along to my racing heart against my goose-bump-prickled skin. I'm captivated, though fighting to stay in the present. I can't stop the mental drift to *The Child*. To my mother.

"If this truly is the fourth Leclerc . . . well, I don't need to tell you what this means, Tilly." No, he doesn't. This is a once-in-a-lifetime opportunity.

I'm so engrossed in Cecil's message that I don't notice Isla, my apprentice, sliding a cup of coffee onto my desk, like she does every morning. It's not part of her job, but Isla is the ambitious sort who looks for every opportunity to stay top of mind. However, today I'm startled by the mug's sudden appearance and throw out my arms, sending it careening across my desk.

"Oh shoot!" I jump up, grabbing my tablet before the pool of dark, hot liquid reaches it. With my other hand I yank out one of the earbuds.

"Tilly—I'm so sorry! I thought you saw me there."

"It's okay, don't worry," I say, setting my tablet on my chair. The coffee drips onto the floor.

Isla races to the small kitchen halfway across the room, returning with an absorbent cloth. I'm the one who knocked the mug over and should be cleaning it up, but Isla resists my attempts to help. She makes quick work of it.

"That's the talk of the lab," Isla says after wiping up the spill, eyeing the package with curiosity. "Do you know what it is?"

"I do," I reply, but add nothing further. Isla nods, professional enough to not ask any follow-up questions. The aroma of roasted coffee hangs in the air between us, the soaked cloth still in her hand. "Can you have it moved to Room D for me, please?"

She gives me a raised-eyebrow look—she knows Room D is our most secure work area, the place any original artwork goes. The room sits mostly empty these days. The video feed is protected, as is the door code. If you're using it, you're the only person who has access to both.

"You bet," she says. She tosses the coffee-soaked rag into the laundry chute before typing into her phone. "Need any support on this one?" she asks, keeping her tone light and easy.

I shake my head. "Not yet, thanks."

Her face falls slightly. Working on an original piece of art rarely happens, and it's a bucket-list item for most of the young conservators. "But you'll be the first one to know if I do."

Once Isla returns to her own workstation, I go back a few seconds on the audio card and press play again.

"I don't need to tell you what this means, Tilly. Also, there are some strange features of this painting, similar to the others. I'm not sure how much your mother told you about her experience with Leclerc," Cecil says, then pauses. "There's also an NDA, which I'm hopeful isn't an issue for you?"

It's not, and I'm not surprised. Especially with the magnitude of the discovery, and the fact that this painting is part of a private collection.

A loud beeping breaks through, GIA's mechanical mover—a platform with caterpillar-like tracks to ensure a smooth ride—coming toward me.

"I'll look forward to hearing from you," Cecil's message closes out. "Godspeed, Tilly."

The following day I stand in front of the package, doing a quick round of box breathing. I've spoken with Cecil, signed the NDA, cleared my schedule for the rest of the week. I can't wait to get started—the prospect of working, with my hands, on an active conservation thins out my patience. I'm struggling to hold my breath for the allotted time. But I want to be calm when I finally view the piece. My hands as steady as they can be.

In through nose for four, hold for four, out through mouth for four, hold one-two-three-four. Repeat. It's also not easy from behind my face mask, meant to protect me from possible off-gassing once I unwrap the piece. I've turned my watch notifications off to avoid distraction, so there's no vibration, no gold star, when I finish the box breathing.

I've been at GIA for six years, starting shortly after my yearlong maternity leave ended. Once Clementine turned one, she entered the state's subsidized day care program, and I was able to go back to work. I've only been in Room D a handful of times, forgetting how quiet it is, minus the low hiss of the air return. I take in the gleaming stainless steel workbench that hydraulically converts from flat to raised, depending on preference and need. The new and plentiful conservation tools at my disposal. There's also a top-of-the-line portable scanning electron microscope, or SEM, which is highly coveted by conservators.

The last time Room D was used was about two years ago. I think of the tools at my personal workstation—the simple stereo microscope, the many paintbrushes, spatulas, bamboo skewers, and fine-edged blades for precision work, which rarely get used. Hypodermic needles and ancient porcupine quills, which I brought with me when we moved here, long-ago plucked by my mother from some poor porcupine that met its end on a Canadian highway. I have never found anything better for the finest pinpoint work, so they are a treasured part of my conservation toolbox.

Satisfied with my clearheadedness, I step forward and press the air release valve on the package. There's a sound like a balloon losing its air, and the package changes shape. I pinch the zipper-sealed seam at the top to open it.

It has already been scanned with infrared and X-ray. Minuscule flecks from the surface placed under the AI-enhanced microscope have verified material types and other details. I open the file of findings on my tablet, reviewing them again. I've practically memorized the file, having gone over it a dozen times already. But I like to be thorough.

Now I better understand why this piece is believed to be the fourth and final Charlotte Leclerc. It has her markings all over it. No signature, as is typical, but instead a luna moth outline she used as a cipher, hidden underneath a layer of paint and visible only on scans; her preference for oil paints mixed with sand and other natural elements, to add texture and layers to the art; the use of heavily pigmented colors, with favoritism for black; and, a most telling finding—the presence of human blood.

Another Leclerc rumor, which gained traction on unmonitored

art-related message boards, is that she recruited blood donors to her studio. Medical students who needed extra money, for example. Still others suggested she kept it simple, using her own blood. Unfortunately, Cecil said microsampling couldn't produce reliable DNA results, due to degradation from the high heat, so we can't know whose blood she used—only that it's human.

I slide the de-puffed packaging down the boxy frame. A cloudy sheet of biodegradable plastic covers the entirety of the piece, but it separates easily with a cautious slice of my self-retracting knife. When I see the enormity of the damage, I lose my breath. Cecil wasn't kidding when he said this was going to be complicated. The entire canvas is blackened, with a few burn holes near the bottom edge, through the full thickness of the material.

I lean close and turn my head sideways so I can view the planes of the piece. The paint, where I can determine paint, is bubbled and has a greasy black sheen, similar to the way creosote clings inside a chimney pipe. I can't determine artistic composition, the soot layer hiding any clues.

I use a soft-bristled brush in small areas around the edges. No residue is removed, so I shift to solvent testing. The first solvent isn't up to the task, nor is the second. Holding a cotton swab firmly in hand, I test a small area (less than a half inch), starting at the bottom left corner. Every conservator has her own process for approaching a conservation, and my preference is bottom to top. That way I won't get bleeding down the length of the painting, on the rare occasion a solvent drips.

With steady, gentle pressure I apply the solvent-dampened cotton in short rolls. Black comes away on the cotton, and with a surge of panic I quickly turn on my Luminara glasses. The paint underneath the soot is a different shade, and I breathe a sigh of relief.

Suspecting I have the correct solvent, I test four other spots on the canvas to be sure—top right, two in the center, bottom right. Satisfied with the result, but the composition still a mystery, I decide I'll work across the painting. Left to right, bottom to top. It's going to be tedious work, but the thrill is worth the eyestrain. Solving a puzzle and uncovering art is the best high I have ever found.

I glance over at the X-ray image on my tablet. With a gentle, glove-covered finger I touch the canvas at the exact spot Leclerc's cipher—the luna moth, with eyelike markings and dangling tails from the hind wings—glows on the X-ray image. Bottom right, a standard placement for an artist's mark.

Later, while researching the cipher, I'll learn the vibrant-green luna moth is one of the largest in North America. Its pupa stage lasts for an incredible nine months, the same as a human's gestation, and then ten days after hatching it dies. Depending on which internet source you ask, this moth symbolizes transformation and new beginnings. I also find another meaning: for some, the luna moth represents the brevity of life.

Right below the luna moth, in fine, white-inked cursive writing (the artist's own, I presume) is the title of the piece. *The Mother.*

I squat a few times, trying to dissolve the tension from my legs. I shift my Luminara glasses to "harsh, waking light" mode, allowing my gaze to soften as I lean over the piece, looking again for shapes or patterns within the blackness. But there are none I can discern.

"Let's see what you've left for me, Charlotte." I sit on the wheeled stool, using my heels to roll closer to the workbench. I cast my eyes down, being cautious I don't knock into anything, but when I raise them something shimmers across the painting. It's subtle, like a ripple from a raindrop in a glass-surfaced pond. I stop abruptly, the soles of my shoes squeaking loudly against the flooring. Squinting, I search the blackness for signs of movement, but there are none. It's still, unlike my pounding heart.

Charlotte Leclerc is not going to give up her secrets easily. The fire damage is terrible, the conservation made trickier by the artist's use of black oil paint as background. The painting remains flat because I find it easier on my neck and shoulders to work this way.

"What happened to you?" My face is inches from the surface as I gently roll the swab over a one-by-one-inch blackened spot. My voice echoes in the room, the air return distracting. I set my earbuds to noise-canceling mode.

Unlike me—I prefer a pin-drop-quiet workspace—my mom loved playing music in her at-home studio while working on freelance projects. I found the music disruptive so would watch her instead of doing my homework. Her confident hands moved across the art with such control. Now, seeing my own hands, I'm momentarily halted by how similar they look to my mother's. Long fingers, prominent knuckles, veins beginning to peek through the fascia as my age creeps up.

After the cleaning session, when I remove a narrow band of soot along the bottom, I spend the rest of the day meticulously documenting details. Rereading the notes on previous Leclerc paintings, which Cecil sent in a second file.

I already know most of the lore, but some of the particulars are new to me. Including the musings of a journalist who gained access to the Leclerc art, under the condition that she would keep the collector's name and location anonymous. In the article—published in an art and design magazine about seven years ago—this writer speaks of being overcome with deep melancholy; a sense of "impending doom, like a terrible fate was coming my way" is the exact phrasing she used, upon viewing the pieces at the collector's home. Hanging original art in homes is highly unusual nowadays, due to flood and fire risks. A few photos are included with the article, and I flip through those.

The "Leclerc" room is described as "large, windowless, and nearly empty." I take in the white walls, high ceilings with elaborate crown moldings, and gallery-style lighting. There is one round burgundy-velvet bench in the room's center, its pedestal feet resting on a herring-bone parquet floor. Three of the four walls hold Leclerc paintings.

The Healer. The Dreamer. Then the third piece, believed to be the artist's last, *The Child*—the painting my mother conserved, which is the one most familiar to me. Seeing the artworks together again allows me to appreciate the similarities. Each piece showcases her preference for memento mori, which translated from Latin means, "remember that you must die."

"Edvard Munch, Vincent van Gogh, and Rembrandt, to name a few, have applied this style to their work," Mom explained when I asked her what "memento mori" meant. We were at the dinner table, and it was early in her conservation of *The Child*. Mom typed something into the search bar, then turned her laptop around and pointed to the images on the screen. "See here, and here? Artists use elements like skulls, decaying flowers, hourglasses, clocks, and even bubbles, integrating them into the tableaux. Memento mori is meant to represent the fleeting nature of life, Mathilde. It's very powerful."

The Healer features a sole female subject on a black background, one half of her dressed in a doctor's lab coat, the other half a bare skeleton. A tiny clock rests where the doctor's right eye should be, the hands set to midnight. The woman in *The Dreamer* is in repose, nude and flat on her back, surrounded by dark vertical slashes purported to be trees in a night forest. Her one visible eye is rolled to the back of her head, her hands in prayer position on her chest, clutching a bouquet of wilting sunset-orange blooms. Marigold flowers, something I learned when researching Leclerc during graduate school; it was a pet project, not part of my official studies, and it was slim pickings. Charlotte Leclerc the artist was like a ghost; hardly anything had been written about her with much authority. But it made me feel closer to my mother, even though my research never revealed the answers I sought after her death.

When I shift my gaze to *The Child*, my throat tightens. I think of Clementine, only a couple of years older than Charlotte Leclerc's daughter was when she died. The grief in the piece is palpable, discomfortingly familiar, even though the art is more jovial and vibrant than her others. But there is something deeply tragic about it; something difficult to put words to.

The young girl in *The Child*—her cheeks rose colored, a yellow polka-dotted dress tied with a bow at the waist, red patent leather Mary Janes—is skipping rope. The rope's handles, upon close examination, have skulls sculpted into them. In the top right corner of the piece a subtle, ghostly image is visible within the clouds. It appears to be an exact replication of the skipping child. *Though one could argue the brain is mirroring the shape into the cloud's formation*, Mom told me, showing me a photo of the finished conservation. Both then and now I believe Leclerc meant it to be an echo, the image purposeful.

The skipping child blows a gum bubble, which is glossy and pink. The ground under her is pitch black, though there is visible texture this journalist describes as "impressions of flower petals." I close the file.

The next photo is of a typewritten card, declared by police to be a suicide note despite being unverified as written by Leclerc. It was found in the room where she died. I study the photo, reading the four sentences out loud.

"If you're reading this, it means I am dead. I promise that I tried. I hope it was enough. I'm sorry, my darling, if not."

A hard shiver moves through me. I've not seen the specifics of the note before, never released to the public, from my recollection, and it unsettles me more than the paintings themselves. I click over to the next series of photos that Cecil included. One of Charlotte Leclerc's medical school graduation, another from the archived website for the hospital where she worked as a surgeon, both of which I have seen. The photos are grainy and small, showing Leclerc as an attractive woman with shoulder-length blond hair, blue eyes, and thinnish lips.

I have a desperate longing to call my mother. I'm ever surprised by how close to the surface her loss remains; one small scratch, and the wound weeps.

I click into my personal folder, turning up the volume. "Mathilde, it's your mother," she says. I smile, remembering how she always started her messages like this, as though her voice wasn't as familiar as my own.

"Please send me your Christmas list pronto, or you'll get toothpaste and laundry soap in your stocking. See you soon, ma belle fille. Je t'aime."

"Je t'aime aussi, Maman," I whisper. I never did send my list, and four weeks later she was dead. I click play again, and again. And again.

During my short walk from the train station home, I mentally compartmentalize my day to create space for my family once I walk through the door. I wonder how Clementine fared at school with her history presentation, if Wyatt was able to secure permits for his latest project, how Shelby's maintenance neurotherapy session went today. Turning onto Oglethorpe Avenue I see the iron gates of the Colonial Park Cemetery up ahead. I'm almost home.

Our town house is half of what used to be one of Savannah's grand estate homes. Most homes have been refurbished to manage the climate migration pressures, which have forced us closer together. While the interiors are extensively renovated to suit families' needs, the homes' exteriors remain traditional. The wrought iron railings frame staircases and second-floor Juliet balconies; wooden shutters and vine-covered bricks provide ambience; ivy climbs on gates and lampposts; and most every front door is painted red, a nod to the Civil War days when red-door homes signified a safe haven.

I'm ducking under the draping Spanish moss of our oak, starting up our front steps, when I see it. Innocently sitting outside my red front door.

The air leaves my lungs in one great whoosh right as our neighbor's door opens. She pops her head out, noticing me. "Oh, hi, Tilly! I had a delivery notification and . . . Oh, there it is."

Becca Woodward steps toward me. She's wearing a beige linen jumpsuit, which looks chic on her. Her long dark hair is swept into a smooth ponytail, seemingly untouched by Savannah's near-constant humidity. I think of my unruly curls, gathered in a messy bun.

"They must have confused our doors." Becca smiles, having no idea what's happening inside my body. No clue about the searing pain in my gut brought on by seeing that box outside my door.

"Congratulations, Becca." I plaster a smile on my face even though I want to cry. "Are the boys excited?"

"They sure are! But we all hope it's a girl this time. Lucky number five, maybe?" She crosses her fingers, then picks up the box from outside my door. My uterus contracts with a cramp.

The box now in Becca's hands is the size of three shoeboxes, the cheery yellow logo bright against the white background. NOURISHBOX, the logo reads, with the slogan "Nurtured by Nature." I know one of these boxes will show up weekly until Becca is six months postpartum. I'll have to find a way not to feel like I've been stabbed in my stomach each time it does. The program's name is written on the tape sealing the seams in a continuous loop, taunting me. *MotherWiseMotherWiseMotherWiseMotherWiseMotherWiseMotherWise . . .*

Becca shifts the box to get a better grip, and something shiny slips out from her T-shirt's neckline. I glance at it, and she notices.

"Almost time for another ring," she says, her tone bright. Another sharp cramp in my abdomen. I can only wave in response to her "see you later, Tilly" as she takes her NourishBox inside, leaving me alone on our shared front stoop.

Of course Becca is cheerful. She's doing what every woman is supposed to do—boost the population, one baby at a time—while being nicely compensated for her efforts.

I know her fifth necklace ring, each representing a living child, won't arrive for a few months yet—midway through her third trimester. The gold rings are worn by mothers, silver "legacy" rings by grandmothers. It's a foundational element of the MotherWise program, the rings both practical and symbolic: the jewelry is tied to program incentives but is also a societal signal of success.

Each gold ring comes with a minuscule tracking device, scanned when you walk into a store, and provides family discounts on everything from groceries to baby clothes. The more rings, the higher the savings. Though the pilot program was still months away when I became pregnant with Clementine, MotherWise allowed new mothers who were a year or less postpartum to sign up retroactively. Which I did, eager for the savings and the quite pretty jewelry that was becoming commonplace on new mothers.

Poppy's ring was delivered two weeks after she died. I never corrected the painful error, never told Wyatt—or anyone else—about it. I waited with bated breath for someone to show up at our door, owning the mistake. *I'm very sorry, Mrs. Crewson, but MotherWise needs to reclaim the ring, as there is no longer a pregnancy.* But no one arrived, and the ring became proof Poppy had been real—*MotherWise would never have sent it otherwise!* I was desperate in those earliest stages of grief for something to acknowledge her.

At first I only wore it around the house, when I was alone. The two rings dainty, pretty, and golden against my neck. As the months, then years, passed, I wore it more often. Though rarely in public. No one ever came back for that ring, and it seemed an administrative error that got lost in the shuffle of the program's multiphase rollout. Now I have a fierce, familiar urge to race to my bedroom, to the dresser drawer where I've hidden the second gold ring in a jewelry box tucked inside a pair of balled-up wool socks I'll never need in Savannah.

"Patience, my darling."

My mother's voice, as clear as if she's right behind me. My fingers fly to my neck, to Clementine's ring, nestled in the hollow of my throat. Safe, legitimate, a grounding talisman.

"Mom?" I whisper, before whipping around. But I'm alone. The moss sways with a sudden gust of too-warm breeze, and I shiver despite the oppressive heat.

I still, my heart racing.

My watch buzzes an alert.

The moss stills too, the breeze gone as quickly as it came.

Shaking hand on the doorknob now, stepping inside the house before quickly shutting the door behind me. Locking it, for good measure.

My mother's voice continues echoing in my ears, like sound waves bouncing off a rocky cliff face. The echo persists, even after I've greeted my family, while I prepare dinner, as I'm reading with Clementine before bed.

"Patience, my darling . . . patience, my darling . . . patience, my darling . . ."

"Let's get everyone checked in," the tautly lean woman, who is not one of our usual instructors, says, standing at the door to the community center's health studio. I attend a breath work class weekly with my two best friends, Maeve and Katrina. We alternate studios, because Maeve's community center is two neighborhoods over from where Kat and I live. Today we're at Kat's and my local health studio, and first in line. I'm at the front of our group, so I give the woman our names.

"Tilly Crewson, Maeve Milford, and Kat Rojas." The instructor touches her tablet's screen, checking us in, then says, "Welcome, ladies. I'm Beatrice, filling in for Ellis S. today. You've been here before?"

We nod. "We're regulars," I reply.

"Excellent. Then you know the drill," Beatrice says, smiling before turning her attention to the next woman in line behind us. The room is lit in a soft, golden glow, meant to mimic near sunset, and we each take one of the VR headsets hanging on wall hooks. The mats have already been laid out, and we choose three in the last row. There's a faint scent of lavender, infused into the space to promote relaxation.

"We have . . ." Kat looks at her watch, sets a timer. "Eleven minutes.

So we each get three. Maeve, you're first." Kat used to be an elementary school teacher and is now at home with her four children. The need to organize remains strong, so Maeve and I are happy to indulge her. Sometimes it's nice to hand over the control to someone else.

"As you both know, I was at a conference last week," Maeve says. She ties her ponytail lower to accommodate the headset. She has a new watchstrap, transparent except for tiny flecks of gold—it reminds me of the jelly sandals of my youth. I've been looking at a similar one, though flecked with white, but it has been out of stock.

"'The Role of Neuroaesthetics in Treating Mood Disorders,'" she adds, before glancing at me. "With a focus on creating visual art as therapy, so I'm going to want to pick your brain later, Tilly."

"Happy to have my brain picked," I reply. "Besides, I owe you about a hundred thousand dollars' worth of therapy at this point."

Kat raises her hand. "Another fifty thousand at least from me."

Maeve laughs, then shares that her partner, Jenn, an emergency-room physician who travels often for humanitarian work, is up the coast in Maine.

"There was a lot of displacement with this one, and injuries, Jenn said," Maeve adds, referring to the most recent hurricane, only two weeks prior, more devastating than initially predicted. "I'm going to join her next week."

Jenn and Maeve are child-free by choice, neither possessing the "mom gene," as they put it. MotherWise, and society in general, isn't sure what to do with women like Jenn and Maeve, and they are mostly left alone. Though there are whispers that MotherWise, and the government at large, is considering disincentives for this childless group.

Along with servicing disaster zones, most of Maeve's therapeutic work focuses on dismantling this concept of "unquestioned procreation," supporting women who either choose not to become mothers or can't due to a variety of circumstances. It's how I met her—she was leading a workshop on secondary infertility, and my therapist at the time suggested I attend.

Kat, who is married to Wyatt's high school best friend, Nick, devotes her update to her kids: Lola, Jose, Ana, and the baby, Rachael, who is finally sleeping through the night. Nick is a former city councilor now tasked with growing the MotherWise initiative, and this occasionally creates friction. I'm more moderate on nearly every issue and am often the peacekeeper between the two. They are as opposite as can be, both in appearance, with Maeve blond and athletic and Kat dark and willow-thin, and in personality. Our friendship has remained solid regardless.

"Okay, so I have a top secret project right now," I say, lowering my voice. I tell them about the mysterious delivery in the vaguest terms possible.

"I can't share more than that for now, I even had to sign an NDA, but I'll say this: it's the project of a lifetime. A true 'pinch me' moment."

There's a hit of anticipation in my belly; the promise of unearthed secrets under the black soot makes me itchy with impatience. Underlying that is a thread of disquiet, as I remain troubled by hearing my mother's voice on my front stoop last night. Plus, Wyatt and I have decided to do a course of privatized IVF, in part thanks to the Leclerc and its bonus fee. I'm both excited and overwhelmed about the decision, which I hope is the answer to our at-the-moment unsolvable problem.

All this to say, I'm counting on tonight's class to rebalance my nervous system.

"Sounds exciting!" Kat says, ever enthusiastic the way only a former elementary school teacher can be. "I'm thrilled for you."

"Me too," Maeve adds. "I can't wait—"

Whatever she's about to say is interrupted by Kat's watch alarm. "Time's up, ladies. Are we doing dinner after?"

Maeve shakes her head. "I have clients this evening."

"I'm out too," I reply. "Work stuff."

"I don't miss that." Kat shakes her head. "I mean, I still *work*. Four kids under seven is almost equivalent to a full-time job."

"I'd say more like a job and a half," Maeve replies, and I murmur my agreement. Raising another human being is the hardest job there is.

With a stab of sadness I think about my recent failed month. I told Maeve, because she checked in on me, knowing test day was coming. There's little I don't share with her, particularly in this arena, but I haven't said anything to Kat yet. It's likely I'm not giving her enough credit, but she can be myopic about motherhood and I don't need cheerleading on the issue.

Beatrice's voice fills the room, coming through speakers that line the ceiling. "Headsets on, folks. We're going to be starting in a minute or so."

I slide the virtual reality goggles onto my head, the glass eyepiece a stormy gray color that's semitransparent. The headband is soft and stretchy.

I click the on button at the side, the device comes to life, and my vision fills with the TAKE A BREATH logo and a glowing yellow sphere that pulses like a slow heartbeat.

Choosing "Hawaiian Beach" for my setting—my usual (Maeve prefers snowy mountainous settings, and Kat wide-open fields of wildflowers)—I cross my legs, resting my hands on my bent knees in a sort of lotus position.

I'm now in Maui, on the beach. The mat is warmed, and I can almost convince myself it's sun-drenched sand under me, the seabirds chirping above the continuous roll of ocean waves. A pod of dolphins swims by, jumping and frolicking among the waves, and I smile. Then a twinkling light pierces the center of the scene, and I watch as it grows to four times its original size, then retreats back to a pinpoint.

My vitals are recorded in the upper left corner of the screen, and I see my heart rate has come down five beats a minute. Feeling chuffed, I take a deep breath in through my nose, then slowly release it through my mouth, as per Beatrice's request. The lavender scent is pleasing, and I take in another deep nasal breath, happy to see the twirling gold star beside my vitals.

"We're going to start the session now." Beatrice's voice is whisper soft, like the gentle breeze the seabirds I'm watching float upon. My heart rate comes down another two beats. "Breathe in through your nose for four . . . now hold for seven . . . release for a slow eight. That's it, everyone. Well done. And again, here we go . . ."

The first time I visit Savannah is when I come home with Wyatt to meet his parents, one month into our relationship. Yes, it was fast. No, it didn't *feel* fast.

Savannah was a very different place then. Before the flood that forced the city to get creative about space, before bicycles and trains replaced cars, before climate migration shoved everyone closer together. Savannah's town squares, each of which used to showcase statues depicting historically significant figures, have been transformed. Repurposed as community gardening hubs, gathering spots for residents to socialize, places for children to play together.

What hasn't changed are the city's massive, century-old oak trees, whose branches hold swaths of Spanish moss, drooping in soft, dove-gray cascades. Some low enough that you can reach up and graze them with your fingers. "It's so romantic," I say to Wyatt as we walk along a quiet street heading to Wright Square on that first trip.

I have never been anywhere like it—Savannah has a heartbeat, pulsing gently, *alive*, especially after the sun goes down. The cicadas buzz loudly in the trees, the males singing mating calls.

"I can't imagine growing up here. These oaks, and the moss . . . what is it, exactly?"

Wyatt holds my hand as we stroll toward the square. Our fingers are sticky with sweat in the August heat, but neither of us cares to let go. "It's a bromeliad. Same family as the pineapple. And it isn't anchored to the tree in any way, so it's more friend than foe. The French colonizers called it 'Spanish beard.'"

"It does look like a long beard." I tilt my head back to gaze up at the moss. The sky is charcoal, stars beginning to pop. "How does it survive?"

"It gets nutrients from the air. It loves Savannah's high humidity and temperatures."

We arrive at Wright Square, essentially the center of the downtown area. Wyatt has a surprise—*something super touristy*, he warns, but also a fun way to learn about one famous aspect of Savannah's history.

"Welcome to Savannah After Dark, and thank you for coming out this evening," the tour leader, a middle-aged woman named Sharon with pink hair and an "I see dead people" tattoo on her forearm, says. I wonder if that tattoo came before or after she started leading ghost tours.

Seems I'm not the first to ponder the question.

"The tattoo came first, before anyone asks. It's what led me to a ghost-tour-leader career. The pink hair after, because it's all about balance, right?"

The group, around twenty of us, chuckles as Sharon hands out headphones and the audio devices, so we can follow along.

"One of Savannah's most notable ghost stories—and, trust me, we have a lot of them—begins here in Wright Square, which is also where our tour begins." Sharon has us stand in a circle. Then she tells the tale of Alice Riley, an Irishwoman who arrived in Savannah in the 1730s to work as a servant, alongside her husband, for a cattle farmer named William Wise.

"Residents here were not fans of Mr. William Wise," she continues. "He would have been accused in the 'hashtag MeToo' movement, if you know what I mean." There are nods all around.

"One day, nasty William Wise ends up dead, his head submerged in a bucket of water, and Alice Riley and her husband are nowhere to be found. Willy Wise was declared Savannah's first murder victim, and with the unfortunate but rampant anti-Irish sentiment here at the time, Miss Alice and her hubby were found to be guilty of their boss's murder. They were sentenced to a public hanging."

I shiver, even with the stifling heat, and Wyatt rubs my arm. "Are you scared of ghosts?" he whispers with a smile.

"You have to believe in ghosts to be scared of them," I whisper back, laughing a little to dispel the odd chill. But then tears prick at my eyes, and, horrified, I realize I'm about to cry. My mom has been gone for years, but some days it's as though it happened yesterday. I wish I believed in ghosts—maybe then I could spend time with my mom, outside of my memories.

I crouch, retying the laces on my sneakers. The knots haven't loosened, but it gives me a moment to compose myself. A minute later I'm in control once more, and I smile at Wyatt when I stand. He returns it, no idea—thank goodness, because we are in the early days of love, when you want to appear flawless—about the emotions churning inside me.

"Now, there's a kink in the 'hang in the square' plan, because turns out Alice is pregnant, with Willy-the-Worst's baby. This is where the story breaks off into a few paths. Some say she was hanged pregnant, and so now her ghost follows mothers with infants and pregnant women, because she wants to take their babies as her own. Another version is that she was a witch, and cursed all Savannah's residents, and this hex is the reason Spanish moss—which as you've probably noticed is on all the oak trees in this city—doesn't grow on that particular tree."

Sharon points at the great oak near us, and we all look up into the dark branches. Sure enough, there appears to be no moss hanging. Someone gasps, and there is a murmur of agreement among us that, yes, that *is* a bizarre thing.

"The most likely version, at least in my opinion, is that they imprison her until her baby is born—a boy named James, who sadly later dies—and then she's hanged, the first woman to be hanged in the square . . . right in that spot there." She points again, this time at a plaque right under my feet. I step back as though the ground is about to give way.

"Some say the reason Spanish moss isn't found here is because it can't grow where innocent blood has spilled, meaning that Alice Riley was not a murderer after all."

Later, over drinks, Wyatt and I talk about the twenty or so ghost stories Sharon delivered on the two-hour walking tour and about the fun of being a tourist in your own city, and how strange it was that at various moments on the tour we both felt cold shivers, even with the evening's warmth.

Wyatt jokes that one of the ghost tour providers probably skulks around in the middle of the night with a ladder to remove any Spanish moss that tries to take up residence in that oak. Otherwise, the ghost story of Alice Riley lacks the pizzazz and impact it needs to continue to be retold night after night, tour after tour. Half-drunk and giddy with our newfound love, we laugh imagining that stealthy guy and his ladder.

On my way home from my breath work class I stop at Wright Square, a place I visit often. Usually I sit on a bench, staring at the spot where Alice was supposedly hanged, now covered by a small splash pad for children, the concrete lining painted bright blue, with smiling cartoon sea turtles and big-eyed puffer fish. The plaque is long gone, but the air here feels unsettled, heavy with something best described as melancholy.

The splash pad has emptied, all the young children home and tucked into bed at this hour. I think again of Alice Riley and imagine a different reality, one where Alice raised her son, James, and where I'm watching Clementine and Poppy play together in the splash pad—two gold rings proudly displayed on my necklace. Indulging in this fantasy is like pressing an angry purplish bruise, but it's pain I revel in. I'm not a religious person, and this ritual is the closest to atonement I have.

I stare up at the same oak tree from that ghost tour, years ago now. The branches are wider, the canopy fuller, and yet, it remains the only tree in the square that's free of Spanish moss. I shiver, thinking of Alice Riley's execution, the spilling of "innocent blood."

Layered over the pain of losing Poppy is a heavy blanket of guilt I've wrapped tightly around myself. When I saw the pregnancy test—the blinking results window announcing five weeks with a smiling face—I couldn't believe it, my first emotion regret, and it filled me to the brim. It wasn't planned, and I didn't want to be pregnant again so soon after Clementine. She was barely four months old! I was overwhelmed with new motherhood, and I missed my work. Wyatt, by comparison, was thrilled. He saw only the positives, his body and brain still his own. Under his complete control.

I've never told anyone about my dark, unconscionable thoughts surrounding that pregnancy, and how *for a moment* I wished it all away. Until I shared it with an AI therapist named "Paige," thanks to a mental wellness initiative GIA implemented as part of a new benefits package, and a weak moment of wishing to expel my guilt. At the time, I hadn't considered the ramifications of sharing my shameful secret, confidentially, I believed. But that was before infertility, before the MotherWise IVF subsidies that required a deep dive into my health records—all of which Wyatt, as the expectant father, would be privy to.

A couple walks into the square, holding hands, laughing about something. They see me, and the woman waves and smiles. I smile back, quickly gathering my things as I note the time on my watch. I've been here too long. I need to stop coming here.

Something flutters nearby, and I'm startled, my bag slipping from my hand.

"Oh!" I whisper, my voice low but sharp with a tiny burst of fear-laden adrenaline. *Is that a bat?* I duck slightly, looking around. But then something lands on the bench, beside where I sat moments ago. At first I think it's a butterfly, but, no, it's a moth. A large one, with wings an ethereal pale green and delicate dangling tails.

A luna moth.

Shock moves through me in rippling waves. Luna moths aren't exactly rare, but seeing one is—especially here in Savannah. I've only seen a luna moth once before, back home when Mom and I visited the cottage of a friend of hers. It rested on the screen door, attracted along with the bugs and mosquitoes to the small porch light, hauntingly beautiful.

What are the chances?

I'm about to snap a photo with my watch when the moth lifts off, soon a small speck of paleness against the dark sky. "Shoot," I whisper, disappointed to not be able to show Clementine such a rare thing.

There's a sudden soft breeze against my neck, the whisper of wings, and my mother's voice comes to me again—but this time it's from a memory.

Did you know all art is made by the dead, Mathilde?

It was early evening, the fading light filtering through the conservation room's tall, arched windows. A half dozen canvases, each in various stages of treatment, were clasped on nearby workstations. The room smelled lightly of acetone and the navel orange I'd recently peeled.

We were alone, the last of her museum colleagues leaving as we arrived. Mom had missed most of the afternoon because I had an unfortunate run-in with a field hockey stick during gym class. I sat on her stool, spinning it slowly in circles, nibbling a sweet orange wedge as she gathered the files she needed for that evening's work session. I was impatient to leave, the way teenagers get with any plans other than their own, but kept busy sharing photos of my three stitches and black eye on Snapchat.

A moment later I realized how quiet the room had gone and glanced up from my phone. Mom stood at the end of her workstation, across from where I sat, staring over my shoulder.

"You good?" I asked, raising one brow, then wincing at the pain. I followed her gaze to the item behind me. Leclerc's *The Child*, and Mom's current project. I couldn't see much of it, the painting draped in protective plastic. "Mom, is everything okay?"

"Did you know all art is made by the dead, Mathilde?"

"Huh?" I remember feeling confused at first, then concerned by her odd question and the flat tone of her voice. "You mean, all the art *here*?"

I glanced around the room then, at the various canvases, thinking about the long-dead artists who had painted them. I got a strange feeling in my stomach and put the rest of the orange down.

"Yes, all this art," she said, a faint smile tugging one corner of her mouth. Her eyes seemed unfocused, and too much of their whites showed. Like they'd rolled back slightly.

Is she having a stroke? I tried to remember what we'd learned in health class about the signs of a stroke but could only bring to mind the acronym FAST, though not what it stood for.

"Every brushstroke, every line, all made by hands that no longer move," Mom continued, one hand rising as though painting strokes into the air. "These artists—they're gone now. But the art remains. Don't you see? The dead speak *through* their paintings."

Something went cold in my center then, and I shivered hard. I slid from the stool and tucked my phone into my sweats' pocket. I was definitely ready to go home.

"Morbid much, Mom?" I heard the slight shake in my voice, tried to hide it with a chuckle. "And you give me a hard time about listening to those true crime podcasts."

But Mom remained rooted in place, her eyes back on the Leclerc. "My job, Mathilde, is to bring these paintings to life. Removing imperfections left by time, the elements. Repairing accidents. Cleaning others' mistakes. But this work, it can . . ." She shook her head, then sighed.

The chill left my center, crawled up my spine. My hands were in tight knots and a headache was forming behind my eyes. Mom lowered her voice to a near whisper, and I had the bizarre thought it was so the paintings wouldn't hear her.

"These canvases hold more than just the artists' skill and vision. Sometimes they carry fragments of the artists themselves. Their beliefs, their fears . . . even their obsessions. When we conserve them, we breathe life back into those fragments. And sometimes—" Mom hesitated. My heart fluttered.

"Sometimes what?" I croaked out.

There was a loud bang against the windowpane. Gasp-worthy loud. Left behind, a tiny circle of soft, downy white feathers on the glass. *A bird hit the window,* I thought. *It's only a bird.* I wondered if it was still alive but didn't want to look outside to find it lying dead on the ground.

The bird striking the window seemed to shake Mom out of her bizarre reverie, and she cocked her head at me. "What, honey?"

I muttered in annoyance, though it was really a cover for how rattled I felt. "Can we just go?"

"Yes, I think I have everything I need." Mom thumbed through her file folders, nodded, smiled. "How's the head?"

Touching the bandaged spot I said, "I have a headache."

With a final glance around, Mom tucked her files under her arm. She turned out the lights and held the door, waiting for me to go first so she could engage the keypad's lock.

But right before I stepped out I heard something—a dull swish, or sweep. It was rhythmic, every two seconds or so, and filled the room with an echo.

"Do you hear that?" I asked. I held my breath, listening. *Swish . . . sweep . . . swish . . .*

It sounded familiar, and yet at the same time eerily unnatural.

"I don't hear anything," Mom finally said. "Maybe it's that headache?"

"Maybe," I replied, without conviction.

Clementine has been sick for two days. Vomiting, fever, zero energy. The sort of illness that takes a bright-eyed, bouncing seven-year-old and reduces her to a pale, limp, sad-sack version of herself. We set her watch to rest mode, which is recommended during illness.

I take one day off work, Wyatt the other, and Shelby fills in the gaps—laundry, warming up soup, mixing cups of electrolyte drinks. It's nice to have a third set of hands on days like these, and I know Shelby likes being useful.

Kat, when I send her and Maeve a note that I won't be at class, tells us three of her four are coming out of a fever cycle. She proudly declares that she and the baby remained healthy, citing her iron-clad immune system thanks to years of marinating in the cesspool of school germs, and breastfeeding. Double up on your zinc and vitamin C, she says, before wishing Clementine well. A gift card for takeout arrives in my inbox about fifteen minutes later from Kat and Nick, which we put to good use that evening.

On day three Clementine wakes up hungry, and I'm relieved. Her fever is gone, her energy back with no signs she was ill, except for a slight hollowing in her cheeks. You don't realize the relief of having a well child until you've had days with a sick one.

Then, on day four, I wake up and immediately know something is off. Specifically, my stomach.

I bolt to the washroom. It comes on so fast, so furiously, that by the time Wyatt gets out of bed I've already flushed the toilet and am spreading paste on my toothbrush.

"You okay?" He comes into our small bathroom, rubbing the sleep out of his eyes. He sets his other hand against my back and rubs gently.

I spit out the toothpaste, another wave of nausea cresting that thankfully doesn't escalate. "Think I caught Clem's crud."

"Back to bed," Wyatt says, shushing me when I protest that I'm too busy for that luxury. "I'll bring you some ginger tea and toast."

I murmur my thanks and oblige, not having the energy to do much else. The nausea is better, but the fatigue is brutal.

Once in bed I click "health check" on my watch, waiting the few seconds for the data to load. Temperature: 97.5 degrees, the screen reads. Resting heart rate: 65 bpm. Oxygen saturation: 98%.

Everything looks normal, my heart rate only slightly elevated. I frown, wondering how I can be so sick with decent vitals. I tap the button to take a second reading. The numbers come out essentially the same. I fall back asleep before Wyatt returns, but wake a couple of hours later to find breakfast left on my nightstand, the tea cold, a heart-shaped dollop of strawberry jam congealed on the toast.

The following day begins much the same way. Shocked awake by a cold sweat and impossible-to-ignore nausea. Throwing up so hard a few tiny blood vessels break around my eyes.

Wyatt and I go through the routine again. Back to bed, I'll get you tea and dry toast, but this time he adds, Think you should make an appointment?

No. I'm fine. The virus working its way through, I'm sure I'll be better tomorrow. Begrudgingly staying in my pajamas, in bed, trying desperately to keep the toast and tea down. Thank goodness for

Shelby, who takes over, helping Clementine before and after school, handling meal preparation, the house tidying. The tedious daily tasks that must be done but that bring no gold star upon completion.

There's never a good time to get sick, but I'm on the cusp of some exciting revelations with the Leclerc. I've recently finished cleaning the bottom half of the painting, and the composition is finally coming through. The subject appears to be female: curved hip, pinched-in waist, a soft pouch of belly below the navel. She's nude from what I can tell so far, though it's still early days. The thought of not being able to work on it again today makes me antsy. However, no one else needs this stomach bug.

After the third morning of this routine—waking up and throwing up—Wyatt insists I make a doctor's appointment.

"But I'm mostly fine," I protest, flushing the toilet. And I (mostly) am, minus the nausea. My temperature, heart rate, oxygen levels, have all stayed steady and normal.

Wyatt raises an eyebrow, one half of his face still covered in shaving cream, the other side smooth and bare.

"Projectile vomiting at six thirty in the morning shouldn't be called 'fine,' Tilly," he says, going back to shaving the other side of his face once he's sure I'm okay. He tugs the skin taut, and his tongue presses into the side of his cheek, helping to direct the blade neatly over his skin.

I sit on the now-closed toilet lid, waiting for him to finish with the sink so I can brush my teeth. My mouth tastes bitter, and there's a cloying thickness at the back of my throat.

"Make an appointment," Wyatt says, tapping his razor against the side of the sink to release the foam and fine hairs. The metallic clang echoes in our bathroom. He catches my eyes in the mirror. "Today."

With a grumble that I will, I head back to bed. Sliding on my watch, I check my health stats again; it gives three short beeps announcing the data.

"What does it say?" Wyatt calls out.

"Normal." I should be glad, but I'm frustrated. I sigh. "Everything is normal."

As I say it, I realize what *isn't* normal.

My watch. It hasn't buzzed me in days. Wait . . . it hasn't buzzed me in a couple of weeks, now that I think about it. How am I only noticing this now?

"I think something's wrong with my watch."

Frowning, I touch the watch face, scrolling through the menu. The notifications icon has a slash through it. "Oh, for the love of all things," I mutter, tapping the icon to turn the notifications on.

"What's wrong?" Wyatt asks, coming into the bedroom, wiping a towel across his chin and cheeks.

"I can't believe it," I say. "I turned off my notifications. When I was working. I didn't want the distraction, but I forgot to turn them back on."

A moment later my watch starts buzzing. Notification after notification loads onto the screen. My eyes scan the list, starting from the oldest to the most recent.

Time for breath work, Tilly?

Your heart rate is slightly above normal range. Time for breath work, Tilly?

Your basal temperature is elevated. How are you feeling?

You hit your sleep goal again. Well done!

Your resting heart rate is higher than normal. Time for breath work, Tilly?

And then . . .

Your period is due in 24 hours, Tilly.

Your period is 1 day late. Tap to record your period.

Your period is 2 days late. Tap to record your period.

Your period is 3 days late. Tap to record your period.

This morning's notification:

Your period is 7 days late. Please take a pregnancy test, Tilly!

I think I might throw up again, but instead I start crying.

Wyatt, getting dressed, stops midway through pulling on his pants, alarm on his face. "What's going on?" he asks. "Are you okay?"

I'm crying so hard I can't speak, so I hold out my watch, my other hand covering my mouth. Wyatt's khakis pool around his ankles, and he kicks them off hurriedly. His fingers encircle my wrist as he turns my watch, reading the most recent notification.

"Son of a gun," he says, crouching in front of me. I take my hand from my mouth. The shock on his face matches my own. "Tilly . . . are you pregnant?"

After more than four years of trying, I am, in fact, pregnant.

"How?" is the question, because we had sex twice last month, and only once during the "high fertility" days noted in our joint calendar. I had my notifications turned off so had no idea what my basal temperature was. No clue when I ovulated. The calendar is based on my cycle, my watch a critical partner to keep things updated in real time.

I'm happy, though full of nervous energy and deeply felt fear. After losing Poppy, I find it impossible to trust that being pregnant means staying pregnant. Wyatt, on the other hand, is ecstatic. It's not that he didn't grieve alongside me, or experience the disappointment every month since when my period arrived. How do you explain to someone who doesn't have a uterus what it's like to go through the routine of physical loss every month?

Unexplained secondary fertility was my official diagnosis, coming two years after Poppy was born at almost twenty-nine weeks, still like a doll, covered in soft down. Her actual arrival so much quieter than the chaos, agony, and panic that preceded it. It was unnatural to have such silence at birth, and I'll never forget the awful stillness of the hospital room when I delivered her. Of holding her in a soft pink blanket, willing her to move even as I knew she never would. I had no risk factors, except for slightly elevated blood pressure, which we were assured was unrelated. We were never given an official reason for my early-term labor. Simply told, "Sometimes there's no answer." That's the sort of thing that can make a person go mad.

"This is good news, Tilly," Wyatt reminds me about an hour later, as I sit on our bed, holding the pregnancy test, which is undeniably positive ("Pregnant—5–6 weeks"). I've stopped crying now, am in a state of disbelief.

"Is it, though?" I ask, my voice catching. "Oh my god. *We had wine the other night.*"

"One glass. It's fine." He smiles at me, the front of his hair flopping over his forehead. He hasn't yet put hair product in. I like shaggy Wyatt—it reminds me of when we met, back when we were in our mid-twenties. Me training under Cecil at the Art Gallery of Ontario in Toronto, Wyatt in town for a job interview. His hair was even longer back then, and I remember running my hand through its silkiness the first night we made out, which also happened to be the night we met. At a hotel bar downtown that served the best chicken wings, and dill pickle ranch dip to die for. Back when wings still came from farmed chickens and not the lab, back when business travel was normal and pandemics were theoretical possibilities.

"Now you need to make a doctor's appointment," he says. I nod, gulping back a sob.

Wyatt glances at his watch, gives a frustrated sigh. "I have to go, babe. Are you okay?" Again, I nod. Wyatt kisses me deeply, twice, and I try to absorb his sense of optimism.

"Wait—don't tell your mom or Clem, okay?" I clutch his hand to prevent him from pulling away. "Or anyone else. Until we get confirmation. Make sure everything is fine."

Wyatt tilts my chin, holds my gaze. "Everything *is* fine. I'll make sure of it."

I smile, focusing on *everything is fine*. Only later do I revisit his declaration of *I'll make sure of it* and feel something akin to ire at my exclusion. In the moment, however, I'm grateful for his sense of control and decide I'll borrow from that confidence.

Everything is fine. *We'll* make sure of it.

I break my own request to keep the news between us, calling Maeve the next morning from a bathroom stall at GIA. I'm already crying when she picks up. When she asks, "Tilly, what's wrong?" I cry even harder. Soon I'm a mess, hiccupping and gulping too much air, and I can't get my breath and my ability to speak aligned. I'm mortified at the idea that someone might walk in and hope my coworkers are busy with coffee and start-of-day chitchat.

Maeve shifts into therapist mode, her voice firm but soothing. "Tilly, I want you to breathe with me. Let's do it together. In for four . . . hold . . ." I'm trying to hold the breath but a ragged hiccup breaks through.

"Now out for a slow count of four, through your mouth. Picture the beach. It's sunny. There's a rainbow. You can smell the salt of the ocean and the sand is warm between your toes. You are content, and you are safe." After another round of this I've stopped crying, have better control over my diaphragm. The bathroom thankfully remains empty.

"Now, tell me, what's going on?" Maeve asks.

It's almost nine, and she has clients soon. I get right to it. "I'm pregnant."

There's a brief pause, and then: "Wow, Tilly . . . Okay, and how do you feel about that?"

By her controlled tone and question I know I'm still talking with therapist Maeve. I wish friend Maeve would hop on the line, with a boisterous *WHAT?! Congratulations! This is the very best news!*

"I'm shocked, thrilled, sad because of what had to happen for *this* to happen . . ." *My sweet Poppy.* "Also, I'm terrified. All of it at once, which is overwhelming."

I reach for a tissue to wipe my eyes. "Maeve, I have no idea how this happened. Honestly, how did this happen?"

At this she laughs. "I am certain you have some idea, but I understand what you mean." And she does, because she's been with me through the years of heartbreaking infertility.

To be honest, I was content with only Clementine. I didn't initially yearn for motherhood the way other women seem to, at least not when I was younger. Maybe it was because of my own upbringing. My mother was honest about how splitting oneself into parts isn't easy. But after we lost Poppy everything changed. I became obsessed with the sense of the incompleteness of our family, as well as my inability to fix it.

"Tilly, my first client just arrived, but this is great news for you and Wyatt, my friend," Maeve says.

I smile through a fresh wave of tears. "It *is* great news. Oh, and we haven't told anyone else yet, so maybe pretend like we never had this conversation?"

"My lips are sealed, but let me know when you're ready to shout it out, and we'll plan a dinner or something. To celebrate properly. Okay?"

"Okay," I reply.

Love you, and then *love you too, Tilly—I'll call you later.* I hang up, flushing the toilet even though I didn't use it. In the mirror above the sink my eyes are bloodshot, my face blotchy.

Allergies—must be a high pollen day—and I forgot my antihistamine, I tell Isla when she asks if I'm all right. I decline the small white pill she offers, saying *It's already getting better, but thanks anyway.*

I find the first sliver of fingernail a few inches above the subject's navel.

A tiny half crescent moon, a deep red hue that is almost black, embedded in the paint layer. At first I'm not sure what it is, the round of it so precise, until I maneuver the benchwork SEM into place—directly above the crescent—to get a better look.

Part of my preparation for this conservation was familiarizing myself with the more common elements Leclerc used in her art. I viewed countless slides of microscope-enhanced human skin, blood, bone fragments, and hair. This nail sliver, once magnified, reminds me of the finely knit pattern of a natural sea sponge. Or the split antlers Stanley loves to chew—porous, with intricately connected chambers, similar to how a bone looks after it bleaches in the sun.

There's a flutter inside my belly. It's excitement, as I'm now one hundred percent certain this is the final Leclerc piece, but it's so similar to quickening I have to remind myself it's too early for that yet.

I roll my stool over to the small desk, to jot down a few notes about the fingernail, when I hear something behind me. A wet pulling away, like a suction cup being dragged off shower tiles. I turn on the stool, toward the strange sound. Discomfited, I take in the space around me.

Everything seems to be in place. Except then I glance at the painting . . . and I see it. Some sort of thin ropelike thing, jutting out from the bubbled black paint above my most recent work area.

What is that?

I shiver, a chill reaching the bare skin of my neck under my zero-contamination suit. I stand, walk over to the painting. My eyes widen as I try to understand *what* I'm seeing.

The three-inch dangling tendril isn't one, singular rope—there are multiple strands, some finer than others, tangled together. I'm reminded of Clementine's garden project from last year, when she grew an avocado plant from a pit. The sinewy roots that sprang from the pit, reaching down into the glass jar of water, had a similar look to these tendrils.

I slowly reach out a gloved finger to touch the nearest strand. Letting it rest on my finger, I shift closer, squinting to get a better look. The strand is brittle and dry, like a twig separated from its living branch. It shouldn't float like it does, flaccid and soft. It lacks the pliancy to do so.

"What the hell?" I murmur, tilting my head to the side to try to follow the strand up through the damage. The soot remains thick, and I can't find where the strand begins. I should get the SEM, to see what this thing looks like magnified. But before I can, the strand . . . *retreats.* Pulling away from my finger and back toward the canvas, like a fishing line being reeled in. So slowly it takes a moment to understand this is real and not my eyes playing tricks on me.

I blink only once, and the tendril is swallowed into the painting.

Like it was never there.

"Tell me again," Cecil says, patience infusing both tone and expression. I'm at my workstation now, the rest of the lab quiet and empty, Room D secured for the evening. My fingerprint is the only way to unlock the door, so I know the painting won't be disturbed.

I video call Cecil right after the tendril reintegrates into the paint, leaving no trace behind. Part of me believes my eyes *were* playing tricks on me. Some sort of pregnancy-related spell. The demands of the fetus overriding my brain, or something. But I don't tell Cecil I'm pregnant—almost seven weeks now. I haven't told anyone yet, except for Maeve.

"I was taking a few notes when I heard this *sound*. Like something was being suctioned? When I looked back at the canvas, there was this . . . thing sticking out from the middle of the painting, right above the cleaning line. It looked similar to a bundle of plant roots."

"Did you get it under the SEM?" Cecil asks.

"No," I reply. "I was about to and then it disappeared."

"Disappeared? Hmm. And no one else has been in there? Nothing has contaminated the room? An errant thread from your lab coat, perhaps?"

I shake my head. "Nothing I can think of. I'm the only one who has access, and I've been wearing the protocol suit." The anti-contamination suits left over from MorA have been repurposed in a variety of ways, worn by medical staff, workers in the protein-growing labs, and conservators at GIA.

He scratches his white-bearded chin, leans back in his chair. "So it's likely some sort of fiber or natural material that's native to the painting," Cecil says. I don't remind him that I saw it move, then vanish—

"And when it comes to Charlotte Leclerc, that means it could be anything, including something biological."

I nod, a strange feeling settling into my stomach, like I drank a glass of something bubbly too fast. I don't want to think of the wet suction sound, but it becomes intrusive and my mouth fills with saliva. My watch taps me, my heart rate rising along with the nausea.

"I should sign off, Cecil. But I'll send you the video feed, and then we can regroup. Sound good?"

We exchange goodbyes. I hit "end call" on my tablet, then quickly reach for the wastepaper basket under my desk before being violently sick into it.

The nausea is odd. I had morning sickness with both Clementine and Poppy, for the first eleven weeks, after which it disappeared seemingly overnight. I would throw up once, first thing, and then feel great for the rest of the day. This time is different. It comes on at work—typically at the end of the day, immediately after my conservation sessions—with little warning. A brief moment of that bubbly stomach feeling and then BAM. I've started carrying emesis bags in my pockets.

"It's probably a boy," Shelby says, when Wyatt and I tell her about the pregnancy, the evening after our first ultrasound. We'll wait a touch longer to tell Clementine. "Because you feel so different this time. That's my guess."

Everything in me tells me I'm carrying a girl. *Mother's intuition*, I surmise. Or perhaps it's merely fervent wishing; the universe rectifying a wrong. Regardless, the sickness is different, and different isn't reassuring.

Later, after Clementine is in bed and Shelby and Wyatt are watching a movie, I retreat to my studio to review the work session's video. I remain troubled by the errant fiber, or whatever floated up from the painting's surface. Not only because of its presence, but also because of its just-as-sudden absence.

I've moved the bioluminescent fig plant into my studio because the glow of it was too bright for our bedroom. The studio is dark except for the low light of the fig leaves, and I slide in earbuds and open my tablet. Sitting at the small desk, I press play, zooming in on the painting—getting as tight as I can to the area where the strand appeared. I switch my glasses to the low-light, infrared setting.

I can't see myself on the screen, as I'm off to the side and out of frame. There's no sound, thankfully, so I don't hear the suctioning that made me turn in the first place. That made me vomit after I hung up with Cecil. But as I zone in on the canvas, I see the tendril release and jut out from the painting—gently swaying. Right above the subject's waist. Hitting pause, I zoom in again, but it doesn't provide a clearer view. So I drop the image into GIA's AI program. The tendril is magnified, but it's too pixelated for the program to identify.

Frustrated, I push back from my desk, the way I would if trying to get a wider view of an impressionist painting, changing my perspective until the shapes and colors become a familiar pattern or figure. It doesn't help. I'm no closer to understanding what released from the painting. Also, I blocked the camera when I hunched over the canvas, not thinking about the recording at the time. Because of this I don't see the tendril retreat on the video.

I keep trying different angles until my eyes burn from the strain. I need to go to bed. Wyatt called more than an hour ago, and my watch has been buzzing me every fifteen minutes, reminding me that my minimum seven hours of sleep goal is at risk. At this point I'll only get six, maybe less if I don't fall asleep right away.

I'm so focused on the screen, on those pixelated images, the flicker in light barely registers. Until it happens again, drawing my focus away from the screen. Then one side of my fig plant shifts strangely—a section of leaves darkening, as though shadowed. I pause, staring at the plant, but the glow is restored. *Tired eyes,* I deduce, powering down the tablet before heading to bed.

If I had looked closer, I might have seen the southern flannel moth caterpillar, covered in beige down like a teardrop-shaped toupee, nibbling the edge of a leaf. Southern flannel moth caterpillars were native to Georgia but have been mostly eradicated to protect the oak trees—their food of choice. The caterpillars are also highly venomous, and if touched the soft hairs leave spikes in the skin, causing headaches, nausea, shocklike symptoms. *Good riddance*, Shelby said when the news reported their diminished population.

By the time this southern flannel caterpillar transforms into a moth, I'll have solved the mystery of the floating tendril. Things that turn out to be much more ominous than they sound.

The fetus needs me to eat every couple of hours.

If I do, the nausea stays away. I've replaced the emesis bags with snacks and haven't had any incidents since. I feel mostly healthy and energetic.

"This agrees with you," Wyatt says, hugging me from behind while I brush my teeth. I lean into him as he nuzzles into my neck. "Can I tell you you're glowing without you rolling your eyes?"

"You can," I say, through a mouthful of toothpaste. I spit and rinse, then pull my nightshirt over my head. I'm wearing nothing underneath, and raise an eyebrow in the mirror as I bend forward, my forearms resting on the countertop. My libido is back with a vengeance too.

Wyatt, grinning, drops his pajama pants and presses into me from behind, his hands and fingers roaming gently.

He knows what I like after all these years. It's been a long time since we've enjoyed each other without the burden of an outcome. The sex is good, great even, and I'm not quiet when I come. Wyatt loves it when I vocalize how much I'm enjoying myself, but with Clementine and Shelby in the house, I usually muffle any sounds with my pillow.

"I'll say it again," Wyatt whispers in my ear, still inside me. I shiver as his lips and warm breath caress my sensitive skin. I'm drenched in sweat, my forearms slipping on the bathroom counter. "This agrees with you."

I smile at him in the mirror, and he closes his gorgeous, long-lashed blue eyes, which I hope the baby inherits, before moving his lips back to my neck.

Are you both still good for Saturday night? I ask Maeve and Kat at our weekly breath work class. Wyatt suggested we have my friends and their significant others over for a belated birthday dinner celebration. It can be hard to get our whole group together, between work and kids and life, but we try every few months. My friends say they're looking forward to it and ask what they can bring. *Just yourselves. Wyatt's handling things. I don't even know what the plan is!*

Wyatt surprises me with a dinner reservation for our party of six at Ciel de Terre, a French restaurant in the city I've been dying to try, with a monthslong waitlist. Dale and Curtis know the owner, as Curtis used to work with her, and apparently pulled a string or two.

"We should celebrate properly, Tilly, with everyone who loves you," Wyatt says when I protest the cost. Going out for dinner to a place like Ciel de Terre is not a regular line item in our budget. "You're worth it."

Clementine is dramatically devastated to not be invited. "But I've never been to Ciel de Terre!" she exclaims, as Wyatt and I are getting ready to leave.

"Briar has already been *two times*." She holds up two fingers, pouting for good measure. Her petulance reminds me we are not far from the preteen phase.

"Well, I'm thirty-nine and a grown-up, and I've never been either," I reply, setting my purse over my shoulder.

"Me neither," Wyatt adds. Shelby suggests a girls' night in, with caramel popcorn and whatever movie Clementine wishes, and then Wyatt and I head out.

On the train into the city I make him promise this is only about my birthday—I'm not ready to share the pregnancy news yet—and he assures me that's all this is. I send Dale a note of thanks, and he quickly responds with You're welcome! Curtis says you have to get the tarte tatin. Nonnegotiable. I promise I will.

Like many restaurants, Ciel de Terre uses augmented reality to enhance the dining experience. Tonight Wyatt has requested a "Musée d'Orsay" table, as a nod to my love of the famed Parisian gallery. I once visited Paris with my mother when I was eleven; she had to accompany a painting being loaned from Toronto's museum to the Musée d'Orsay. As the gallery's senior conservator, she was responsible for the safety and well-being of the art, from packaging it for travel to its installation in the Parisian exhibit.

I roamed the gallery alone, my mother occupied with work, in awe of the art housed in the beautiful old train station. Mesmerized, I spent hours with Edgar Degas's statue *Petite danseuse de quatorze ans*, Claude Monet's *Femme à l'ombrelle tournée vers la droite*, Auguste Renoir's *Bal du moulin de la Galette*, Vincent van Gogh's *Vaches dans un pré*. My favorite was a piece titled *Fleurs étranges*, by French symbolist artist Odilon Redon. By the day's end I told my mom I wished to live at the Musée d'Orsay, and she laughed, her Parisian colleague stating, "Telle mère, telle fille." *Like mother, like daughter.*

"A toast to my beautiful wife and another year around the sun," Wyatt starts, holding up a glass of deep-burgundy Bordeaux. He's ordered two bottles for the table. I'm having nonalcoholic champagne, which is delightful and barely distinguishable from the real thing.

Everyone raises a glass.

"Everything that's good in my life is because of you. You've made my dreams come true, and you've done it with such strength, determination, and grace," Wyatt continues.

I tear up, emotion welling inside me. With a small laugh I wipe at my eyes with the napkin Kat hands me, embarrassed by the display even among dear friends.

"To Tilly," Nick adds. "Happy birthday, and *happy baby*!" He winks at me, claps Wyatt on the back with his other hand. There's a moment of surprised silence, and then everyone is talking at once at the unexpected reveal.

Happy birthday, happy baby! they repeat, clinking glasses around the table, offering me and Wyatt congratulations. I don't know what to do with my face, my anger all-consuming and surely darkening my expression. I can't look at Wyatt, my hand holding the champagne glass quivering, as I *clink, clink, clink.* I only manage a smile when Maeve's hand reaches my leg under the table, giving a small squeeze of support.

"I'm going to bring you the ring myself," Nick says between bites of his mile-high mille-feuille dessert, the custard dotted with bright red raspberries.

"What a great idea," Kat says, slicing her fork into the dessert they're sharing.

My insides constrict at the mention of the ring. I don't tell them I haven't yet signed up for MotherWise. *This week, I promise,* I told Wyatt when he brought it up, again. How can I explain the superstition that has gripped me? With Poppy, once my perspective shifted on the pregnancy, I couldn't wait to make that call. This time . . . whenever I think about MotherWise I hesitate. I'm not ready, and besides, there's no rush. I technically have until thirty weeks to sign up.

"That's a long way away," I say to Nick, taking another bite of the tarte tatin even though I'm full. The caramelized apples are perfectly spiced, nestled into a buttery crust that melts in my mouth. Wyatt catches my eye, and I can't read his face. Later, he'll confess he told Nick when they played pickleball the day after the positive test, unable to hold back his excitement. My anger lessens, because I also told Maeve. It isn't only my news to share, though I wish Wyatt had asked Nick to use discretion. It is decidedly not *his* news to share.

"It will be here before we know it," Wyatt says, and Kat murmurs how true that is. I try to swallow the tarte tatin, the bite glomming in my throat.

"You're catching up to us, Tilly," Nick says. "But we're not done yet, so best keep at it, you two." Kat smiles in a way that makes me wonder if there's more to that comment.

"I'd love three. Maybe even four," Wyatt replies. My tepid smile wanes, for this should be our third baby. *Why does it feel like I'm the only one who remembers that?*

"Who wouldn't?" Nick says, going back to his dessert.

"Me. I wouldn't." Jenn raises one hand and sips her coffee. She often pushes Nick on this topic whenever we all get together. They are polarized on the program, and for Jenn, the main issue comes down to overreach. "The government shouldn't be this involved with our uteruses" is a statement she has made more than once.

"Well, luckily you're in the minority, Jenn," Nick says, forking an icing-sugar-dusted raspberry before shifting the conversation back to me. "We're working on more incentives, including a six-month extension for NourishBoxes. It will be up and running soon—well before you deliver, Tilly. People are excited."

"Another six months is a big deal. Nick's been instrumental in getting it to this point," Kat says, glancing at her husband. They exchange a smile before she turns back my way. "I've loved the boxes, personally. And the program. Just wait, Tilly. You'll see."

"You can dress it up in whatever costume you want, Nick, or add a dozen new incentives, but it's still about control," Jenn says. "We should all stay vigilant, if you ask me. These things have a way of snowballing."

Nick sighs quietly, and I see Kat nudge him gently. The waiter arrives then to check in on dessert and coffee refills, thankfully inserting a break in the conversation before it can escalate.

"He makes it so easy," Jenn whispers my way, after Maeve mouths—for Kat's sake, and also probably mine—for her partner to leave it be. She smiles then. "But fine. I can play nice. It *is* your birthday, and I love you."

Jenn is petite with fiery red hair, which also matches her personality. I adore Maeve's partner of three years, finding her both refreshingly different from many of my women friends, as well as incredibly empathetic. *She's the ride-or-die sort*, Maeve told me after her first few dates with Jenn had gone well. *You know that's my love language.*

For this reason alone Jenn will always get a pass with me, even when she's needling Nick at my birthday dinner. I don't disagree with her take on MotherWise, but I also know I'm biased, as a newly pregnant mother. The perks *are* tantalizing, and the benefits hard to ignore.

I also know that Nick is a wonderful husband to Kat and father to their kids, and that she's as happy in her marriage and family as one can be. Not to mention, my husband values his long friendship with Nick. Both reasons I typically give Nick a pass for his insensitivity and at times clueless remarks.

"Jenn, you keep telling us you never want kids, but how does the saying go?" Nick asks, scraping his fork through a swirl of custard on the plate. He grins at Jenn. "Thou doth protest too much."

"'The lady doth protest too much, methinks,'" Kat says. "From *Hamlet*. That's the line."

She sips her water before giving Nick a pointed look. "Let's leave Dr. Jenn be, babe. She's busy saving the world."

"So are you, Kitty-Kat. One precious baby at a time." Nick kisses his wife's cheek. Her four gold rings shine brightly against her neck.

At our second ultrasound with Dr. Laura Fillia, my ob-gyn, I watch the fluttering heartbeat on the screen. *Please keep going, please keep going, please keep going,* I think. Dr. Fillia, who knows my history, is quick to tell us everything looks "perfect—right on track, Mom and Dad."

Wyatt takes a clip of the video where the fetus appears to be waving, adds a text tag that reads, "Hi, Mommy!," and sends it to me later with a simple Love You, We've Got This message. I feel the warmest of glows for my husband and our little bundle. That afternoon I disclose the pregnancy to GIA's HR department, my colleagues, and Cecil. Luckily the lab already has high-level health-and-safety procedures in place, so nothing has to change in terms of the conservation.

Wyatt's not only excited but also impatient for me to register for MotherWise. He keeps referencing Nick's comments about the improved benefits and perks. I try, and fail, to find a way to explain my anxiety about making that call. Superstition trumps logic, it seems.

"You'll have on-call, top-of-the-line medical care at your fingertips, twenty-four seven, Tilly," he says. I'm grateful he's spared me from having to speak the worry out loud. "And don't forget the Nourish-Boxes, which Nick said are worth hundreds of dollars a month."

Still, I'm not ready. "Give me another week," I tell him. "Then I'll register. Promise."

"Okay, one more week," Wyatt replies. I appreciate his patience with me, and tell him so.

"How are you feeling?" I ask Kat as we walk down York Street, which is shaded by both the oak trees and today's cloud cover. I miss the changing seasons back home. When the air begins to crisp and the maples are crowned with vibrant red, orange, and yellow leaves. Here in Savannah it's still summertime warm this time of year, everything green and lush.

"Decent," Kat replies, holding a decaffeinated iced tea in one hand and a bright red apple in the other. Her stroller is on hands-free mode, seven-month-old Rachael napping as we walk. "As long as I keep food in my stomach, I'm okay." She bites into the apple, the crunch of it audible.

I was right to wonder at my birthday dinner if she and Nick had news. She'd waited a few days to tell me, not wanting to shift focus away from my celebration. Our due dates are only one week apart.

"Same here." I had a snack not long before our walk. "I've been craving popcorn. The old movie theater kind, dripping with fake butter. What's funny is that I never liked movie theater popcorn."

"Bet you need sodium." Kat sips her iced tea, the stroller continuing its leisurely pace mere inches ahead of us. "I had a wicked craving for bananas yesterday, and like five minutes later my watch sent me a low-potassium alert. Our bodies know what we need—just have to listen to them. That, and pay attention to this." She raises her arm, showing her watch.

We turn up Abercorn and walk past the Owens-Thomas House,

impressive in stature, the green shutters the identical shade from when I first visited Savannah with Wyatt. The old colonial mansion was featured on our ghost tour and is supposedly home to many spirits. Most notably the Lady in Gray, believed to be the ghost of former owner Margaret Thomas. Like many of the estate homes in downtown Savannah, the Owens-Thomas House has been refurbished. I wonder what happened to the Lady in Gray once the renovations started.

A cool breeze tickles my arms as I stare up at the top-floor windows, the shutters closed against the heat. I have the oddest sensation I'm being watched, despite the shuttered windows. Goose bumps rise on my arms, and I'm about to ask Kat if she felt the breeze, but Rachael has begun to fuss.

"I need to feed her. Let's grab a bench in the square," Kat says. The breeze and goose bumps disappear, and I chide myself for letting my imagination control my nervous system like that. I do a round of box breathing, Kat oblivious, busy with the stroller.

There's plenty of activity today in Oglethorpe Square, with a seniors' group doing tai chi and a gaggle of kids enjoying the splash pad.

We settle onto a bench, and Kat pulls out a mesh breastfeeding sling. "These are life-changing," she says, settling Rachael into the sling. "Ideal position for nursing, gives me my hands back, but cool enough so Rae doesn't overheat."

The baby latches quickly. "MotherWise will send one in your welcome basket. Have you signed up yet?" Her tone is light, but I can tell the question isn't hers alone.

I raise an eyebrow. "Did Wyatt say something?"

Kat smiles, caught. "He chatted with Nick about it." She glances down at Rachael, nursing contentedly. I rest a hand on my mostly flat belly, imagining the two of us sitting here in some months, nursing our newborns together.

"It's best to register early, Tilly. You won't believe all the great stuff you can access now."

"So I've heard," I reply, a band of tightness settling over my stomach. MotherWise was in its infancy when I became pregnant with Poppy. Bare-bones, compared to now. NourishBoxes weren't added until the pilot program's second phase, about a year later. "I'm going to register. Soon."

Kat nods but seems distracted. "Listen, can I talk to you about something?"

I'm concerned by her cautious tone. My shoulders tighten. "Sure. What's up?"

"Have you spoken to Maeve? Like, in the past few days?"

"No." I haven't spoken with Maeve in a week—she's been away with Jenn. "Why?"

"She was weird when I told her Nick and I were expecting again. Like, she seemed happy for me . . . *you're such a good mom, Kat, this is exactly what you and Nick wanted, congratulations* . . . but it seemed put on."

Rachael is in a milk haze, half-asleep at the breast, her cheeks rosy and mouth slightly open. Kat glances down at the baby, smiles, then adjusts her top to cover herself.

"I'm sure she was happy for you," I say. "She's probably tired—you know how much she works."

"I know. I know." Kat sighs.

"Or it might be related to one of her clients? Remember, she spends hours listening to women who desperately want this"—I gesture to Rachael—"and can't have it."

Kat nods. "True. But don't you ever feel judged for wanting to have more kids when you're with her and Jenn?"

She turns toward me. "Also, isn't it strange she's chosen to work in the field she does, with the women she does, when she doesn't want a baby? Or to be a mother?"

I've considered this. Especially after a conversation we had years ago. But I've never asked her outright. It seems one of those things she would offer up if she wanted to.

Besides, if given the choice, I would be conserving original art rather than virtual exhibits, and Wyatt would be designing new buildings versus working on refurbishing already existing ones. We do the work that's available, because bills need to be paid and being idle is not an option. It's more than possible that Maeve does what she does because that's where the opportunities exist.

"I don't know. But it's awkward sometimes," Kat says. "Somehow when I talk about my pregnancies or my kids with her, it's like I'm boring her to tears. As if being a mom—and being able to do so, which of course I'm hugely grateful for—makes me less interesting or something."

"You know that's not true."

"I do! And I'm confident in my decisions," Kat says. "I do wonder . . . maybe Maeve wants kids after all? Maybe Jenn's the one driving that decision?"

"Maybe . . ." Maeve has never once talked about wanting to be a mother. But that doesn't mean it isn't true. "I suppose we can't know for sure."

"I suppose not. Besides, it's none of my business." Kat sets a sleeping Rachael back into the stroller. "Okay, time for a new topic. Something fun."

Baby settled, she sits beside me again. "Are you getting the tattoo?"

I laugh. "You think getting a tracker injected counts as 'fun' on any level?"

Kat laughs as well. "Maybe 'fun' isn't the right word. But it's a quick way to see all is well with the baby. My nervous system is steady as a rock, as you know, but I still like the reassurance of it."

"I haven't decided," I say. "But, as you know, I *do* suffer from anxiety, so maybe I should? I guess you're getting another one, then?"

"Already done. This morning, actually." She shows me the inside of her forearm, where three glossy dots form a small triangle near her wrist crease. The skin is slightly red, the smallest hint of swelling. "Don't overthink it, Tilly. You'll appreciate the peace of mind. Trust me."

After I get home, tucking the few groceries I picked up into the fridge, I decide to register for MotherWise. Kat and Wyatt are right—I'll appreciate the benefits. I'm still unsure about the pregnancy tattoo, though. It isn't mandatory, as long as you're in good health.

"First of all, congratulations on your pregnancy!" the customer service person, Angela, says. I hear the exclamation point in her voice and wonder if it's real or trained. "Secondly, this call is being recorded for quality and educational purposes. May I proceed?"

"Yes, thanks," I reply.

"Excellent. Now, let's see if you're already in our system, Tilly. What's the spelling of your last name?"

"C-R-E-W-S-O-N. But it has been years since—"

"There you are!" The woman's voice is bright and cheery. "Mathilde 'Tilly' Crewson, over on Oglethorpe?"

"Yes, that's me," I say.

"Seems you were last active . . . oh, it has been a few years, I see." Angela's tone changes. I know she's likely looking at my cancellation, and the reason why.

"That's why I wasn't sure if I would . . . still be in the system," I reply, clearing my throat. My watch buzzes. Time for breath work, Tilly?

"We keep all registrants in our database," Angela says. "It's easy to reactivate, but in your case that doesn't seem necessary."

"What doesn't seem necessary?" I hit ignore on my watch.

"You've already been reactivated, Tilly. It looks like this current pregnancy was registered by a Mr. Wyatt Crewson. Is he your husband?"

"Yes, he is." I swallow hard—there's a bad taste in the back of my throat. "Can I ask . . . when did he call to register me?"

"Let's see here . . . yesterday, actually. Is there an issue, Tilly?" Angela's cheeriness has dimmed a couple of degrees.

"No issue. I'm, uh, just surprised. It was on my to-do list, but we must have gotten our wires crossed." So much for Wyatt giving me another week. I'm fuming, though I can't sort out what I'm most angry about.

"Happens more often than you would imagine; everyone is usually so darn excited!" Angela says with a laugh. Cheerful again. "Welcome back to MotherWise, Tilly Crewson and baby. We're thrilled to have both of you."

Initially I rail at Wyatt for registering me without my knowledge. I'm annoyed he went back on his word to give me more time. I'm not sure who I'm most angry with . . . Wyatt? MotherWise? Our pregnancy-obsessed society? Irritated to be fighting about this at all; guilty that my gratitude at this privilege isn't front and center.

"I have a right to the program too, Tilly—this isn't only about you," Wyatt says, at the boil-over point of our argument. He's not wrong. MotherWise has a complementary program for fathers-to-be, offering support groups and workshops.

"I know it isn't!" I shout back. Clementine comes into our room to find out why we're yelling, and that pops the balloon of tension. We apologize for our words, our tone of voice, though I note that Wyatt doesn't apologize for registering me. I let it go, for Clementine's sake.

Resolved to move forward, I text Kat that I registered (I don't share that Wyatt beat me to it), and we sign up for a MotherWise meditation pod class the following evening.

"You're going to love it," she says. "Better than a full night's sleep!"

Wyatt and I share news of the pregnancy the following morning with Clementine, over breakfast, now that my first NourishBox is on its way. She's unfazed but pleased.

"I hope it's a boy," she says. "I'd like a brother. Don't find out, okay? I want it to be a surprise." I don't tell her I'm sure it's a girl, and promise to keep the sex a secret until the baby is born. It's sweet she wants to wait, even though the rest of us will find out in advance.

"You'll be the best big sister ever," I tell her.

The Leclerc conservation is another story. It's tedious and slow-moving. I try not to get frustrated but am on edge as soon as I walk into GIA. The breath ball on the elevator door does little to settle me, and my short-temperedness follows me to my desk.

"How about a hot tea?" Isla asks, right after I snap at her for something unimportant (*Where did the new brushes get moved to, because someone moved them and it wasn't me . . .*). MotherWise has sent a box of supplies to GIA, including an herbal tea meant to enhance the parasympathetic nervous system, specially formulated for working mothers-to-be. Isla has excitedly—kindly—unpacked it for me.

I force my shoulders down. "Tea would be great. And I'm sorry for snapping. I'm in a mood today."

Isla smiles the apology away. "You have every right, Tilly. You're growing a person in there." She gestures to my belly, the barely there bump hidden under my dress. "I can't even imagine what it's like, being pregnant."

She has a look on her face I recognize—delighted anticipation, without a hint of concern.

Isla is only twenty-three. Like so many young people who have yet to be let down by life's travesties, she sees only the upsides of pregnancy, of MotherWise.

"I forget that sometimes. Yes, I am growing a person! No wonder I'm so exhausted and short-tempered." I give her a wry look and she returns a warm smile before heading off to make my tea.

Gathering up my tablet and Luminara glasses, I decide I don't have the patience to wait for the beverage. So I take the long way to Room D, stopping by the kitchen. "Hey, mind if I cancel that tea order? I'm anxious to get started."

"No problem." Isla swiftly dumps the water into the filtration system that will recycle it for later use. I haven't adjusted to how they make tea down here. *In a microwave!* My mom would have shaken her head at this southern quirk. I brought my mom's well-used kettle with me from Toronto when we moved, but it's gathering dust in a high-up cabinet in the kitchen.

I'll pull it down tonight, I think, as I get my suit zipped up and my mask on, clicking it to the highest filtration setting. *I should drink more herbal tea.* I'm lost in thought, placing my fingertip to the lock pad by rote, and so initially don't notice what's different about Room D. I have an unobstructed view thanks to the wall of glass that turns from opaque to see-through when the lock is disengaged, and yet my mind is elsewhere. The door opens with a satisfying click. I step inside the room, then abruptly stop.

The canvas—the final Leclerc—rests on the floor, face down. The protective, air-pocketed cover I place over it at the end of each session rests nearby, deflated.

My gag reflex kicks in, and the mask suctions against my face with the force of my indrawn breath. *This makes no sense.* My brain races to catch up to the overwhelming physical reaction I'm having. I secured the frame anchors myself and check them multiple times during a work session. There's no way the painting simply *fell off* my workbench. Someone other than me must have been in this room. But the lock pad only opens with my fingerprint.

Back in control of my body, I set my things on the table near the door, grab the camera, and move calmly but quickly to the fallen canvas. I crouch, trying to control my breathing. My watch buzzes (heart rate elevated . . . time for breath work, Tilly?) as I snap a few photos to document the scene. Then I stand and walk the perimeter of the painting, stopping now and then to observe different angles. So far it seems fine.

I grasp the top edge of the canvas. Holding my breath, panic deepening, I gently lift it from the ground, leaning it against the workbench.

Okay, it's fine.

I'll have to call someone to help me get it back safely onto the table, but first I scan section after section with trained eyes. It doesn't seem to have sustained any damage.

Crisis managed, my fury builds (*Who was in here, and how did they get in?*). I press the intercom button to call Isla, but she's not at her desk. Next, I call Dale.

"What's up, Tilly?"

I explain the situation as calmly as I can. He's appropriately alarmed at the thought of someone gaining entry to Room D and assures me he'll be right there.

While I wait, I reinflate the cover to place it over the artwork before he arrives. Normally conservators work collaboratively on pieces, but this is a different project. Not to mention the signed NDA, which made it clear the art is to be concealed except when I'm actively working on it. Only Raoul (who is out of town this week), Cecil, and I know what's in this room, and the significance of it. I can't risk it—my fee, and reputation, potentially compromised if anyone else sets eyes on the painting.

I crouch, about to affix the covering, similar to a cushioned, fitted mattress pad, when a flash of movement catches my eye. I pause, cover in hand, and hold my breath, wide-eyed as something emerges from the canvas.

Again, the sickening sound of deep suction. A tendril slips out of the dark layers of soot, appearing to vibrate as it stretches thin, reaching toward me. *Closer, closer*...

I'm rooted in place, not breathing, watching in disbelief. It's identical to what I saw the other night. The tendril quivers, like an inchworm waving in the air as it searches blindly for the next branch. There is a sudden smell of something musky, subtly spicy, acrid. I can't place it, though it's vaguely familiar. Then the thing reaches my containment suit and continues pushing forward. Pressing into the small bulge in my middle, where the fetus nests, with a near-painful pressure.

Like it wants to get inside me.

I wake up two floors below, in our building's medical center.

"Wyatt's on his way," Dale says, his brows knitting together so two lines form between them. He's also smiling cartoonish-wide, clearly forced. His unnatural expression worries me more than the forehead lines.

I try to sit up but am restricted. There's an oxygen cannula in my nostrils. An IV in my arm, delivering fluids. A thin but weighted blanket, used to control temperature, has been placed over much of my body. My dress is on the chair beside the bed, inside out. This bothers me, that it wasn't turned right side out. A physician assistant is at the foot of the bed—a young-looking woman with a blond braid over one shoulder, wearing augmented reality medical glasses.

"Welcome back, Tilly," the PA says. "Lie back. We've got everything under control here." Then she gestures upward with her finger, scrolling the menu of vitals she's tracking with the MedAlert glasses, and I hear heartbeats—one that I can feel, and the other much faster, which I know has to be the fetus's.

"The baby!" My throat is dry and it comes out as a whisper. I realize this is the first time I've referred to the fetus as such.

"Is just fine," the PA says. She turns the bedside monitor toward me and points to the screen. The baby's heart rate and mine are there, running in parallel wavy lines (my rate is 73 beats per minute, the baby's 130).

I settle then, allowing my body to sink deeper into the gurney's mattress. "What happened?"

"I don't know," Dale says, frowning now. "When I got to the room you were passed out on the floor. I had to use the emergency override to get in."

Right. The emergency override program. Whoever had accessed Room D and knocked the canvas off the workbench could have used that fail-safe.

Wyatt rushes in as I'm about to ask Dale if he knows who else used the override in the past twenty-four hours—it would have been logged.

"Babe, are you okay?" He grabs my hand, kisses my knuckles. "What about the plum?"

"Are we doing this again?" I manage a smile. Our MotherWise literature compares the size of the fetus to a fruit, updated week by week. I'm eleven weeks pregnant, and the fetus is apparently about the size of a plum.

"Wow, a plum! We're on our way," Wyatt announced at dinner last night after reading the email. Proudly, as though he was the one growing the baby. It was sweet, if not mildly annoying to hear the royal "we" used. "Lime is next, babe. I'm thinking virgin margaritas to celebrate . . ."

This is also why Clementine is named Clementine. When we had our twelve-week ultrasound, the technician said she was about the size of a clementine orange, and that became her nickname. Then when she was born, it was the only name that fit.

At four weeks a fetus is the size of a poppy seed. I wish I had the chance to tell Poppy how she got her name.

"I'm good. And the plum is too." I shift my eyes to the monitors, Wyatt following my gaze.

"All good, Dad. Measuring eleven weeks, two days," the PA says, giving Wyatt a confident smile. He visibly relaxes, his shoulders dropping, his face loosening.

"All right, okay," he says, returning the PA's smile before turning to me. "You scared the hell out of me. What the heck happened?"

"Dale found me. Guess I passed out?" I shiver, thinking of that wiggling tendril. The way it stretched out, glistening black, straining to get closer and—

"Out cold. Couldn't wake her up, so I called Medical," Dale says, the forehead lines back. My shivering kicks up a notch, but no one seems to notice.

"Thanks, man. Glad you were there." Wyatt claps Dale on the shoulder.

"I'm going to head back up to the lab, give you two some time," Dale says. "And before you ask, Tilly, Room D is secured. The piece is stable—and, no, we didn't take a peek." He's read my mind. "The cover was already on it, so Tony and I set it back on the workbench, all anchors double-checked." Tony is Dale's apprentice.

"Thank you," I reply, before adding, "Wait. You said the cover was on it?"

He nods. "You just worry about getting well, okay?"

"I will, thanks again, Dale. And thank Tony for me," I murmur, as Wyatt walks Dale out of the room to say goodbye. I watch them from my bed, can see they're talking but can't hear anything.

"I don't know how the cover got on it," I say once Wyatt returns. It's disturbing, because the cover was absolutely *not* on the painting when I passed out. If I didn't cover it, and Dale and Tony didn't . . . then who did?

"Cover?" he repeats, but he's distracted. Running his hand through his hair the way he does when he's thinking through a problem. I wonder what he and Dale were discussing.

“Never mind. It’s not important.” I turn to the PA. “So, when can I get out of here?”

“Waiting on some blood work, and then you’re cleared to go. *Home*,” she adds, with some emphasis. “This pregnancy needs to be your number one priority. At least for the next couple of days.”

“Naturally,” Wyatt says, nodding. His mouth is tight when he smiles at me. “Number one priority, right, Tilly?”

I nod and murmur yes, understanding that’s the correct answer. But my thoughts stray back to Room D. To the Leclerc. To the inexplicable tendril I decide to keep to myself for now, at least until I have a reasonable explanation.

A short time later, after I’m discharged and am changing back into my dress, I see something curious on my stomach. A small purplish bruise, dime-size and in the shape of a circle.

That night I dream of Charlotte Leclerc. She’s in a lab coat, covered in luna moths, whose wings beat softly, in unison. We’re in a cold, gray cinder-block room—a single metal gurney in its center.

“Where are we?” I whisper, then notice a disembodied hand on the gurney. Holding a . . . *paintbrush*? Suddenly, the hand comes to life, dipping the bristles into the pool of blood under it. Sinew and skin hang from the stump, flapping with the motion. Disgust fills me, and I recoil.

“Follow me,” Leclerc says, her voice different from what I expect. Low and deep, but crystal clear. I’m grateful to follow her, to leave the macabre hand behind.

With a single finger she beckons, down a long, dark hallway lined with steel doors, each bearing a symbol. A one-handed clock. A broken matchstick. A tipped-over hourglass. Then a shattered mirror. When I look into it, my eyes go wide. The shriek burns my throat but is halted at my lips, which are curved into a smile. The moths flutter chaotically, a stomach-churning kaleidoscope in the fragmented mirror. A metal name tag is pinned on my white lab coat, iridescent in the darkness. DR. CHARLOTTE LECLERC.

"Come out, come out, wherever you are," this image of me says. "We've been waiting."

Who's been waiting? For what? My mind screams, but my face—Charlotte's face—bears no sign of alarm.

There's a sudden pressure behind my eye, dull but relentless. I blink, then press my fingers against it. Something's tickling my eyelid from the inside, pushing into my fingers. Slowly, I let my hand drop as a tendril—*the tendril*—pulses from the inner corner of my eye. Making the white sclera bulge as it resists. The tendril stretches farther, as though reaching toward the mirror, about to make contact and—

My watch wakes me up, buzzing due to my sudden elevation in heart rate. I rip it off my wrist. My throat burns, like I have a bad case of strep. Swallowing convulsively, I force myself to breathe deeply through my nose. *It's just a dream, Tilly. Just a dream.* Eventually I fall back asleep.

By the next morning—a Saturday—I'm exhausted from my sleepless night, but the bruise has faded to a barely noticeable yellow dot the size of a pea. By midday, around the same time my first NourishBox arrives, it has entirely disappeared. I'm glad, because that bruise unnerved me. Obviously enough to cause a nightmare, whose terror and details have been somewhat neutralized by the daylight.

The experience of the tendril has similarly dimmed. Still, lingering questions—my pregnancy, my mental state, the oddities of Charlotte Leclerc's paintings—haunt me, resisting logic. I want to believe it a delusion, brought on by my supposed dehydration (yes, I know the recommendation is one cup of caffeinated coffee per day), which led to me passing out. Except there *was* a mark left behind, even if it's now gone.

My watch alerts me to the delivery I've been waiting for. I'm quick to open the front door, an overwhelming sense of anxiousness that if I don't hurry someone might take it away.

The white box, with the sunshine-yellow font, sits outside my front door. Waiting for *me*—I can see my name printed on the label. At the same moment the neighbor's door opens. It's Becca—she's quite pregnant now, her stomach like a bowling ball inside the fabric of her dress. With some difficultly she bends, trying to pick up her own NourishBox. She hasn't noticed me yet and is grunting with the effort.

"Becca, hey!" I walk over, enjoying the ease with which I can still move about. "Let me get that for you."

I am supposed to be resting, as per doctor's orders. Not doing anything strenuous for forty-eight hours. But being a good neighbor is important, and besides, I feel normal.

Crouching, only a slightly restrictive pressure of my waistband against my stomach, I pick up Becca's NourishBox.

"Thank you, Tilly. You're a sweetheart." She then sees what's on my doorstep, and her mouth forms into an O shape. Swatting playfully at my arm, Becca grins. "Congratulations are in order, I see. Wyatt must be thrilled!"

"He is. We are." This is the narrative that plays out these days, if a pregnancy occurs: be sure the dad gets recognized for his efforts.

"Come on in for a minute. Can I get you anything? Tea?"

Back home if someone offered me tea it would be piping hot and unsweetened. Here it's cold and, in my experience, sugary enough to make your teeth ache.

"I'm good, thank you," I reply, impatient to get back to my NourishBox. "Let me bring this inside for you, though."

Becca's home is similar in layout to ours, with a central kitchen and a vertical vegetable garden, a family room to one side of the kitchen, and a small dining room to the other. A main difference is the color—our walls are painted a pale blue, Becca's a soft beige. The bedrooms are all on the second and third levels, depending on the family's needs. My studio will likely become Clementine's room after this baby is born. I'll miss my own space, but the reason is well worth it.

"Just set that on the island, hon." Becca gets a pair of scissors. "Is that your first box?"

"It is, and I should get back to it."

"I am tickled for you and Wyatt. And Miss Shelby and Clementine too! It will be so nice for her to have a sibling. And for you to get that second ring—I remember it well, though it feels long ago now."

I nod, but my smile wanes. Becca and Chip weren't yet living next door when we lost Poppy. I'm muzzled by a wave of grief, though my thoughts race on. *Fuck you and your plethora of rings, Becca.*

I'm instantly horrified by my secret vitriol, my unkindness. I would never wish on anyone what we went through. I do wish, however, to be naïve like Becca. I don't want to understand how cruel the quest for motherhood can be.

"Yes, it will be nice to have that second ring," I reply, my tone flat even as my smile holds.

"You bet it will." Becca beams at me before slicing open the packaging on the NourishBox. "Enjoy every bit of this, Tilly. It goes way too fast."

My NourishBox is identical in weight to Becca's when I pick it up off my doorstep. I'm excited to see what's inside the first one. There's an exterior chilled compartment for the protein—chicken, beef, or fish, from the top protein-growing lab in the country—along with an inner box for the microbiota-friendly teas, pregnancy supplements, and healthy snacks, among other goodies.

I set the box on our kitchen's island and relish the moment. Tears prick at my eyes, and I realize how low my expectations had sunk. I truly believed Clementine would be our only living child.

Picking up the kitchen shears, I gently press the sharp blade into the taped seam of the box. I'm careful not to go too deep and pierce anything inside. There's the satisfying sound of the tape releasing, the pop of the cardboard edges coming apart. I'm about to open the flaps, to take stock of the contents, when Stanley begins barking.

At first I think he's barking at another dog walking by, or a delivery drone, whose whirring noise he hates. A quick glance out our front window shows neither—only the Spanish moss–draped oak tree and an empty sidewalk. Then I realize he's barking at the kitchen island. Or more specifically, at the NourishBox.

"Stanley, no barking." I infuse sternness into my tone. But he's locked in and continues with the sharp yips, one after another.

Shelby strides into the kitchen, VR headset in hand, and I know her neurotherapy session has been interrupted. She's recently started a specialized program called Memento, which was newly released and prescribed for the sixty-five-plus crowd. The incident when she mentioned my mother's name, which prompted us to sign her up for Memento, feels long ago now. Luckily, nothing similar has happened since.

"Sorry, Shelby," I say. "I didn't mean to disturb your session."

"It's fine, honey. I haven't left for the store yet." One of her regular exercises with her AI memory coach, "Diane," is to create a short shopping list, then go to the virtual grocery store without the list to see how many items she remembers.

She snaps her fingers at the dog. "Stanley!"

He instantly stops barking and sits on her foot. Shelby reaches down to rub his ear. "I'm sorry he's being a menace. Not sure what he's getting on about."

Then she sees the box, and her eyes light up. She touches her necklace, with one silver ring, for first grandchild Clementine. I know she's thinking about her second legacy ring. Poppy died before Shelby's ring was delivered—those don't arrive until the baby is born.

A smile passes between us, and she says, "I need to get back to Diane. But I can't wait to see what's in there."

I wave at her. "Go, go. Don't let me keep you."

"I'll take him with me. Stanley, *come, darling.*" The dog trots after her, though he gives one last glance and low growl toward the island. A moment later I hear Shelby talking to Diane in the voice she uses for therapists—pleasant and patient, as though she's helping Clementine with a homework problem or chatting with an elderly neighbor at the community garden. I chuckle, knowing that while AI-generated Diane doesn't require this nicety, Shelby is a southern woman to her core.

Alone in the kitchen again, I'm about to open the box but pause when something shifts inside. A gentle scuttling, then a rhythmic scratching. My hands still and I listen intently.

There's an almost mechanical fluttering sound, reminding me of old-fashioned alarm clock bells. *Fast. Urgent.* Something smacks the inside of the box and the fluttering stops. The step I take back is involuntary.

Whatever's inside wants out, and the fluttering intensifies again. A black needlelike thing suddenly pokes up between the flaps where I've cut the tape. The thing moves back and forth, like the arm of a metronome. A moment later, another identical black needle pokes through and moves in a similar back-and-forth pattern.

The flap shifts and a palmetto bug, a flying cockroach, soars out of the box. I let out a yelp, then shudder as I watch it land on the countertop. Reaching for one of Clementine's books, the closest thing to me, I raise it high and swiftly bring it down onto the bug. There's a sound that is both *squish* and *crunch*, and a jolt of adrenaline courses through me, raising the hairs on the back of my neck.

Carefully lifting the book, which has bits of the crushed exoskeleton and a smear of guts, I see the cockroach is flattened. One wing has detached and is lying beside the insect's body. An antenna twitches, but I'm pretty sure the cockroach is dead.

Letting out a ragged breath, I reluctantly nudge the smashed cockroach with the book's edge. It doesn't move. I'm about to grab a tissue to sweep it from the countertop when I hear the same soft scuttling.

I recognize it now: insect legs scratching the cardboard. I don't even have time to slam the box flaps closed before a stream of cockroaches pours out, a sea of brown scales and wings covering the island, black antennae stretching up from the twitching mass in every direction. Some of the insects take flight while others shuffle haphazardly across the countertop, crawling over one another, their movements frenzied and unpredictable.

I want to get away—I want to *run*—but fear and disgust root me in place as the palmetto bugs tumble off the countertop, then begin streaming across the floor toward me. I only have time to make note that it's happening before they're upon me. As the first dozen reach my bare foot, the barbs on their spindly legs prick into my skin, and the *click-click-click-click* sound of their wings becomes deafening.

Shelby finds me writhing on the kitchen floor, screaming, "Get them off me!" I'm frantically scratching and clawing at my legs, out of my mind with panic. My confused and alarmed mother-in-law kneels beside me, trying to help.

"But . . . there's nothing there, Tilly!" she says. Her hands touch my arms, my legs, but they miss the insects. "What is it? What is it, honey?"

A second later the room goes quiet. No mass fluttering of wings. Stanley stops barking. The cockroaches, every last one of them, are gone. Disappeared in a poof, as though by magic.

I whip my head around, looking for the insects. Shelby's distress at finding me on the floor like this is evident: eyes wide, mouth pulled tight, a slight tremor in her hands.

"I'm sorry, Shelby. I don't know what happened. There were . . . bugs, cockroaches! Flying around the . . . in the box and then . . . Wow, I must be dehydrated again. I'm okay."

I'm rattled, all over the place with my explanation. I'm also hyperventilating, which makes each word come out in a forced staccato.

Shelby helps me up from the floor and into a chair, then gets me a glass of water. I apologize again for not making sense, and beg her not to tell Wyatt. She finally agrees, though it's reluctant.

But I should have known it was a promise only to soothe me in the moment. After all, she was there when I collapsed at twenty-nine weeks with Poppy. On this same kitchen floor. Surely she remembers the blood as well as I do. So Shelby was always going to tell Wyatt about this. In her shoes, I suppose I would do the same.

"Please, Tilly, let's get you and the baby checked out."

Wyatt leans against the island, watching me. His voice is low, so as not to be heard over Clementine's music. Clara the Cloud released a series of sing-along songs, and Clem has been playing it nonstop.

I'm tossing the salad and have already told him, three times, I don't need to go to the hospital. The health check on my watch came out normal, and my heart rate has stabilized. It's been hours since the incident.

"There's no need," I say again. "Please drop it, okay? There's nothing to worry about."

He presses his lips together, and there's a mild hollowing out of my insides. We both know that "there's nothing to worry about" is true only once the baby arrives earthside, pinked up and screaming her little lungs out.

I don't want to think about sad, awful things tonight. Besides, I'm still trying to reconcile what happened. Wyatt's concern, and scrutiny, is adding to my apprehension.

Turns out there were no cockroaches in my NourishBox. Or anywhere in the kitchen, or on my body. Even Clementine's book holds no sign of the crushed insect when I inspect it later. Regardless, I call MotherWise to report "a cockroach inside the box . . . yes, it was highly upsetting . . . ," wanting this particular NourishBox out of my house. The service replaces it immediately, no questions asked. The drone has already made the switch.

Walking around my still-worried husband, I place the salad bowl on the table, which Clementine is setting. She hums along to the music—Clara is singing about how a cumulus cloud can both float in the sky and weigh hundreds of tons. I'll end up humming this tune for days.

"We need knives, Clem." The fish fillet is broiling in a baste of avocado oil, fresh lemon, and dill and parsley from our garden. I'm so hungry I'm nauseated, and want to focus on getting dinner on the table versus what happened earlier. I can't think about it without a full-body shudder, my gag reflex kicking in.

Close the door. Turn the lock. Walk away, I think, visualizing leaving the cockroach nightmare behind that door. It's a trick I learned from Maeve to deal with ruminating thoughts. It works about fifty percent of the time, which isn't great, but I'm desperate for a reprieve.

"Okay, Momma," Clementine replies, opening the silverware drawer. "And spoons for dessert?"

"Yes," I reply, applying a mental padlock to the door in my mind for good measure. I smile at my daughter, and she grins back. Clementine loves dessert, and Shelby's rhubarb custard—on tonight's menu—is a favorite. Rhubarb is drought-resistant and easily grown in most gardens here. We like it Nana-style: stewed with honey, nestled over vanilla custard.

"Tilly." Wyatt's sharp tone forces me to look his way, thoughts of sweetly honeyed rhubarb instantly replaced with scurrying cockroaches. *Damn it.*

"Wyatt," I reply in the same tone. Then I offer a tepid smile, the best I can do.

Close the door. Turn the lock. Walk away. "The plum is good, I promise. Let's eat."

"Did you lose consciousness?" Jenn asks. She's taking my vitals with her MedAlert glasses. Wyatt's cleaning up after dinner but listening closely to our conversation.

"I think she did," he says, then calls over his shoulder. "Mom, did Tilly pass out?"

Shelby's playing cards with Clementine and Maeve in the living room.

"No, not really," she replies.

"Go fish," Maeve says, after Clem asks if she has a queen. My friend glances over at us and gives me a reassuring smile. I explained how unnecessary this visit was when I called her.

Wyatt won't leave me alone about it, I said. *Is Shelby's rhubarb custard enough to make a house visit worthwhile?*

Dessert is a bonus, Maeve replied, after conferring quickly with Jenn that they could pop over. *We'll be there in fifteen.*

"'Not really' or 'no,' Mom?" Wyatt's tone is harsh, and I shush him with a quiet "Stop it, Wyatt."

"She was awake the whole time, Wyatt," Shelby says. "Confused but awake."

"Do you have a ten?" Clem asks.

"I do, you lucky girl!" Shelby hands her the card.

"Before everyone else weighed in on my experience"—I roll my eyes for Jenn's benefit, and she chuckles—"I was about to say, no, I did not lose consciousness."

"Okay, good," Jenn says, scrolling through the vitals reflected in her glasses. "Everything looks great to me, Tilly."

"Did she tell you she passed out yesterday? At work?" Wyatt wipes his hands on a tea towel, then sits at the island across from me. I think about this counter covered in cockroaches and resist the shudder. *Easy, Tilly. There were no bugs, remember? It was a hallucination.*

Like the tendril. A dehydration-induced hallucination. Nothing more.

Lock the door, lock the door, lock the door . . .

"Yes, she did," Jenn says. I didn't tell her, but I appreciate the little white lie. Besides, I gave Jenn access to my chart, so there was no need to relay yesterday's incident. "Notes here say it was dehydration related?"

Jenn looks at me over her glasses, and I nod.

"That's what the PA said," I reply. "Too much coffee and not enough water."

"Well, I don't see anything concerning." Jenn turns off the Med-Alert glasses. "Likely a holdover from yesterday. Sometimes our system takes a couple of days to get back online. You've upped your water, had some electrolytes?"

"They sent me home with a few packets, and I got more in my delivery."

"Anything else we should do?" Wyatt asks. *"We" again.*

"Relax? That's my professional opinion." Jenn stands and puts an arm around Wyatt. "I'll write her a script for forest bathing. She can even do it VR, if you guys don't have time to take the day trip."

Wyatt gives Jenn a look that says he doesn't appreciate the humor. But it's mostly put on, and I can tell he's more at ease after her assessment.

"Seriously. She's okay, Wyatt. I would send her in if I thought otherwise. I'm more stubborn than she is." Jenn smiles my way, and I return it.

"See, babe, I'm fine. Dr. Jenn says so."

He nods, sighs deeply, and offers a half smile. "I really appreciate this, Jenn," he says. "I just needed to be sure."

Jenn squeezes Wyatt into a side hug. "I would expect nothing less."

"Now, how about some sugar? I think we could all use a dopamine hit, and Shelby's custard and rhubarb is a surefire way to get that flowing." I wink at Wyatt, and he lets out a small laugh, raising a hand.

"You had me at sugar," he replies.

"So, who else wants dessert?" I ask the group, and a gleeful Clementine shouts from the living room, "Meeeeeeeeeeee!"

We all sit down, and Shelby doles out custard and stewed rhubarb while Wyatt makes another pot of coffee, for the "nonpregnant adults." I dream of sneaking a cup of it later after everyone's in bed, imagine guzzling it down cold, the lovely lift of caffeine.

Clementine keeps up nonstop chatter with Maeve and Jenn, who indulge her like they always do. I sit, smiling as I listen to Clementine, sipping a barely palatable herbal tea that tastes like bark and blueberries. My other hand rests under the table, unseen, absentmindedly touching the spot on my stomach where the bruise used to be.

Wyatt fully relaxes by the time Maeve and Jenn head home, after which he makes me an electrolyte-infused water I'm unsure I can drink, my stomach full of tea.

Can't have you dehydrated, Tilly, he says, handing me the glass.

Jenn also suggested revisiting my supplements with Dr. Fillia, in case some minor deficiency is to blame.

My supplement bottles are on the bathroom counter, and there are many. It seems a lot to take, except they're small—about the size of a baby aspirin—and dissolve on my tongue, leaving no aftertaste behind. I gather tonight's supplements in my palm.

Calcium, choline, C vitamin, D vitamin, folic acid, iron, omega-3 fatty acids . . .

I soon realize the bottles are lined up in alphabetical order. I didn't do it, so Wyatt must have. A wave of irritation rises as the pills dissolve on my tongue. But then I tell myself he's merely looking for ways to help, letting me know he's thinking of me and the baby. At this stage of the pregnancy, there isn't much he can contribute.

Gratitude, Tilly.

"Coming to bed?" Wyatt calls out, already under the covers. I look to the bottles again.

"In a minute," I reply.

I move the folic acid to the front of the line and shuffle a few other bottles so they are no longer in alphabetical order. Then I feel it—an itching, burning pain near my ankle. I don't see anything at first, but when I run my fingers along the spot, a tiny but sharp something snags on my skin.

"Ouch," I murmur, though it doesn't exactly hurt. More like when you pull off a burr, and one of its hooks sinks into the top layer of skin.

Setting my foot on the closed toilet lid, I twist my body to better evaluate the skin around my ankle. Squinting, I see something the size and shape of a sliver, dark brown against my pale skin. With steady fingers I grasp the sliver with my tweezers. It comes out easily. When I run my finger over the spot again, it's smooth.

Holding the sliver up to the light, I see minuscule spikes running its length. They're uniform and remind me of tiny thorns. *What the hell?*

All of a sudden, I know what I'm looking at. My stomach clenches and the electrolyte water and tea threaten to come back up.

It's not a sliver; it's the slim, barbed leg of a cockroach.

I don't mention the sliver. I scrub an alcohol pad across the tiny indentation in my skin, reassure myself it can't be a cockroach leg. *A remnant of a stick that Stanley loves to carry on his walks. A fibrous-stalk sliver from one of our garden plants, perhaps.* I expect I'll have nightmares, cockroaches all I see every time I close my eyes. The click-clack of their exoskeletons rubbing together in the swarm, their oily, musty smell that still lingers in my nose. Miraculously, I have one of my deepest sleeps in ages.

You hit your sleep goal, my watch buzzes in the morning. A gold star appears on the screen, spinning in circles. Well done, Tilly!

We have a nice Sunday. Clementine is invited to a classmate's birthday party. Wyatt and I brainstorm plans for the studio conversion. Shelby and Stanley attend a seniors' meetup at a local coffee shop. By Monday, I'm well rested, clearheaded, and ready for a productive workday. It's easy enough to blame dehydration for the unpleasant events earlier in the weekend; I'm glad for the extra electrolyte packets.

I feel good.

While I get ready for work I mull over the tendril, and likely explanations. Perhaps a minuscule tear in the canvas, and it came loose . . . Room D's robust air circulation causing the flap to lengthen, then lift from the surface . . . an illusion of purposeful movement. Definitely possible. *Don't overthink it, Tilly. You need to focus. The painting needs your best work.*

The house is quiet—I'm the last to leave this morning. Tugging on my underwear and bra, I hear something unfamiliar. Not the usual creaks and sighs our old house makes, but a sound that reminds me of a straw broom brushing across a wood floor. *Swish . . . swish . . . swish.*

I pause, listening closely, holding my breath. Then I realize the swish, or more accurately a rhythmic *whoosh* sound, is coming from inside me—it's my heartbeat. Strange to be so aware of it, but I know that during pregnancy the amount of blood pumped by the heart increases by thirty to fifty percent (it was in last week's MotherWise e-zine). I tap my watch, checking the rate. Seventy beats per minute, the tiny red heart on the screen pulsing in time. Nothing to worry about.

When I get the call, I'm still only half-dressed, in the bathroom running a brush through my damp hair. My phone, resting nearby, flashes the incoming call. I touch the speaker icon.

"Hello?"

"Hello there, is this Mrs. Mathilde Crewson?" *Mat-hildEE.* The voice is male, friendly. Southern, and based on the name he uses for me, someone I've never spoken to before.

"Speaking." I rub in the SPF moisturizer I've dotted onto my forehead and cheeks.

"This is Mack Jenkins, from the medical center? I'm with the MotherWise program."

"Oh, hello, Mr. Jenkins. What can I do for you?"

"Just so you're aware, Mrs. Crewson, this call is being recorded for quality and educational purposes. May I proceed?"

"Yes," I reply, my answer rote. The statement is ubiquitous—everything is recorded.

"Excellent. I'm not sure if you remember me from the other day? You were in a bit of a woozy state when you were brought in, and I wanted to check in on how you're doing."

I have no clue who Mack Jenkins is, or any recollection of meeting him. But faking recognition seems the best approach.

"Oh, I remember," I reply. "I'm doing well, thank you for asking."

I rub the moisturizer in circles until it disappears into my skin, only half-listening. Then I dab some on my ears and the back of my neck, knowing that I no longer have time to style my hair. A low bun it is.

"I am sure glad to hear that, Mrs. Crewson," Mack says, his already energetic tone ticking up another few notches. "Now, I've got a couple of things to send over to you. Your follow-up appointments. Your first momma meeting location. We need you to fill out the list for preferred times for—"

"That all sounds great, thank you. And please, call me Tilly." I cut him off, as I still need to put on pants and makeup. "I'm racing to get ready for work. Can you send it through and I'll respond when I get a moment?"

"Oh goodness. We must have our wires crossed!" Mack laughs and I join in, though it's only to be polite. I'm irritated with Mack Jenkins and his inability to get to the point. I miss the days of communicating exclusively by text, or email, or even with a direct message on social media. Our phones were used sparingly as actual telephones then, most often to speak with those who never fully embraced digital communication. Aging parents. School administrators. Insurance companies.

"You're on home rest, Mrs. Crewson—*pardon me*, Tilly."

I stare at the phone. "I'm sorry, what?"

"You've been placed on home rest." Mack's voice slows, and he enunciates *home* and *rest*. "Says here your blood pressure was a tad higher than we like to see, and your husband—I presume you're married to Mr. Wyatt Crewson?"

"I am." My watch buzzes. Time for breath work, Tilly? My heart rate is up to eighty-one beats now.

"I have a note here that Mr. Crewson requested additional support for your pregnancy." There's a pause. I almost hear a *tsk-tsk* in the silence. As though this Mack Jenkins person thinks Wyatt shouldn't have had to make the request; as though I should have been more careful in the first place about my blood pressure, so he didn't have to ask.

"So doctor's appointments, meetups with your MotherHelper group, and daily neighborhood walks are the only approved outings you'll be enjoying for a time. Breath work and meditation classes can be done at home, for now."

I start sputtering a response, and he interrupts me. "This is temporary, Tilly. Until we're sure here at MotherWise that you and that little nugget of yours are healthy as can be."

"But I am healthy! And so is the plum."

"The who?" he asks.

"The baby. We call it that because . . . It doesn't matter. The point is, we're doing really, *really* well." I try to relax, to make my voice sound smooth and unbothered. But I'm upset, especially by the news that Wyatt is the reason for this. "I'm confident I don't need to be on home rest, Mr. Jenkins."

Was this what Wyatt was speaking with Dale about? In the medical center Friday, when they were outside the room and my earshot. Asking Dale's opinion, perhaps, about how Raoul might respond to this home rest request?

"Mr. Jenkins, can I ask when my husband called in for this extra 'support'?" My annoyance rises along with my heartbeat. Time for breath work, Tilly? I touch the ignore box on the screen.

"Hmm, let's see here. Looks like Saturday evening, eight twelve p.m."

Saturday evening. After Jenn and Maeve's visit, after he ran me a bath, before saying he had an email to send and would be right back.

"I'm feeling great." I stare at myself in the bathroom mirror, notice the new lines at the corners of my eyes. "Can't I just . . . cancel this home rest, or something?"

"I am sure glad you're feeling well, Tilly, but these are your ob-gyn's orders."

"Dr. Fillia?" Again, why has no one told me anything about this? Not to mention, I'm her patient, not Wyatt—so why didn't I get a notification from the office about this change?

There's a clicking of computer keys. "Oh, Dr. Fillia isn't in the Enhanced Care program, Tilly. You've been assigned to Dr. Rice. Lovely man. He took care of my wife. You're in great hands."

More key clicking. What is he typing? I envision the note in my file: *Mrs. Mathilde Crewson appears resistant to her home rest order . . . regular check-ins to ensure compliancy are strongly recommended . . .*

"Since you had two spells in a row, Dr. Rice wants you to prioritize rest," Mack says.

Two "spells." *Damn it.* Also, who is this Dr. Rice now making decisions about my ability to work?

"Mr. Jenkins, is there someone I can speak with? I have an important project at work right now, and it's impossible for me to be away."

"I can ask Dr. Rice to call you, Tilly, but I'll let you in on a teensy secret." Mack Jenkins lowers his voice. "It won't make a lick of difference. The MotherWise guidelines are there for a reason, and I've rarely seen exceptions made."

His intonation changes on the word "guidelines." "Rules" would be a more accurate term. Mack Jenkins has likely been trained on using "sensitive" language, for everyone's comfort.

"All we want is to take the best care of you and the baby. That's MotherWise's only goal. I'm sure you want the same thing, Tilly."

What can I say to that? Mack Jenkins has my medical file in front of him. He knows about Poppy, or if he doesn't, this Dr. Rice does. I'm infuriated by the restrictions, but I do understand what I signed up for. If I want to participate and reap the benefits, I have to comply. After passing out on Friday, and the hallucination Saturday, it's hard to argue the extra layer of medical care isn't reassuring. This fills me with shame. What sort of mother doesn't put the health of her unborn child first?

But then I think of the painting, in Room D, waiting for me. I can't let anyone else work on the Leclerc. It's not an option. One, the money—we can get by without it, but it's a nice cushion. Two, this is the final Leclerc—there will never be another opportunity like it. Three . . . the painting needs me. This sudden knowing is like when Clementine calls out in the dark, after a bad dream. My presence and whispers of "there, there, sweet girl" the only way to lull her back to sleep. In those moments I'm the one she needs—"Momma magic," Wyatt calls it.

"I'd like to speak to someone either way, Mr. Jenkins. Perhaps your supervisor?" I don't care what he's typing into my file. Call me "difficult" or "demanding"—*have at it, Mack Jenkins.* The painting needs *me.* "Like I said, I have a project I can't leave right now."

It takes another four phone calls and half my morning, but things are set. I'm partially victorious, even though the home rest requirement remains in place.

The Leclerc will be moved to my studio at home. Dr. Rice (who is quite lovely and understanding) said that while I'm on "home rest," I'm not on "bed rest." As long as I do what's required to keep my stress low and have no further episodes, he gladly signs off on me working from home.

"My wife also works out of the home," Dr. Rice tells me during that phone call. "She's a teacher. Passionate about her job. Just try to keep her from her classroom, her students, I always say!"

GIA is fine with the change, once I assure Raoul my studio is set up and ready for the conservation. Thankfully, Wyatt installed climate controls for humidity and temperature when we renovated the house. Cecil only wants me to take good care of myself but agrees the work can be done from home. Wyatt . . . well, Wyatt is a tougher nut to crack.

He thinks rest should look like rest and knows how involved my work can be. He finally admits he was the one who contacted MotherWise, but again doesn't apologize for not talking to me about it first. Wyatt wasn't like this with Clementine, nor with Poppy, which is partly why I'm confounded. I can't leave it alone.

I want to understand; I want him to understand.

"It wasn't your call to make, Wyatt. Not without talking to me first." He holds eye contact, the set of his jaw defiant. "This is our child, yes, but it's my pregnancy—my body. I need to know you understand this. Let me do what's best for me, please."

"I shouldn't have had to make the call, Tilly." Wyatt sighs, his frustration coming through. Running hands through his hair. "The salient question, if you ask me, is, why didn't you?"

We argue. I don't remember arguing this much, ever, in our ten-year marriage, but it's circular and soon there's no energy on either side to keep it going.

I remind him—*pointedly*—that Dr. Rice ("he's the expert here, right?") signed off on me working at home. But it isn't until I agree to get a MotherWise pregnancy tracker tattoo that he gives in. I wonder, as I toss and turn in bed that night, which one of us won the argument and if it even matters.

It's after school and Clementine sits on a pillow on the floor of my studio, my childhood copy of *Nancy Drew and the Hidden Staircase*—before books were printed using water-resistant sustainable "paper"—held carefully in her lap. She has unlimited access to my entire collection, and I have encouraged her to read the books free of worry.

She's read this particular Nancy Drew dozens of times, as it's her favorite of the lot. I said that as long as she could occupy herself, she was welcome to spend time with me while I worked. Not on the actual painting, which is secured under its cover, but while I'm scanning notes or doing other related tasks.

Wyatt and Shelby are out walking Stanley before dinner, the weather most agreeable today. I long to open the window and let a breeze in, but it's not good for the Leclerc, even covered, to be exposed to climate shifts. The studio's relative humidity remains constant at fifty-three percent, the temperature sixty-five degrees, which is ideal for the art. It should also be ideal for my bioluminescent fig plant, but today I noticed a mottling of yellow-brown on its leaves. I need to run an AI plant scan on it after I finish up here.

"Mommy, what happened to her?"

"What happened to who?" I'm focused on my tablet's screen, rereading my last notes.

"The lady who painted the picture," Clementine says.

Setting my glasses atop my head, I turn quickly toward her. "Did you look at it? The painting?" Fear thrums through me. Then hot anger.

"No, I said I wouldn't and I didn't." Clementine pouts. She may only be seven, but she considers herself quite mature and doesn't take kindly to being questioned about following rules or breaking promises. Besides, how would she even get in here, past the coded lock, without me? "But you told me it was a lady artist who wasn't alive anymore."

Right. I did tell her that, seeing no harm in giving those few details when she asked what was on the delivery drone in our living room, awed by the robot's stair-climbing abilities. It's not like Clementine will tell her classmates about the fourth Charlotte Leclerc her mom has tucked away at home. She doesn't even know who Charlotte Leclerc is.

"I'm sorry, Clem. I shouldn't have snapped like that."

She shrugs. "It's okay, Momma. I know you have important things on your mind."

"I do, but so do you." I sit cross-legged in front of my daughter on the floor. The covered Leclerc is on the workbench on the other side of the room. I watch Clem's eyes go to it.

"So, what specifically do you want to know? About the artist?"

Clementine carefully closes the Nancy Drew book. "How did she die?"

I remember back to what my mother told me when I asked a similar question about Charlotte Leclerc. We were tucking into a late dinner of tomato soup and grilled cheese, after leaving the museum. It was the day I got stitches from my run-in with the field hockey stick in gym class—the same evening when Mom said, *All art is made by the dead, Mathilde.*

"She died in a fire," my mom said, stirring freshly ground pepper into her soup. "In her attic studio, where she painted."

"How did the fire start?" I asked then. It felt important to understand this, especially because Mom had a home studio as well.

"No one is certain," she said. "Some say she accidentally knocked over a candle—she liked to paint by candlelight, apparently. Others say she deliberately set the fire because she was heartbroken about losing her only child and no longer wanted to live," my mother explained, as I sat wide-eyed, holding my breath.

I share this with Clementine now, though I hold back the suicide theory. I resist the urge to look at the painting, as the back of my neck prickles with the memory of what my mom said next. "There was one very odd thing, though, about the incident."

"What?" My sixteen-year-old voice lowered. I was still on edge after the whole *all art is made by the dead* thing.

"The flames stayed in about a four-foot radius, in the middle of the room." I stretch out my hands and arms now, as though measuring the space for Clementine. I probably shouldn't share this lore with my seven-year-old, who is prone to nightmares. *Stop, Tilly,* I think. But I'm overwhelmed by a bizarre compulsion to tell her the story. Like I have a delicious piece of gossip to share. "It burned everything in that area. Including, most tragically, the artist herself."

"Oh," Clementine says, before sucking in a breath. "That's sad."

"It is. And also strange, because that's not how fire behaves. Usually it keeps going until it runs out of oxygen."

Clementine chews the inside of her cheek. I note how similar she looks to my mom right now, wistfulness swelling inside me. She picks at her cuticles, chews a fingernail, which tells me she's anxious. *That's enough.*

So I don't mention the supposed suicide note, nor the on-the-fringes web chats of spontaneous human combustion I recently came across. Some speculate, according to my latest research, that Charlotte Leclerc ignited from the inside out. That was why once her body (and everything within a few feet of it) burned, the fire extinguished. The rest of the wood-paneled attic—including the highly flammable paint supplies held in plastic milk crates—was untouched.

"What made the flames run out of oxygen, do you think?" Clementine asks.

"No one knows." I try not to lie to Clementine or hold back hard truths. But what happened to Charlotte Leclerc is full of myth and light on facts. About as verifiable as a campfire ghost story. "Sometimes we can't get to the whole truth of something."

She nods knowingly. "Nana believes that too."

I laugh, because I've mimicked Shelby—after living together all these years, it's bound to happen. "I guess she's the one who taught me that."

My watch buzzes a notification that Wyatt, Shelby, and Stanley have arrived back home.

"Why don't you go help Nana pack lunch for tomorrow? Then make yourself useful for dinner prep, okay?"

"Okay." Clementine springs up, the way only a child can—not using her hands to support her. She sets the book under her arm, waits for me to unlock the door from my watch.

With a click the lock disengages. "Mommy, when you're finished with the painting, will you show me?" she asks.

I nod. "You bet, sweet pea."

Clementine grins, then heads out of the room, shutting the door behind her. I reengage the lock before walking over to the workbench. Something is niggling at my brain—an idea I haven't before considered. I put on my ventilation mask and remove the cover.

It was found gathering dust in an old police evidence room. Sitting there for years, unnoticed . . .

I run my eyes over the painting, split in two by the cleaning line that separates the treated area and the still soot-laden one.

. . . the fire that killed Charlotte Leclerc burned fast and furious. But it only burned Leclerc, some supplies, and the easel itself. Which, apparently, held her fourth and final work of art . . .

Yet, there was no mention in the police report about a painting found on the charred easel, despite its existence in the evidence room. I mentally review items found near the burned area, from the police log: the metal piece that connects the bristles and handle of a paintbrush; a typewritten note, tacked to the far wall, and the four brass thumbtacks used to hold it there; a melted plastic yogurt container, containing black oil paint; one leather sandal, women's, size eight.

This painting must have been on that easel. That's why it's so badly burned. Yet . . . how can a fire incinerate a human body down to bone fragments but leave a canvas—badly burned, but still intact—a foot or so away?

Something pulses inside the paint above the navel, above the treatment line. It's so subtle that if I weren't standing directly over the painting, I wouldn't have seen it.

With resolute calmness, I snap on a glove and hold still—ready. As soon as the pulsing begins again, the paint bulging, I carefully touch the bump with my gloved finger. It's soft, like a water blister you get from ill-fitting shoes. I apply more pressure to the paint blister, and when I remove my finger the indentation fills back in again.

Using a scalpel, I gently push the tip of the blade into the pulsating bump. A clear liquid trickles out, and I catch some in a sample vial I pull from my pocket. Holding the vial up to the light, I try to get a better look at the liquid. It's then I hear the suctioning sound, from behind me.

This time I don't hesitate. I set the capped test tube back in my pocket and, with scalpel in hand, turn slowly to face the painting.

I see it then, the tendril. Slightly opaque, glistening with a blackish fluid, stretching out of the bubble I sliced into. I wait, holding my breath. A static-like sound fills my ears. Maybe a rush of adrenaline, activating fight-or-flight mode to ensure I have the laser focus I need to grab hold of the wriggling tendril.

It squirms in my fingers, as though alive, and I hold it tight. Then I bring my scalpel blade down on the quivering, fleshy bit. There's a split second of tension, like a guitar string tightened to the point of snapping, followed by laxness as the tissue severs from the painting.

"Are you sure?" I can't believe what I'm hearing.

I'm on a call with Dr. Ruth-Anne Torrance, GIA's conservation scientist. Most people don't understand how much science is involved in art conservation. How many compounds need to be analyzed from original artworks. Along with the expected art history or fine arts expertise, this work necessitates knowledge of chemistry, plus a desire to solve complex puzzles.

"I'm sure," Ruth-Anne says.

"So, it's cerebrospinal fluid. But . . . how?" How can this painting, burned beyond recognition, not to mention decades old, be leaking a liquid? Let alone human cerebrospinal fluid? It makes no logical sense.

"I don't have a reasonable scientific explanation for you, Tilly," Ruth-Anne replies. "But science doesn't always have an answer."

"That's true," I murmur, thinking about Cecil and what his take might be.

"But here's the other nutty thing," Ruth-Anne continues. "The tissue sample you sent in?"

"Yeah?" I snap out of my reverie, now thinking about that slice of tendril. As is standard, the sample was permanently cast in a polyester resin, which was then ground and polished for analysis.

"It's connective tissue, from a human nerve bundle. A piece of the palmar branch of the median nerve, according to my analysis."

"The median nerve?"

"It's one of the main nerves in your arm," Ruth-Anne says. "Runs from the forearm to the hand and provides sensation to the palm and up the thumb."

Bile rises; a memory of the dismembered hand from my nightmare, painting with blood, loads into my mind. The tendril-like strands that hung limply from the wrist . . . I swallow hard, forcing the image to retreat.

Former Leclerc paintings have revealed fingernails, eyelashes, blood, skin cells . . . but a human nerve branch? Where did she get it? And equally puzzling . . . *why* did she use it in this painting? Incorporating an element like this would be especially challenging—paint can be finicky, and materials don't always play well together.

"The artist was an adult, right?" Ruth-Anne asks.

"Yes," I reply, my voice unsteady. "Probably around forty."

"Then this nerve isn't hers," she says. "Too many neurons. Probably a child, under twelve according to KIRBI."

KIRBI stands for Knowledge Integration and Retrieval for Biological Inference, a specialized AI tool for analyzing and inferring biological data. It's used frequently in medical and scientific settings, though rarely in our industry. Unless you're restoring a Leclerc, that is.

"A child?" My voice cracks, my mind spinning.

"Yup," Ruth-Anne says. "I don't need to tell you this, but obviously this wasn't an accidental inclusion. You don't just wake up one morning and say, 'I know what this painting needs—a human nerve bundle!' It's pretty morbid, truly."

The dead speak through their paintings, Mathilde. The back of my neck prickles, goose bumps rising on my arms. My watch buzzes a notification, and the creepy-crawly feeling escalates.

"I'd better let you go, but thanks for rushing this," I say.

"Happy to help," Ruth-Anne says. "I've filed the samples here, unless you want them returned?"

"That's fine. Thanks again. I appreciate both your speed and discretion."

My fingers tremble as we hang up. I shake them out, trying to prepare for my next meeting, which is in ten minutes. I'm not looking forward to this one.

The MotherWise tattoo technician uses an alcohol swab to clean the inside of my forearm, resting on the kitchen table between us. There's a rush of coolness, which increases when he fans the area with his gloved hand. I look away, toward the glassed-in vertical garden on the other side of the kitchen. There are newly blooming squash blossoms, a pretty bright yellow color.

Earlier, Shelby mentioned wanting to batter and fry them up for dinner—*I'll trim them after this is over.*

I'm not distracting myself with thoughts of deep-fried squash blossoms because needles bother me. They don't. But I remain prickly about the soon-to-be tattooed tracker, and my turned-away glance is one of annoyed acceptance. However, the technician—young, long hair gathered in a bun at the nape of his neck, a name tag that reads ALEX R.—clearly interprets it as squeamishness.

"How are you with needles, Mrs. Crewson?" He's getting the tracker tattoo ready, opening packages and laying things out on a sterilized pad.

"Fine," I reply. "No problem at all. I've had many."

I turn back to watch the procedure, proving I am, in fact, fine with needles.

"Okay, great! You'll only feel a minor prick, then a touch of warmth, then all done. It's highly tolerable." Alex sure is enthusiastic, or enthusiastically following a training manual he's memorized. I wonder how he knows that it's "highly tolerable" and how he can declare that with such confidence. I'm confident Alex here has never had a MotherWise tracker tattooed under *his* skin.

"Good to know." I glance at my disinfected forearm; the spotlight from Alex's headband light shines a pale blue circle the size of a quarter onto my skin. This marks the spot for the tattoo, he tells me.

Alex puts on his glasses, tapping the right arm. A green light illuminates near where he's tapped. "If you could relax your hand, Mrs. Crewson, that would be fantastic."

It's not intentional, but my hand has clenched into a tight fist. I release it slowly, watching the tendons and ligaments move under my skin. I know that with the glasses on, Alex can see right through my skin to the structures underneath. I consider asking to try them on, the glasses, so I can see what he's seeing. I think back to my conversation with Ruth-Anne. To the piece of a child's nerve bundle I sampled from the painting. Asking myself, again, *Where did Charlotte Leclerc get a palmar median nerve bundle?*

A crazy—truly, insane—answer comes instantly to mind: *She harvested it from her own daughter, after she died.* I nearly laugh at how absurd and impossible that would be. But then . . . Charlotte Leclerc was a renowned surgeon at the time her daughter died. She had privileges at the hospital, and maybe, somehow, obtained access to her daughter's body.

I let the story take shape. Perhaps it was a professional kindness extended her way, granting her privacy to sit with her child alone in the morgue, post autopsy. All she would have had to do was ask the right person. Dr. Leclerc also had the skill to remove a nerve branch from a corpse, her scalpel working with quiet efficiency, the body bloodless by then. Half-mad with grief, maybe Charlotte Leclerc did something no one else could understand.

Is it possible? I wonder. I want to call Ruth-Anne back, to find out if she can narrow the age window of the nerve. *Could it be from a, say, five-year-old?*

I'm distracted from my thoughts by Alex, who is re-swabbing my arm with another alcohol pad. It's unnecessary, which tells me he's nervous, despite his steady hands and all-seeing med-tech glasses. "So, how many weeks along are you, Mrs. Crewson?"

Small talk. I'm unsure if he's trying to distract me or himself. "Almost fourteen."

"You must be excited. Your husband too," he says.

I nod. "We are."

He picks up the tattooing device. It looks like a steel ballpoint pen with two flat ends. He clicks something on the bottom of the device and a trio of quarter-inch needles pops up.

"See?" Alex says, showing me the needles. "Super tiny, right?"

If you connect the dots these needles will make on my skin, you'll get a triangular shape.

"As promised," I reply.

Alex smiles, and with another click on the device the needles retreat.

"All set?" he asks, looking up at me. The headband's light hits my eyes, and I squint against the glare.

"Ready whenever you are." I watch the blue circle reappear on my forearm, about two inches from my wrist crease. He sets the needle end of the device onto my skin, double-checks the parameters to ensure the circle lines up, then says, "Take a deep breath, Mrs. Crewson. One, two . . . three!"

On three he clicks the end and there's pressure and a mild stab into my skin, like I've brushed against the stinging barbs of a plant. Then a brief flush of warmth to the area before he removes the device.

"That's it?" It was fast, like Kat said it would be. Like Alex himself promised.

"That's it!" He smiles and nods before setting a white bandage over the area.

After giving me instructions to remove the bandage the next morning, and to call if there are any issues, like ongoing pain or redness, Alex packs up and heads off to his next appointment.

As soon as he leaves, I remove the bandage, holding my arm up to the light and moving it back and forth to see how noticeable the tattoo is. It's the same color as my skin, the three triangulated dots only visible because of a sheer, glossy finish and the lingering redness. They look like dots of the white glue we used in elementary school, which dried clear. There's an uncomfortable ache in my forearm that reminds me of when I've gripped a paintbrush or solvent swab too long. But after I clench and unclench my fist a few times, the ache dissipates.

"Highly tolerable," I murmur, gently pressing my fingertip into each of the glossy dots. Under my finger on the last dot I feel something: a barely there pulsing; it's quick, like a fetus's heartbeat. Then a voice fills the empty room—childlike, seemingly coming from upstairs. *"You shouldn't have done that, Mathilde."*

I hold still, barely breathing. When I raise my eyes from the tattoo to the staircase, I tense but there's nothing there. The faint pulsing under my finger continues as I watch the stairs, eyes watering the longer I refuse to blink.

It's a reaction to the procedure, I tell myself, finally removing my finger from the still-faintly-pulsing dot. *Your inner voice, acknowledging your apprehensions about getting the tattoo.*

"I did what I had to do," I say, out loud to my empty kitchen.

There's no response, and the quiet stretches on.

The treatment continues to be slow, the way this type of conservation can be. I'm fighting restless impatience, removing a narrow line of soot, when my watch buzzes.

> MotherHelper meetup in 30 minutes, Tilly!

I groan—I have too much to do, but I can't blow the meeting off. Besides, a break will be good for me and the plum; I've been at it for some hours now. Though the nausea has finally disappeared now that I've reached the second trimester, I still fatigue easily. It's frustrating, when the fog of exhaustion settles over me, but I'm trying to listen to my body more. To "honor the work it's doing," as this week's MotherWise e-zine suggested.

As I lock the front door, nervous butterflies fill my stomach. Like I'm going on a first date, or heading into a job interview for a much-wanted position. Kat told me her MotherHelper group was her lifeline with her last pregnancy, and the women still get together once a week. Because this is her fifth pregnancy, she isn't required to attend every meeting. Today she's volunteering at a school event, so I'm on my own. I trend introverted, and making new friends hasn't always been easy for me. Unfamiliar groups like this one can be downright anxiety inducing.

I sit on my front steps and do some breath work, reminding myself, the way Maeve would if she were here, that stretching boundaries is good for me. My watch pings a gold star notification, followed by a second reminder about the meetup. I sigh, longing to stay home with the Leclerc instead.

> At MotherWise, collaboration is our doctrine! Both mom and baby thrive when surrounded by a community of caring, like-minded people, from health professionals to educators to peers. Your MotherHelper group is comprised of other pregnant women who live and work in your neighborhood. We encourage you to attend the weekly sessions to get to know these women better and to create a wider support network during your pregnancy and beyond. It's MotherWise's great hope that—

"Hi there, are you Tilly?"

My eyes shift from the handout I'm reading to the woman standing in front of me. She looks to be in her early thirties, with a short bob to her chin and a small gold stud in her nose. Wearing a pair of sage-colored natural-fiber overalls, a fitted white T-shirt underneath, she looks comfortable while still being stylish. I glance down at my simple navy T-shirt dress, see a dollop of dried yogurt from breakfast.

I stand to shake her hand, and she envelops me in a hug. She smells like vanilla and peeled mandarin oranges. My arms hang at my sides because she's taken me by surprise, and I don't have time to embrace her back before she lets go.

"I'm Margie," she says. "Margie Tupholme. I live over on York." About a block from me, which I tell her.

"Oh, I know." Margie smiles. "I'm the lead for this group, so I have everyone's address and other personal details. Welcome, Tilly!" I wonder what other "personal details" she has on me. I see her necklace now, which came out from under her shirt when we hugged. Two gold rings.

Her eyes go to my necklace, easily visible due to my dress's scoop neck. One gold ring.

"So, your second baby, huh?"

I nod, smile politely. Margie lets out a contented sigh.

"Ah, the second one. It's dreamy to bring a sibling into the world for your first, but wow, the workload more than doubles."

"Hmm-hmm. I've heard that." From everyone. Including Kat, just yesterday when she came to my place for my MotherWise-approved, at-home breath work class. I miss going with Maeve and moving about as I wish, but I'm hoping to be off home rest soon enough. I hate hearing about the double-workload thing. For one, it's boring and predictable information that isn't helpful. But also? I should already know this. The plum should be—*is*—my third pregnancy.

"This is your third?" I ask Margie, my tone pleasant and conversational.

"Sure is! I still can't believe I'm going to be a mom to three under three soon."

I hope my smile looks genuine. "So, Margie. What exactly happens at these meetups?"

We're in a room in the local community center near Oglethorpe Square, which also houses a library, a day care facility, a swimming pool, and a small grocery store on the bottom level. Each neighborhood has a center like this one, meant to serve the local residents. It's walkable and well used "from cradle to grave," as they say.

As this room is a multipurpose one, there's nothing descriptive on the walls except one large screen, used to display media for whatever event is taking place. Soft, natural light streams in from the ample windows on one side, and the chairs are cushioned and comfortable. There are snacks out, and I notice the NourishBox-branded packaging tucked off to the side.

Margie starts setting up the drinks station. There's a large jug labeled PEPPERMINT TEA, WITH LOCAL HONEY ready to be poured, which I offer to do. We have five minutes until the meeting begins.

"Each week is a bit different. But mostly we chat, ask questions, seek support on anything we're struggling with. Every few weeks we have an expert in, too, which is great," Margie replies. I nod, continue pouring the cold, fragrant tea into cups.

"It's meant to be social and fun, but there is an educational element too," Margie continues. "At least part of each meeting is focused specifically on the week of pregnancy we're in, and milestones."

"We're all in the same week?" I'm surprised. "How many of us are there?"

"Well, within two weeks, yes. And there's five of us regulars, plus a few semi-regular drop-ins. I think you're friends with one of them. Katrina Rojas, right?" Margie asks, and I nod. "Love her. She's always got great advice."

I smile, thinking of my friend. "That's Kat for sure."

"So out of the five here weekly, three are moms-to-be, like you and me, and one is a surrogate who attends with the intended mother." She lays out a handful of ginger and lemon lollipops meant to aid morning sickness. I have another moment of gratitude that mine has passed.

"It's a nice-size group," Margie says. "Small enough to get to know each other well, big enough to see how common the joys and issues are."

"Sounds great."

"It *is* great. This is the most important time in a woman's life, don't you think?"

I think of the Leclerc, waiting at home for me, and don't respond.

"So you work at GIA?" Margie asks, as though reading my mind.

"I have a cousin there, in the Atlanta division. Not sure if you know her? Jamie Giller?"

I shake my head. "I don't. It's a pretty big place, when you add in all the satellite labs. What about you?"

"I'm home with the kids." Margie smiles. "Best job there is."

I nod, then blush, as though continuing to work outside the home is an embarrassment. Staying home—if possible—is the societal preference.

"Oh, there's Evelyn! She lives down the street from you. This is her second baby, too." Margie waves to a woman walking into the room. She's tall, which helps mask her belly. You can't even tell she's pregnant in her white linen shorts and black tank top, wedge espadrilles on her feet. I recognize her from the neighborhood, though we've never officially met.

"Come meet Tilly, Eve," Margie says. "She's joining us this week."

Once the group begins, I realize these women already know one another well, and I'm ever more the new kid who doesn't know where she fits in. I'm wishing I signed up for MotherWise earlier (I can almost hear Wyatt and Kat's "told you so" in unison).

Turns out all four of the women—including the surrogate, who has three kids of her own—are stay-at-home moms, or planning to be. I'm somewhat surprised the intended mother is at home, with no children in her care yet. This baby will be her first, her necklace only a bare gold chain, and she tells me she left her job as a solicitor to focus on impending motherhood. I long to ask her what her days look like, at home without work or kids, but can't see how to do it without coming across as judgmental.

I don't tell anyone about Poppy, and the group assumes this is my second pregnancy.

As we go around the room, sharing personal details, my mind wanders from the women to the painting in my studio. *The Mother* is as impatient to be uncovered as I am to do the work—I can sense it, the distraction of an open file, the need for resolution.

My tattoo begins to ache, and I touch it with gentle fingers. This time I feel nothing under my fingertips, which is a relief.

"Mine stung for about three days," Evelyn, seated to my right, whispers. Her eyes stay on Margie, who is at the front of the room talking about how at this stage of development the fetus can suck his or her thumb. "Ice helped."

"Good to know," I murmur back. "Thanks."

I try the ice later, which numbs the spot but doesn't dispel the yawning, persistent ache that stretches down into my palm, pinpoint hot in my thumb. *The median palmar nerve.*

It's one of the main nerves in your arm, Ruth-Anne said. *Runs from the forearm to the hand and provides sensation to the palm and up the thumb.*

Before I know it, I'm heading up the stairs to my studio. Unlocking the door, my mind dreamlike (*it's fatigue, Tilly—you should take a rest*). Pulling off the cover, I carefully set a finger against the spot where the tendril was. The slightest depression left behind, waiting to be restored.

I can't afford to rush this. I take a deep breath and close my eyes briefly, using the quiet moment to think through adhesive options. Distracting my mind so I don't think about *why* I need to secure the surrounding paint, to prevent further damage.

Deciding on a cellulose-based adhesive—gentle, organic, reversible, and the type you might use for something fragile (*alive*, I think, the word landing like it was planted in my mind)—I mentally work through the next few steps.

First, the adhesive. From the shelf near my desk I pull down the one I want, mixing it with distilled water. *Next, the application tools.* I choose a fine-bristled brush, narrow enough to apply the adhesive to the minuscule indent left behind. My hands tremble slightly. The ache near my tattoo increases. "Focus, Tilly."

Now apply the adhesive. I gently brush the aqueous substance onto the edges of the depression. My Luminara glasses are switched on and I perch over the canvas. Slowly, methodically, I stabilize the layer of paint. Then I lean back, checking over my work with a critical eye. It's seamless.

Only later will I realize that as soon as the depression was restored, the ache in my arm disappeared.

If you're a mother, you know that the sound of your child screaming—with pure, raw terror—makes you move faster than anything else can.

It's late afternoon the following day, and the house is full again, everyone home from work and school. Wyatt is on a conference call in the living room with noise-canceling earbuds, Stanley snuggled in his lap. Clementine just went upstairs to change out of her school uniform, and I'm unpacking this week's NourishBox with Shelby after locking up my studio for the day. It was a productive, if tiresome, session, removing another thick line of soot. But at least nothing strange happened today. Perfectly ordinary, a welcome respite after recent events.

"Oh, this looks lovely," Shelby says, taking the packaged protein, steak in a chimichurri sauce, out of the NourishBox. "I'll bet we can—"

But whatever she says next is cut off by Clementine's scream. "Mommyyyyyyyyyyyy!"

I don't even think. I drop what's in my hand and race for the stairs. Stanley—startled by the commotion—jumps off the couch, his nails digging into Wyatt's legs as he scrambles. I hear Wyatt curse loudly, though I'm halfway up the first set of stairs by then. Stanley barks at my heels, right behind me.

Clementine stands at the doorway to her bedroom on the second floor. Her back is to me, and at first I don't understand why she's shrieking.

"What is it? Clementine!" She keeps screaming. "Clementine!"

Almost there, almost there.

Finally, I'm on the landing and only steps away from her. If I looked through the doorway now, up at her bedroom's ceiling, I would see them. I would understand. But my eyes are locked on my daughter, on her rigid posture. Her arms are tight to her sides, her hands balled up.

And then she stops screaming. Her body ricochets backward, like she's been hit by something heavy in her center. Without Clementine's screams, I hear another sound, though at first I can't place it. It's rustling, sort of the way sandpaper sloughing off wood grain sounds.

Directly behind her, I'm about to grab her shoulders, but she turns on her own to face me. In horror, I see why she's gone silent.

She's covered in moths. I can hardly see skin. Her eyes are wide with terror, and her mouth—*oh my god!*—is filled with the insects. Pale wings flutter against her lips as they crawl in and out of her mouth.

Clementine reaches for me, a strangling sound leaving her, and a moth crawls from one nostril into her gaping mouth. Her little body heaves, and it's then I understand that she's choking. *The moths are going to kill her.*

I scream for Wyatt, clawing at the moths covering Clementine's face with desperate hands. Trying to get them away from her—out of her—but there are so many.

"It's okay, Clem . . . Mommy's here, Mommy's here . . . Wyatt! WYATT!" I don't sound like myself, my voice high-pitched with fear.

This all happens in mere seconds, and then Wyatt is there. He reaches around me to grab Clementine under her arms, hoisting her against his body and wrapping his strong arms around her middle. He gives a forceful squeeze with clasped hands to her upper abdomen, then once more, and she vomits onto the floor in front of us. A pile of moths struggles through the mess, their wings saturated.

Clementine is breathing again, crying too. *Thank god.* Wyatt doesn't even pause, stepping over the puddle of sick with Clementine in his arms, racing for the bathroom. He shouts at me over his shoulder. "Shut the door, Tilly, shut the goddamn door!"

I watch them go into the bathroom, stunned, my limbs unwilling to move. Wyatt slams the door and the shower goes on. I should be in there, with Clementine, and take a slow and clumsy step toward the bathroom. I can't feel my legs. I look down and see I'm standing in the moth-laden vomit, in my bare feet. A group of dying, wet moths flap helplessly against my foot. I can't feel that either. But then Stanley's barking breaks through, and sensation floods my limbs with an intense prickling that soon moves throughout my body.

"What's happened?" Shelby shouts, coming up the stairs. "Tilly, what's happened?"

"Careful!" I yell, pointing at the mess on the floor. I don't want Shelby to slip.

Shelby follows my gaze into the bedroom and gasps. "Stars and garters!"

I would laugh at this southern curse if things were different. But all I can do is stand in the doorway, shocked silent by the utter chaos in Clementine's bedroom.

"Tilly, my goodness . . . those are southern flannels. But . . . where on earth did they all come from?" Shelby whispers.

Hundreds of moths fill the room. They blanket the floor, the walls, her duvet cover, her desk. So many are in flight that at times you can't see the far wall through the haze of moths. A seemingly organized group of the insects try to get out the window, which is closed. Undeterred, they continue launching their bodies at the glass as though it isn't there, over and over.

Stanley barks furiously into the room, and Shelby picks him up. "Stop, it, Stan." He continues barking in her arms.

"Stanley! Settle!" Shelby commands, which is followed by a shout of pain. I turn to see the dog, still barking, drop to the floor. Shelby looks at her hand, at the fleshy part between her thumb and forefinger. There's a small puncture wound, two spots of blood.

"Did he bite you?" I ask.

She nods, incredulous. "I've never seen him like this. I have no idea what's gotten into him."

Stanley has always been a sweet, mild-tempered dog, though right now he seems anything but. He stands in Clementine's doorway, a low, menacing growl emanating from his quivering little body. The moths get louder, like sandpaper scratching metal now, as still more take flight. Zigzagging around the room, they bang against the window, the ceiling and walls, one another. And yet, not one flies out of the room.

I need it all to stop. Grasping the handle of Clementine's bedroom door, I slam it shut.

Wyatt helps Shelby clean the minor wound Stanley's teeth left in her hand—luckily, he barely broke the skin. Clementine is wrapped in my fluffy bathrobe, which is far too large for her. Only the tips of her fingers, which she uses to tightly hang on to me, are visible from under the rolled-up sleeves. I'm sitting on the edge of the bathtub, Clementine on my lap. The way I used to hold her when she was much younger. Stanley rests at my feet, though he faces the bathroom doorway, his eyes open and alert. His ears are perked up, listening. On guard.

"How are you, sweet pea?" I murmur to Clementine. My watch buzzes continuously.

> Heart rate elevated . . . Heart rate elevated . . . Heart rate elevated . . .

Clementine shrugs against me and gives a loud sniffle, her body jerking involuntarily. The final throes of her panicked sobbing. I've turned her away from the bathtub, which is layered with the now-dead moths. I don't want Clementine to see.

"She can't sleep in her room tonight," I say, to no one in particular.

"No, she cannot," Wyatt replies, his tone grim as he applies a bandage over Shelby's wound. "There you go, Mom."

"Clemmie can stay with me tonight," Shelby says. "We'll do a girls' night! A sleepover party. How does that sound, my sweet girl?"

"Good," Clementine says, smiling at her grandmother. Her eyes are swollen and red, her skin splotchy. My stomach lurches, remembering the moths streaming from her mouth. I inhale sharply, and Wyatt gives me a quick, concerned look. I shake my head.

I'm fine, I mouth at him. It's a lie, but I'm also a mom to a traumatized kid and that takes priority.

I take a quick shower in Shelby's washroom before helping Clementine change into a pair of my pajamas. Shorts and a tank top that swim on her, but they'll do for one night. Shelby takes her downstairs for a cup of hot chocolate, while Wyatt disinfects the floor and bathtub. I sit on the stairs outside the washroom (he doesn't want me breathing in the cleaner, though it's nontoxic) as he cleans, and we discuss what to do next.

He calls a friend, Travis, who has a pest-control company and, based on our description of the moths, agrees we're likely dealing with the southern flannel moth.

"Haven't those been eradicated?" Wyatt asks.

"Mostly," Travis replies. "But we get the odd cluster, every now and then. How many would you say were in the room?"

Wyatt has him on speaker, and we're sitting on our bed with our door shut. I don't want Clementine to hear anything further about the moths tonight. "A whole bunch," Wyatt replies.

"Like, more than ten?" Travis asks.

"Oh, there's more than ten," Wyatt says, chuckling without mirth. "When I say her bedroom is full of them, I mean fucking full, Trav. Like . . . thousands of moths."

There's silence on the other end.

"Travis?" Wyatt asks, and we glance at each other, wondering if maybe we've been disconnected. "You there?"

"I'm here," Travis says, letting out an audible breath. "Thousands? Literally thousands?"

"Thousands, it had to be," I repeat. My voice shakes slightly. Wyatt rubs my shoulder. My watch buzzes. I don't check the notification.

"Well, dang it. That's a lot. An infestation for sure, which means there are eggs and babies around."

Wyatt scowls, mutters, "Christ almighty," and I want to cry, the trauma of seeing Clementine like that still reverberating through me. I press my tongue hard against the roof of my mouth, which is a trick I learned after my mom died to keep the tears at bay. It works.

It's late and Travis has a sick kid at home, so he says he'll come to our place first thing in the morning.

"Keep the door closed and maybe put a rolled-up towel against the bottom, to make sure nothing can get out," Travis says. "I know I likely don't need to say this, but I wouldn't go back in there tonight. You don't want to give those moths a chance to head anywhere else."

"Don't have to tell us twice," Wyatt replies.

I whisper to Wyatt that I'll get a towel from Clem's bathroom. I don't want to use our good ones for this. He nods, and I head downstairs, averting my eyes from Clementine's shut bedroom door.

Choosing an old towel from under the vanity's sink, I'm about to leave when something catches my eye. On the floor, mostly hidden under the corner of the cabinet. It's small, beige colored. Maybe one of Clementine's hair barrettes?

I crouch to get a closer look and suddenly the thing moves. No, it *flutters*. It's one of the moths, somehow still alive.

My body recoils, and I fall hard onto my hip and arm on the tiled floor. The needles of pain take my breath away. The buzzing against my wrist becomes constant, and I glance at my watch. Elevated heart rate, Tilly. Time for breath work. I touch the OK button and try to breathe only through my nose. My eyes dart back to the moth, which is clearly struggling. I see now that one of its wings is broken.

I crawl forward on my hands and knees, reaching out for the moth. It resists my finger at first, but then climbs onto it like one might a life raft in the middle of a vast ocean.

"There, there," I say, my voice low. Only for the moth. I stand, holding it at eye level. The moth's one good wing flutters.

"You are a pretty thing." And it is. Lovely golden down covers its body, with antennae that look like tiny feathers. Black-tipped furry legs, and these fuzzy, patterned wings that evoke a desire to pet them. "But I can't let you live. Not after what you did to Clementine."

I catch my reflection in the mirror over the sink. There's a pallor to my skin that's concerning, dark hollows under my eyes. I don't look like myself. I don't feel like myself. The dreamlike, heavy-limbed sensation is back. As though I've drunk too many glasses of red wine, too quickly. All thoughts a slurry, except for one that is so clear it's impossible to ignore.

"You know what you have to do."

Is it a thought, or a voice? I don't know. It doesn't matter.

Holding the moth close to my cheek, I watch it move from my finger to my face. Struggling to get a grip until it finds the top of my lip, where it rests. Flapping one wing against my skin. It tickles but I hold still. The moth begins crawling again, across my lip. The tickling is almost unbearable. I slowly open my mouth, and the moth seeks the opening. I don't move. I don't even blink.

An image of Clementine, with dozens of these creatures inside her mouth and throat, sparks. My gag reflex kicks in but an instant later it relaxes. I'm oddly calm, my heart rate steady and slow. My watch buzzes and I recognize the pattern: a gold star, for a one-minute meditation and lowered resting heart rate.

The moth leaves my lip and crawls deeper in. Its good wing flutters against my soft palate, tickling pleasantly now. The body nestles between the top and bottom rows of my teeth, I see in the mirror. One spindly black-footed leg remains behind, hooked at the corner of my mouth. I feel warm, peaceful. I begin humming softly, the vibrations holding the moth in place between my teeth.

I bite down as hard as I can.

The next morning Travis shows up at seven sharp. I've checked in on Clementine multiple times already—she's fine, said she isn't scared anymore because she had a dream she opened the window in her bedroom, and all the moths flew out. "They wanted to be free, Mommy. They weren't trying to hurt me."

I'm grateful she's doing okay, though I don't understand how.

I am definitely *not* doing okay.

Shelby helps Clementine get ready for school and will take her so Wyatt can be home for the extermination. I brew an extra-large pot of coffee before Travis arrives.

"Count your blessings," I murmur, anticipating the imminent hit of caffeine. It's something my grandmother used to say, and I smile at the memory of her. My mother's mother, who was warm in all the ways my mother wasn't, regularly made salted-caramel popcorn balls and called them "dinner," and unfortunately passed away from a stroke when I was only twelve.

"That smile's a sight for sore eyes," Wyatt says, kissing the side of my head. He's joined me in the kitchen, has a mug at the ready. "One hell of a night, huh?"

I nod, holding the smile with effort. "You can say that again."

Travis arrives then, Wyatt's watch buzzing the notification. I'm glad when he leaves to answer the door and let my smile drop.

Shortly after Shelby and Clementine leave for school, Wyatt, Travis, and I head upstairs. Travis, who has taken the lead, asks if we've seen any other signs of the moths, prior to last night's incident.

"None," Wyatt says, then over his shoulder asks, "Tilly? Anything?"

"No. Nothing." It's then I realize I have no clue about signs of a moth infestation, aside from the obvious. "But what sort of signs?"

Travis starts up the second flight of stairs. "Caterpillars, for one. They're real furry, like a teardrop-shaped hairpiece. Or eggs, but those are tiny. Pinhead size. Hard to spot."

No, we haven't seen any caterpillars, nor eggs.

"Okay, good. The puss caterpillars are super venomous. Glad you didn't run into those."

We're at Clementine's bedroom door now, and I'm breathing heavily. I'm not yet pregnant enough to experience real breathlessness, but the exertion of the stairs, plus fear of what we'll find when we open the door, has made me short of breath. Like I said, I am not okay.

"In here?" Travis stands in front of the still-closed door.

I glance at the rolled-up towel. A wave of nausea moves through me and I put a shaky hand over my mouth. Remembering how when I bit down on the moth, the dreamlike haze evaporated. I became hyper-aware of the crushed furry body in my mouth, the bitter taste of its slimy innards coating my tongue. The panic that the moth was venomous and I had just poisoned myself and the baby.

I vomited into the sink, running the water in the hopes no one would hear. Then brushed my teeth three times using Clementine's cherry-flavored paste and an extra toothbrush from under the sink. Furiously enough that my gums bled. Flossed, too, because I kept picturing bits of the moth's body, a filament of its fine hair or a leg, caught in the crevasses of my teeth. Then I used the towel to wipe my face before I rolled it up and stuck it under the bedroom door.

The worst part? I can't explain what possessed me to let that moth crawl on my face, into my mouth. There was the voice, or thought—again, I can't be sure what it was. *"You know what you have to do."* I felt drunk, soft-minded, and yet the idea that I had to kill that moth—even though it was near death anyway—and in such a gruesome way, became like a blinking neon sign in my consciousness. I literally couldn't turn away from it.

Am I losing my mind? I think of the tendril, wriggling out of the painting. The swarming cockroaches. The half-dead moth, sticky between my teeth. I set a hand against the wall, leaning into it, overcome by the horror of last night and the sickness in my stomach. I regret the coffee, am afraid I'm going to throw up on the recently disinfected floor. At least Wyatt and Travis are focused on the door and don't see my semi-collapse.

"Yep, in here. Clementine's bedroom," Wyatt replies, though Travis and his family have been to our house before and so he knows this. Clementine and Travis's son, Ford, are the same age and have played together many times.

Travis sets an ear against the shut door, listening carefully.

"I can't hear anything," he says. He raps on the door, five times and with force. I jump, my spine going rod straight with the adrenaline, but I'm still behind them so it goes unnoticed.

Still, nothing happens. Silence, except for my whooshing heartbeat, which is so loud to my ears I can't believe Wyatt and Travis don't hear it.

"I'm going to take a peek," Travis says. Then he pauses, gestures away from the door. "Might want to give some space."

Wyatt and I step backward, until he's against the wall and I'm on the second-to-top stair, clutching the handrail whose installation I insisted on. It's not a lot of distance, but I'm glad to not have a front-row view of whatever's happening behind that door. Everything inside me feels ready to snap.

I picture Clementine covered in the insects, the desperate way she looked at me as they choked her. I shudder from head to toe, and gag, though I try to hide it with a cough. The jerky movement and sound catch Wyatt's attention. He reaches for my hand and squeezes. I swallow the sourness, then squeeze his hand back.

Travis turns the handle, slowly, then opens the door a crack. Still nothing. No sounds, no fluttering, no moths trying to escape the room.

"Well, I'll be damned," he says, sticking his head right in. My muscles tighten up, preparing for an onslaught. My fingers tingle with the anticipatory fear of what's coming. But then Travis swings the door fully open and I see why he's unconcerned.

The floor of her bedroom is inches thick with moths, every last one of them dead.

Travis calls a team to come and dispose of the insects. Wyatt takes his meetings via conference call, in our bedroom. I stay downstairs, both to keep out of the way and to avoid watching the shovelfuls of moths tumbling into the disposal bags. I'm queasy and unsettled, still unable to shake the sense that this moth infestation is more sinister than it appears.

At least we have a clue about where the moths originated—my fig plant. Travis found evidence of caterpillar "activity" on a few of the leaves (they had been partially eaten), and some eggs as well. Clementine had secretly taken the plant to her bedroom, wanting to nurse it back to health as a surprise for me. I hadn't noticed it was missing from the studio, single-mindedly focused on the Leclerc. Wyatt's annoyed with himself for not being more careful when he chose that fig for my birthday. Not that he would have been able to tell, Travis reassures him, especially if there were only eggs present.

"Like I said, so tiny they're nearly impossible to spot," Travis says. "Also not unusual to see a bonus caterpillar hitch a ride on a house plant."

But the sheer volume and the rarely seen type of moth remain a mystery.

"I can say this. It's the worst I've seen in all the years I've been doing this," Travis says. "How they replicated at this rate, and so fast, is beyond me."

It's after ten a.m. and I haven't yet gone up to my studio. I want to get to work, but I'd rather not walk past Clementine's room. I pour a second cup of coffee, then reconsider. I need to watch my caffeine intake and avoid dehydration.

"Good morning, Shelby. Are you ready for today's Memento session?" My mother-in-law's suite door is open, and therapist Diane's voice streams into the kitchen. Shelby's long back from dropping Clementine at school and walking Stanley. I glance at the mug in my hand. *Maybe Shelby could use an extra coffee for her session.*

AI Diane is on the screen—a forty-something "woman" wearing a floral blouse with a silky necktie, seated on a cushy-looking upholstered chair. She's wearing glasses, amber frames that match her eyes, and smiling. "So, tell me about the weather today."

"Rain with a chance of rain," my mother-in-law replies, and Diane laughs. Shelby has yet to put on her VR headset, so I'm able to catch her eyes. I raise the mug and my eyebrows, keeping the ask silent. Shelby smiles a thank-you. I set the coffee on her dressing table.

As I'm leaving her suite, I hear Diane ask about last evening, breezily, the way a friend who's called to chitchat would. I pause briefly to listen, hidden by the door so she doesn't know I'm still there. Shelby mentions the sleepover with Clementine but says nothing of the moths.

Back in the kitchen I stir an electrolyte packet—watermelon flavor, not my favorite—into water and wonder, with some concern, if the harrowing event has somehow slipped her mind. Panic rises for a moment as I think about Shelby's lucidity and how we let her take Clementine to school this morning. But it's silly to worry now. Drop-off went "splendidly" according to Shelby, and I've checked Clementine's location—she's in class, where she's supposed to be.

I consider maybe Shelby left the moth fiasco out of her session preamble on purpose. Even though Diane looks and sounds like a live person, she's an avatar. Anything Shelby shares is recorded and analyzed by both the Memento program and her doctors. My mother-in-law is protective of our family's privacy, and of Clementine in particular, which would easily explain the omission. I choose to believe that's it, reminding myself that simply because I'm feeling something doesn't make it a fact.

Time to get to work. I've procrastinated long enough. My breath hitches as I climb the stairs. I can't resist glancing into Clementine's open door, seeing with relief the job is nearly done. A man around my age and a younger woman are cleaning the room. The woman, whose aqua-streaked hair is visible through the mask of her protective suit, looks up as I pause at the doorway. She's holding open a disposal bag for the man, who sweeps a pile of moths onto his shovel.

"Another ten minutes or so," the woman says, her voice slightly muffled by the suit. "We'll run the disposal unit after this to pick up dust and any remaining fragments."

"Thanks so much," I say. The man doesn't look up, focused on the task of dumping the swept-up insects into the bag. Though each moth must be featherlight, a pile of them carries enough weight to make a distinctive sound when dropped into the bag. Another wave of nausea hits. My watch buzzes repeatedly.

Heart rate elevated, Tilly. Time for a rest?

My finger hovers over the ignore button.

It's more important than ever to pay attention to your body's cues. Your watch will be your best friend, Tilly, Dr. Rice said on our call. The subsequent literature that arrived about the home rest protocol also made it clear that if I ignore the notifications I risk the restrictions being escalated.

With a resolved sigh I touch OK, then sit on the top step, out of view of the young woman and man, and do my breathing exercises. I repeat them until the watch stops buzzing. A vibration pattern tickles my wrist, a gold star spinning on the screen. Satisfied, I head up to my studio, eager for the distraction the Leclerc offers.

I enter the code on the door's alarm pad. The light turns green, the lock disengaging. I take in another deep breath. My time is limited this morning, so I need to be focused and efficient. But I am not prepared for what I see—*or don't see*, more specifically—when I open the door.

I've flipped upside down; at least that's how it feels. Like a loop-the-loop rollercoaster ride from my youth, or when you're pushed so high on a swing you experience a second of weightlessness. Then the glass drops from my hand. It bounces off my foot and then the flooring, made of shatterproof glass so at least it doesn't smash into shards. My slippers are soaked from the spilled water.

None of this registers immediately, however, including the sharp pain in my baby toe, which takes the brunt of the hit. All I can focus on is the painting and what's missing.

While conservators focus on areas of loss, replacing missing elements, one needs to avoid altering the artist's work. Sometimes you add to the painting, your own brushstrokes becoming part of the story—ideally done in a skillful way to match the artist's style, allowing the original vision to remain intact. A conservator's goal is replicating with precise detail; to be an invisible partner to the artist.

So you spend as much time looking at what is there as searching for what isn't. However, usually what's missing is only a tiny fragment of the story. Something discrete—a corner of a pillow on a settee, or maybe the edge of a flower petal. Perhaps a sliver of chin, the missing top of a pointer finger, the heel of a shoe. Most of the time you have enough to work with and can visualize the story the artist was telling in the composition. You see the path through the conservation.

Now, as I stand in my studio, drenched slippers and throbbing toe, I stare at the painting and wonder, for the second time in as many days, if I'm losing my mind. For real this time.

I press my fingers against closed eyelids, count to five, then blink a few times to clear my vision. Cold vines of dread spread through me, and I'm dimly aware of my watch's incessant vibrations.

I can't explain it. Nothing about this makes any sense. The painting is . . . blank.

I'm half-done with the surface cleaning—managed to clear the soot to a good three inches above the belly button during my last session. There, I've uncovered something that looks like the base of a triangle, sitting below the subject's rib cage. The shape is heavily streaked with fine black lines, the paint thickly applied to create an intricate crosshatch pattern. For now it's unclear what the shape represents, but excited by the discovery, I took dozens of photographs of the finding.

But now the newly uncovered crosshatched section is gone. So is the entire bottom half of the painting I've already cleaned. The navel, where I found the fingernail fragment, is nowhere to be seen. All that's left behind is the black background.

Either someone got in here and covered the canvas with black paint, or the subject simply disappeared from the painting. I know the first didn't happen—I've been the only one in the studio. Which leaves the impossible as the stronger option.

Am I breathing? Barely. Am I dizzy? Yes. Do I understand what I'm seeing? *Fuck, no.*

I take a couple of steps backward and press my body against the closed studio door, my breath releasing in a wheeze. I frantically glance around the room, looking for what, exactly, I don't know.

Take a photograph.

This thought breaks through my confused panic. *Yes, a photo!* Maybe the light is doing something odd. Maybe the stress of what happened yesterday has caused a brief lapse from reality. Maybe I'm dehydrated, delirious, again?

I turn to get my camera from the desk, fingers shaking. I keep my movements slow and deliberate, as though trying to cue my nervous system to relax. Or maybe it's that I don't want to scare the missing subject, if she's (somehow, somewhere) in the room with me.

I freeze, my quivering fingertips mere inches from the camera. I'm paralyzed with fear because now I have the sense I'm being watched. As though thinking about the subject somehow invoked her.

The hairs on my arms rise.

Trying to calm myself, I take stock of my surroundings. Nothing out of the ordinary. *Feelings aren't facts . . . Feelings are not facts . . .*

It's a sunny day. Light streams through the window, creating dancing patterns on the floor. Everything is as it should be. Those are the facts. (Yet, so is the truth that the canvas is blank.)

"Look up."

The voice is urgent, and I can't figure out where it's coming from. Inside me? Outside me? I shake my head. *No.*

"LOOK UP!" More urgent now, the voice—female, possibly my own—echoing inside me.

"I don't want to," I whisper, shaking hard. The urge to tilt my head, to abide by the voice, is powerful, and despite my great desire not to do so, my chin begins to lift. I squeeze my eyes shut.

Ever so slowly my chin rises, the crown of my head tipping backward. I keep my eyes tightly closed until there's painful pressure at the base of my skull, and I know when I open my eyes I'll be staring straight up at the ceiling.

A scream waits at the back of my throat. My entire being tenses. I wish I had my scalpel, I think, my fingers clenching around empty air.

I open my eyes.

There's nothing but white paint and pot lights in the ceiling above.

The relief is so extreme I start to laugh, head still tilted back, until tears stream out of my eyes. Finally, getting a hold of myself, I look over at the canvas.

The last remnant of my relieved chuckle is lost in my throat. I blink rapidly, my vision tear streaked. Three rapid steps forward and I'm standing directly over the painting. I put my face so close to it, I am nose to canvas. Then I pull back, following the recently uncovered crosshatched section. Gloveless, I air-trace the lines with my finger, following the circle of her navel next.

She's back.

A short time later I sit in the corner of my studio, on my stool. There's as much distance between me and the painting as the space affords. I keep forgetting to breathe. Then I gasp deeply to compensate for the lack of oxygen, and the act of it is violent enough that pain blooms in my chest. I'm reluctant to blink, afraid if I take my eyes off the painting and its subject she'll disappear again.

Mostly, I don't move because my legs are still numb. I have no clue what's happening, within my body or within the art. I can't make sense of any of it.

Paintings, the objects and people captured in them, are static. They *do not move*. Except in the interactive GIA exhibits, when we animate art for entertainment.

Moreover, the subject didn't exactly move—*she disappeared*.

There is something wrong with me. Maybe some sort of mental break, caused by my raging pregnancy hormones? I wish I could ask someone without drawing attention to the why. Maybe Maeve knows about this, if it's a thing that can happen. I consider how to pose the question. "Hypothetically speaking, Maeve—related to the conservation I'm doing, and its artist—is there such a thing as pregnancy-induced psychosis?" However, I know I can't ask Maeve—she'll see right through the "hypothetically speaking" bit.

A brain tumor? Scary to imagine, but it could explain these hallucinations, and at least there are excellent treatments—cancer is rarely fatal nowadays. This offers a moment of relief, because while a tumor diagnosis would be daunting, losing one's mind is more terrifying for me to consider.

But then, another thought . . . *What if it's not me?*

What if something's wrong with the painting?

My MotherHelper meeting starts in ten minutes and I haven't left the house yet, which means I'm going to be late. It's an add-on meeting to accommodate a guest speaker, a holistic dietician who Kat told me is "amazing . . . her milk-making muffin recipe is a staple." I told Kat I'd attend, and it's too late now to back out.

There's no time to change, so work outfit it is, minus my apron—a short-sleeved cotton dress faded from years of wear, my hair in a finger-swept ponytail, makeup-free. I look disheveled and I don't care. I'm too distracted to worry about my fashion sense.

For the last hour I sat on the stool in my studio, taking shallow breaths, watching the painting with such focus that my eyes ached. Pinging between loosely plausible explanations for what happened, none of which held.

Is it me? Is it the painting? I couldn't make sense of any of it.

I should tell someone what's going on. Wyatt, at least.

I will, I decide—but later.

Now, as I reach for my bag at the front door I see my tattoo—the three dots glossy and skin-colored. No sign of anything amiss; no discernible pain. I'm suddenly glad for the biometric tracker, because it tells me that at least the baby is okay, which instantly brings down my heart rate.

Cutting through Colonial Park Cemetery will be fastest. It's a gloomy day, the air muggy, the sky overcast and threatening a thunderstorm. The type of weather where you can sense the electricity in the air, your fingertips tingling with energy. I love a good thunderstorm in the South. They can get wild, like nothing I experienced back home. But too much rain leads to a host of problems, including dreaded flooding. At least today's storm isn't supposed to be this type of drencher. I don't even bother with an umbrella.

The cemetery saw its first dead buried in the early 1700s but has been a city park since 1896, about forty years after burials ceased. There's a meandering path through its middle, and benches for rest and reflection under moss-draped oak branches. The graves are old, many of the stones crumbling and illegible now. A large number of those buried in Colonial Park Cemetery died from the yellow fever epidemic, which gripped Savannah in 1820.

Clementine and I often walk through Colonial Park, a new grave marker catching her eye each time. "How did this person die, Momma? He was even younger than me!" She finds the idea of being buried—whole-bodied, in a coffin—curious, because that is not how it's done anymore.

Neighborhood memorial centers, designed like beautiful museums, have replaced cemeteries. Here cremated remains (the process evolved to be environmentally friendly) are interred in the wall behind name plaques. Fountains babble and soothing nature sounds stream through speakers, creating a serene place to visit the dearly departed. Poppy has such a plaque—her box of ashes so small it barely took up half the space—beside her grandfather's, but that's not where I go to visit her. I can't feel her there.

There's a sudden loosening of my left shoe and I see the lace has come untied. With a grumble, the community center still a five-minute walk, I sit on the nearest bench and bend to retie the shoelace.

The next thing I know, it's teeming rain and I'm soaked to the bone. I'm seated on the bench. My shoelace remains untied. My wrist—specifically the area where the tattoo is—hurts again, like something is burrowing into my bone. The pain is searing, hard to breathe through. I massage my forearm, which seems to help a bit. My ponytail hangs in a dripping rope.

How long has it been raining like this?

Confused, I glance at my watch. See three calls from Kat and one from Margie. Then I notice the time.

I've been sitting on this bench for more than thirty minutes, but I have no recollection of those minutes passing. My dress clings to me, soaking wet, like a second skin. I'm chilled and shivering, my mind jumbled. Then something rises to the surface of my consciousness. Or rather, *someone* . . .

I wasn't alone on the bench during the rainstorm.

I'm in trouble.

Not simply because I've been hallucinating, about cockroaches and disappearing subjects in paintings. Nor because I sat on a cemetery bench in the pouring rain for half an hour, without any recollection of time passing. Certainly not only because of the unexpected and unexplainable visit from my long-dead mother, who sat beside me on that bench.

No, the most pressing issue at the moment is that I missed the MotherHelper meeting.

Once I'm home and out of my wet things I call Kat to tell her I'm fine.

"An accidental nap," I explain. She promises to send me the muffin recipe, and we make plans for our next breath work class. After I get off the phone with her I call Margie.

"I'm so sorry," I say. My phone is on speaker, and I'm in our bathroom, squeezing water from my sopping hair with a towel. My hands continue to tremble, my heart rate elevated.

“I lay down for a few minutes and then fell asleep. I never used to be a napper before this baby!” I laugh, hoping to keep the conversation short and sweet.

“Oh, I hear you,” Margie says. “Naps can be so nourishing for our bodies. But I hope that doesn’t mean you aren’t sleeping well at night.”

“I’m sleeping well,” I reply. “A touch of a headache this morning. Likely the storm.”

“Hope you’re better now.”

I assure her I am.

“Rest is the best thing for those pesky hormonal headaches,” Margie says. “And peppermint oil on the back of the neck works wonders. Did you get a bottle in your first box?”

I did, and tell her I’ll give it a try. We hang up, and I naïvely believe that’s one problem I’ve successfully checked off the list.

After lunch I clean the kitchen and start a VR meditation, trying (unsuccessfully) to regulate my nervous system. I’m watching dolphins swim when my watch taps me, a notification flashing at the top of the screen. Lifting the headset, I look at my watch and see it’s from MotherWise. I read the message on the family tablet we keep in the kitchen.

> Mathilde Crewson, MotherWise Health Center—location N5,
> 9 a.m. Dr. Alfred Rice

I have a new appointment, which I did not schedule, tomorrow morning. As I scroll through the details I see the reason why: re: headaches.

A burst of irritation fills me, and I calculate exactly how many minutes have transpired between my conversation with Margie and this appointment notification: thirty-eight.

I shouldn’t be surprised. I should *not* have said anything about a headache. MotherWise has clear-cut rules for home rest, which they prefer to refer to as "guidelines." One of which is to attend your Mother-Helper meetings. Why didn't I come up with a better excuse . . . *a headache*? That was sure to raise a flag.

There's a ringing, and I see a video call is coming through. It's Wyatt.

"Hey, babe, how are you?" I lean on my elbows and set my chin on my hands, smiling widely. I'm glad he's seeing me over the screen—it's easier to hide my stress.

"Are you okay?" Wyatt is at a jobsite. There's a robotic crane some distance behind him, a sheet of metal swinging lightly as it's winched into the air. A piece of wavy hair escapes the yellow hard hat Wyatt's wearing. He looks handsome, but also worried. And angry, I see, as I take in the hard set of his jaw.

No, I am not okay. I'm hallucinating. I lost a chunk of time . . . oh, and I saw my mother.

"I'm okay," I reply, infusing brightness into my tone. "Cleaning up from lunch and then I'm going back to the studio to—"

"What's this about headaches?" Wyatt interrupts me.

"What do you mean?" It's a silly question, because obviously he's seen the MotherWise message.

"Tilly, what do you mean *what do I mean*?" He sighs. The crane's beeping punctuates the silence when I don't reply.

"You know the notifications come to our joint account," Wyatt adds.

I do know this. One of the other MotherWise caveats is that a pregnant woman's medical history is not quite private. Wyatt, as the biological father, has the same rights I do to access my health records. At least the ones that relate to this pregnancy.

"I was a bit tired, that's all," I say. "So I took a quick nap before my meeting and forgot to set an alarm."

Wyatt frowns. "Why does the appointment say it's for headaches?"

"I had a *mild* headache—from the storm, I'm sure of it. Nothing a little peppermint oil and a nap didn't fix." I hope to appear at ease. But my heart beats faster. My watch buzzes and I lower my hands to my lap, where Wyatt can't see them. I surreptitiously remove my watch. The last thing I need is another data point for folks to get excited about. "Margie clearly overreacted when I called to tell her why I missed the meeting."

"And you're fine now?"

"Perfect!" I nod emphatically to prove it. "I'm about to call and cancel the appointment. A simple misunderstanding."

"I think you should keep the appointment. It can't hurt to get a checkup, especially because you did have a headache, and you're tired."

"Of course I'm tired." I let out a quick, forced laugh, tamping down the flicker of annoyance. "I'm almost eighteen weeks pregnant, Wyatt. Growing a human inside my body. I'd be worried if I wasn't tired."

"Still, it's already booked," Wyatt says. "Might as well take advantage of the perks, including free doctor's appointments."

"They aren't 'free,'" I reply. The MotherWise program is mostly funded through taxation.

"You know what I mean," Wyatt says, his tone softening. "I better get back at it. And I'll pick something up for dinner on the way home. Why don't you take the rest of the day off and rest up?"

It doesn't sound like a suggestion, the way he says it.

"You're measuring right on schedule, but your iron's low, as we suspected, and your blood pressure is higher than I would like," Dr. Rice says, reviewing my test results. My aching tattoo has also darkened slightly—barely noticeable, unless you are looking at it with a trained eye, which Dr. Rice has. This darkening confirms the low iron, he tells us.

"You had elevated pressure with your last pregnancy, correct?"

"With my first one, yes." I clear my throat. Wyatt takes my hand. He's come along to the appointment despite my assurances it was unnecessary. But now I'm glad he's here, as a few blips have shown up. Maybe enough to explain why I've been off recently.

"Our second pregnancy didn't go full term," Wyatt says. I hear the strain in his voice and press my tongue hard to the roof of my mouth. *Do not cry.* "But Tilly's blood pressure was mostly normal with that one."

Dr. Rice offers a smile, his eyes kind as they connect to mine. He's about my age, maybe a couple of years older. Slight salt-and-pepper highlights in his otherwise dark, closely trimmed hair. Tall and slim. He wears a wedding band, and I wonder how many children he has with his teacher wife. There are no pictures in his immaculate though impersonal office, the white walls containing only framed degrees. "Other than those two issues, which at this point I'm not overly concerned by, everything looks great, Tilly."

"Thank you." I think about Poppy and how beautifully that pregnancy was going, until it wasn't. My stomach twists uncomfortably.

"So, let's continue on as we are," the doctor says. He shifts in his chair, and the slight movement makes me strangely queasy. "Home rest; we'll add twice-daily blood pressure checks to your protocol so we can keep an eye on things."

Wyatt stands when Dr. Rice does, and shakes his outstretched hand. "Thank you, Dr. Rice. Appreciate the thoroughness."

I'm about to do the same—stand and shake the doctor's hand, which he extends my way—when a woman steps into my peripheral vision. She's behind the doctor, to his left, dressed in a familiar outfit. The same one she was wearing when I saw her at the cemetery. A short navy-blue lab coat over a white T-shirt and dark pants. Her hair is pulled back into a low bun, reading glasses perched atop her head.

"Mathilde," she says, saying my name exactly as it is supposed to be said. *MAH-tealed.*

But the tone is different from how I remember my mother sounding. Her voice had a musical lilt to it, as though she sang in a choir in her free time. This version of my mother has none of that lilt, her tone flat and lacking warmth. Also, there's something odd about the way she's holding herself, her head tilted sharply right, at an angle that isn't natural.

My throat closes. I cannot speak; I cannot breathe. I don't hear Wyatt or Dr. Rice calling my name, though later, when Wyatt recounts this story, he tells me they were practically shouting at me. "It was like you were just . . . *gone*. It scared the shit out of me."

"The work doesn't like to be kept waiting, my darling," my mother says in that strange voice. We lock eyes, and her gaze penetrates deep into me. *"It isn't wise to keep the artist waiting."*

"Tilly, Tilly! Okay, babe . . . *Christ* . . . take it easy. That's it, deep breaths."

Wyatt's crouched in front of me, hands on my arms, squeezing them too hard. I'm breathing heavily, and it takes a long moment for my eyes to focus.

"What are you doing?" I ask, confused about why he's gripping me this tightly. It hurts.

"What am *I* doing?" He glances over my shoulder. "Dr. Rice, she's back."

I'm aware of a commotion behind me. My eyes dart to Dr. Rice's now-empty chair and to the space behind it. No one is there. My mother is gone.

A machine beeps loudly, and something slips over my pointer finger. Someone presses a mask to my face and I breathe deeply, as instructed. The fogginess fades.

"How are you feeling, Tilly?" Dr. Rice steps into view, and Wyatt stands to get out of the way. I look at the finger sleeve, see the MotherWise logo and a series of small blinking lights. The beeping is incessant.

"I'm fine," I reply, my voice muffled behind the oxygen mask.

"Are you cold?" Wyatt asks. I nod, trembling with shivers that course through me every few seconds. It's as though the temperature in the room has dropped twenty degrees in seconds.

"Can we get a warmer, please?" Dr. Rice says, and soon a thin silver sheet is draped around my shoulders, the heat of it instant. My shivering subsides. Wyatt paces back and forth, casting a quick glance my way with every turn. He can't stand still when he's nervous.

"I suspect it's the low iron." Dr. Rice checks my vitals through his

MedAlert glasses. Wyatt finally stops pacing, crosses his arms over his chest. But his fingers tap in a continuous rhythm, which tells me he's still keyed up.

"My wife had the same issue with her pregnancies," Dr. Rice says, addressing Wyatt. "She would get dizzy if she stood up too quickly."

"How many children do you have?" I ask.

"Three, with another on the way," Dr. Rice replies, smiling. "Two girls and a boy, so far. We've been blessed."

He scrolls through my vitals, then picks up his tablet. "I'm going to order you a heftier iron supplement and make a few changes to your NourishBox program. We'll boost the vitamins and minerals mostly through diet. If that doesn't do the trick, we can move to infusions. But let's see where we get with this first."

Wyatt lets out a long breath. I smile at him, but the oxygen mask prevents him from seeing it. "Can I take this off now?"

"As long as you're feeling steady," Dr. Rice replies. I remove the mask and the hiss of oxygen stops. "Let's take one last pressure and oxygen saturation, and we'll send you on your way."

Thirty minutes later Wyatt and I are heading up the town house stairs. He was supposed to go straight back to the worksite, but after what happened at the appointment he insists on seeing me home. It's sweet, and I appreciate the concern, but I'm tired of answering questions about how I'm feeling.

I want to be alone so I can figure a few things out without being under his watchful eye.

My mother's words and her voice, in that strange tone, echo through my mind, crowding everything else out. *"The work doesn't like to be kept waiting. It isn't wise to keep the artist waiting."*

I need to get back to work.

Wyatt finally leaves to get Clementine from school. Shelby is out with a friend, doing some early Christmas shopping, even though we're still a month away from celebrating. I insist that Wyatt not call her. *I don't need a babysitter,* I say. *Let's not make this a bigger deal than it is.* How ironic that he's suggesting Shelby keep an eye on me, versus the other way around. Eventually he lets it go, after I promise to call him every fifteen minutes until he's back home. Finally, I am alone.

I head to my studio the moment the door closes behind him. Once inside, I take a look around. Everything is as it should be; everything is where it should be.

My relief is short-lived, however, because on the heels of it comes the memory of seeing my mother at the clinic. Let's hope this is truly as simple as a low-iron issue, but even as I think this, I understand it can't explain everything. Not even close.

It isn't wise to keep the artist waiting.

Again, my mother's words infiltrate my mind and my hands begin removing the painting's cover. I watch in awed confusion as my fingers peel away the cover, corner by corner. I can't feel my hands or the rest of my arms, all the way up to my shoulders. It's as though they're under another's control. As though they belong to someone else.

The cleaning is nearly two-thirds finished, the subject (another hit of relief, seeing her in place) exposed up to her neck. I know the final third will be difficult—the fire damage more extensive toward the top of the painting. It's going to require a delicate, steady approach.

The feeling suddenly returns to my arms and hands, the pins and needles all-consuming. I shake them out, grimacing with the pain, until the tingling eases.

Do not think of her, Tilly. Do not think of her.

How can I not think of her?

I was twenty-one and home from Queen's University in Kingston. I was halfway through my third year of a four-year bachelor of science degree, with an eye toward becoming a conservator, like my mother. So far the break had been about sleeping in and spending time with my mom.

We visited the Distillery's Christmas market, went to see the decorated windows downtown, had a festive-themed high tea at the Royal York hotel. There was a big snowfall, something that was becoming a rarity with the current climate woes. Out of childhood nostalgia I convinced my mom to build a snowman with me on the front lawn. She tied one of her painter's palettes onto the snowman's stick arm, and then we dressed it as a Parisian artist, complete with a beret and mustache made of hairs from an old brush. Though Mom had no French heritage, she was a self-proclaimed Francophile. After that we made salted-caramel popcorn balls and ate them for dinner, in honor of my grandmother.

It was a wonderful holiday.

Then, two days before Christmas, I met friends downtown for brunch. We had mimosas and caught up on gossip and news, after which I meandered home tipsy. Mom was taking advantage of the quiet house to put final touches on a presentation for a CAC—Canadian Association for Conservation of Cultural Property—conference two weeks later.

I let myself in the back door. I didn't want to disturb my mom, but I also didn't want her to know I was day drunk. Even though we were years past lectures about such things.

Everything appeared normal at first, though in retrospect I remember thinking the house felt oddly empty. Too quiet. But Mom was upstairs in her studio with the door likely closed, as it often was. I paused, listening closely, and heard something faint through the ceiling . . . as though someone was sweeping the hardwood floors above. Maybe she was tidying up her studio.

I shuffled into the kitchen and poured myself a glass of water, then grabbed a sugar cookie from the batch we'd decorated the night before. It was a holiday wreath with bright green and red icing, and silver candy balls. My plan was to chill on the couch until Mom came downstairs, maybe scroll through my phone for a social media dopamine hit while the mimosas wore off.

But I never made it to the living room.

Three steps out of the kitchen I stopped abruptly, staring uncomprehendingly at what lay on the floor a few feet away. The cookie and glass dropped from my hands, and for a long moment I stood still as a statue. Then I screamed.

My feet were like concrete blocks as I closed the gap between us. I didn't know what to do. I was crying, then choking on the bite of cookie caught in the back of my throat. My eyes watered as I gagged.

My mother was on the floor at the bottom of the staircase. Flat on her back, her head tilted to the right at an unnatural angle. She was motionless. No rising chest, no twitch of a finger, no signs of life whatsoever. But her eyes were open, staring unseeing toward the ceiling. Her expression was not one of surprise or terror. Her face appeared . . . strangely relaxed. Resolute.

I was afraid to touch her and so hovered my hands over her body, as though that might somehow patch her back together. My tears dripped onto my mom's blouse, my panic rising. I shouted her name, again and again, sobbing over her lifeless body. Finally, I called for help.

The police and ambulance arrived quickly. I sat on the bottom stair, my knees pulled up to my chest as I shook uncontrollably. My house was considered a crime scene until proven otherwise, so I stayed with a friend for a couple of nights. I have very little memory of the weeks after my mom died. My brain went offline, likely to protect itself.

Officially, her death was the result of a broken neck. An accident, the police investigation soon concluded. She died instantly, the coroner's report stated. It was speculated her foot got caught in the fabric of her long skirt, causing her to lose her balance at the top of the staircase.

I hadn't noticed the skirt when I found her, but later, when I read the report, I couldn't move past that detail. See, my mother never wore skirts. Didn't even own one, as far as I knew, her closet filled with fitted trousers, leggings, one pair of skinny jeans she wore on Sundays. Mom found dresses and skirts impractical for her type of work. All that extra, unnecessary material piled around her legs while she sat on her work stool. "So fussy," she'd say when I asked why she never dressed up. "Who needs it?"

I had no idea why she was wearing a skirt that day—white, billowing fabric, paint-spattered, returned to me with her other belongings from the hospital—and would never be able to ask. But it was odd, out of character. It unsettles me to this day.

"A tragic, horrible accident," her colleagues and friends, as well as my friends, kept repeating at the funeral. They clutched my arms in sympathy, offered tight hugs that stole my breath. I longed to run away, but to where? Even then I understood grief follows you everywhere.

A couple of weeks after the funeral I returned to university, then the house was sold, and I went backpacking in Europe with two school friends for the summer. My grief came with me, my constant companion, but somehow I kept my head above the surface. Until we arrived in Italy, where I saw a familiar saying on an apron, of all things. Hanging innocently in a tourist shop near the Stazione di Venezia Santa Lucia—Venice's central train station.

Non tutti le ciambelle riescono col buco.

(Not all doughnuts come out with a hole.)

My mom was trying to tell me she was with me, would always be with me.

I bawled like a baby while I clutched the apron, scaring the hell out of my friends and the shop's owner, who insisted on giving me a steep discount. I still have that apron—I wear it in my studio, and every time I tie the strings around my waist I think of my mother.

But I never thought I would *see* her again. Not in this lifetime, anyway.

It's three a.m. and I can't sleep. Every time I close my eyes my dead mother is there. Standing beside Dr. Rice, head tilted hard to the right as she watches me. This leads me to the horrible memory of finding her at the bottom of our staircase, in that skirt I had never seen before. The subsequent cresting grief and panic inside me won't relent, and I try to visualize a breath ball. It's useless. I can't lie in bed a moment longer.

Wyatt sleeps soundly as I creep out of our bedroom. First, I go to the kitchen for a glass of water, adding one of my electrolyte packets. I stir the mixture with my finger and head back up the stairs, tiptoeing past my bedroom and Clementine's. The moon is nearly full, and it glows through the window adjacent to my studio's door, illuminating a rectangular patch of light on the landing. Typing in my code to unlock the door, I cringe as the alarm pad beeps loudly three times, granting me entry.

Slipping inside, I turn on the lights and then squint with the sudden brightness. My watch buzzes. Switch to red-light filter for optimal circadian rhythm management? I touch the ignore button, the bright lights remaining as they are. I won't be going back to sleep tonight.

Blinking to help my eyes adjust, I look at the painting, which remains covered on my workbench. A chill moves through me, goose bumps rising across my arms. There's a cardigan hanging on the back of the door, and I slide it on before sitting down at my desk.

I sip my electrolyte water as my personal tablet comes to life, and then take a notebook and pen from inside the desk's drawer. Normally I'd use my GIA-issued tablet, but I don't want a digital trail for this search. I'm not sure exactly what I'm looking for, or what I'll find, but I have the sense I'll want to keep it to myself.

Welcome back, Tilly! A search bar appears below the greeting message, and a virtual keyboard lights up under the tablet. Setting my hands on the lit-up keys on my desk's top, I start typing. "Margot Milton, Painting Conservator, Toronto, Canada."

A list of hits runs along the side of the screen, with another search box popping up in the center to help narrow the findings. For a moment my fingers pause on the keys, my chest tight. Then I type, "The Child + Charlotte Leclerc." Six references are highlighted along the side, and I touch the first one.

It's an announcement of *The Child*'s procurement, which I've seen before. The details are limited, and the collector is mentioned as "an anonymous admirer of Leclerc's art." I close it, then scan the next few references. A website link for the Art Gallery of Ontario. A HoloLex—the modern version of Wikipedia—page on Charlotte Leclerc, with optional hologram features if you have the technology at home (we don't). That article by the journalist from a few years back, with the teaser headline . . . A TERRIBLE FATE WAS COMING MY WAY. The fifth reference is blocked, a red-bordered box popping up when I click it, asking for an Advanced EduNet passcode. This article is behind a security wall, meaning it can't be viewed by the general public. The screen is fuzzed out for privacy, so I can't even read the synopsis.

I hesitate, as entering my GIA code will automatically flag a connection to Charlotte Leclerc. I was given strict instructions to keep the nature of this conservation private, the signed NDA top of mind.

I decide it's worth the risk. After all, who's going to go looking through my search history? Raoul knows what I'm working on, and I can't imagine anyone else bothering to check. I enter my password, and the screen comes into focus.

> **Charlotte Leclerc:** *TRAGIC CHARACTER OR AVANT-GARDE ARTIST?*
> The Child, *A CONSERVATION.* By Margot Milton, Principal Conservator—Paintings, Art Gallery of Ontario

It's my mother's presentation. The one she was working on the day she died and never had the chance to deliver in person. I can't believe this is the first time I'm seeing it. Then I check the upload date—only a month ago, for a CAC conference session about some of the museum's most enigmatic artists and projects. That explains why it wasn't in the package I received from Cecil when I started my conservation.

I race through the presentation, which is verbatim and many pages long. I'm breathless by the time I reach the end. Then I reread her closing paragraph, and a shiver moves through me.

I've learned three things.

One, *The Child* was as disturbing and curious a piece of art as the one currently in my studio. Two, my mother was deeply affected by this particular conservation, noting how Charlotte Leclerc "wormed into my subconsciousness, whether or not I was actively working on the piece, and at times made me question where her brush ended and mine began."

Three, while it was her self-professed "project of dreams," my mother posed a final question in her presentation, and reading it now makes my blood run cold.

"When we restore art—breathing new life into the brushstrokes, colors, shapes, and textures—a conservator must ask: have we also brought the artist herself back from the dead?"

I've exposed the subject to the jut of her chin. Because I'm working across the piece, I haven't yet uncovered the right shoulder and arm, nor that edge of her rib cage. That's the next phase of conservation.

From what I can tell at this stage, she's slender, showcased by the light and dark shadows of her external obliques. There is a softness to her belly, however, that doesn't match the tautness of the rest of her. Clearly this is a postpartum body—parts of you never return to the way they were before, after stretching out to accommodate human life. I set a hand on my stomach, rounding out now that I'm nearing nineteen weeks. The quickening has begun—bubbles popping low in my pelvis, a sensation of butterfly wings tickling my insides. I've tried to explain the sensations to Wyatt, who's impatient to feel her movements himself, but it's impossible to do them justice.

Right above the subject's navel is the hourglass-shaped black hole, with the crosshatching, from breastbone to belly. It's another common memento mori symbol, the hourglass, and it looks like it's been carved right out of her chest, due to the artist's use of shading and texture.

Her left hand, the fingers grotesquely long and skeletal, press to her chest above the hourglass shape.

I'm currently working on the edges of the hourglass, specifically on the subject's right side. There's a strange pebbling in the color, which likely occurred after the paint aged versus being original to the piece. I have a theory as to what's happened, and why, but I'll need to analyze a sample to be certain. Using my scalpel, I remove a fleck of the paint from the hourglass and tap it carefully onto a slide for microscopic evaluation.

I'm trying not to think about my mother—or her presentation, whose last line continues to unnerve me—as I work. But today it's impossible not to think about my mother, because she's in the room with me. Standing off to the side, her head hanging precariously to the right, as though the bones are rubber.

"You know what that is, Mathilde," she says. *"You have to trust your instincts more, not rely so much on technology."*

I do know what it is, or at least I suspect I do. *Rust staining.* Usually seen on paper, but it can happen with paint as well. Say, in a case when the paint interacts with the mineral iron . . . which is an essential element in the production of blood.

But I don't respond to my mother's comment, because she's dead and can't possibly be here talking to me in my art studio about rust staining, or anything else. It's best for me to write this off as my overactive, grief-soaked imagination bringing her to life as a comfort. Or the low-iron thing. I cling to these possibilities, even as she continues talking to me.

"Mathilde. Please look at me."

I shake my head, quickly tidying my tools. That's enough for one day. I need some fresh air. I need out of this room.

"I'm sorry, my darling," she says. *"It isn't supposed to be this way."*

I'm suddenly freezing, like I've jumped into a cold lake back home on a late October morning. My breath catches, her words hanging in the room. Squeezing my eyes shut, I continue shaking my head. *No, no, no. NO.*

"Please go away," I whisper. "You can't be here. Please, leave me alone."

The coldness disappears as quickly as it comes, and I cautiously open my eyes. Look to the corner of the room, see that it's empty.

My mother is gone.

I need information and reassurance as urgently as I need an escape. Thankfully, this time when I call, Cecil picks up right away. I'm nibbling some mixed nuts and sipping a hot lemon balm tea, both of which came in this week's NourishBox. The note that arrived with the tea says it's good for "*mom-xiety* and irritability," which makes me roll my eyes, but I still brew a cup. Using the microwave, because I keep forgetting to bring the kettle down. So far the tea has done nothing but make me have to pee.

"Tilly, nice to hear from you. How are you?" Cecil asks. "How's the family?"

I pause, too long.

"Tilly? You there?"

"Yes. I'm here. How are you? How's the weather in Toronto?"

"I'm well, thank you for asking. And it's sleeting, which I'm sure you don't miss. But I have the sense this isn't a social call," he says. "So why don't we get right to it?"

I sigh, wrap my hands around the still-warm mug. A ghost of the chill lingers in my body. "I have a few questions about Charlotte Leclerc, and . . . well, my mother's conservation of *The Child*."

"I'm not sure I'll be able to help," Cecil replies. "I wasn't at the museum when your mother was working on that piece—but let me try."

"I found her presentation on EduNet. The one she was supposed to give at that CAC conference. They just uploaded it recently. Have you read it?"

"I have." Cecil's tone gives nothing away.

"Her experience with *The Child* . . ." I don't quite know how to ask for what I need. How do I explain what's happening with the painting in my studio? With me? "I'm not sure exactly how to put this."

"As plainly as you can, Tilly. Always the best way."

I think back to when Mom was working on the Leclerc. That night in the museum. I lean into the memories, forcing myself back in time.

She was distracted, and consumed by the work. Her clothes baggier, her cheekbones sharper. I was a petulant teenager, preoccupied with my own ego and experiences, so didn't pay much attention to the changes. I don't remember much else about the piece, or her conservation, except for that odd night at the museum, and then later, a strict warning to never go into her studio without her being there. She had never been that explicit, and I remember telling her to "chill, bruh," in my obnoxious teenager lingo, for it seemed overly dramatic.

I wonder now about that warning. Was it about confidentiality around her work, a particular piece resting in her studio? Perhaps, even, *The Child*? It could explain her sudden edginess, though it made little sense. Paintings didn't leave the museum mid-treatment—no one's home was set up for that type of work back then. Mom's studio was a place she practiced techniques, or read, in her off time.

None of this is particularly helpful at the moment, so I focus on the presentation.

"There's a lot in there that's familiar," I say to Cecil. "The use of body-based materials, for one thing. The melancholy of Leclerc's color choices and memento mori style. The sense that what you're seeing is only surface level, and that she's hidden truths within the composition."

I take a breath, pacing around the kitchen. My bladder protests, and I set down my half-drunk tea.

"The last paragraph. The question. It . . . I—" A deep cramp squeezes my lower abdomen. My breath leaves me as I double over. "Oh!"

"Tilly? Are you all right?"

The pain and pressure are gone a second later, though they leave me mildly breathless. "Stubbed my toe, I'm fine." I stretch back—maybe it's round ligament pain, which is common in the second trimester—but feel only a mild tension in my abdomen.

"Anyway, I'm having a similar experience with *The Mother*, and I don't understand it." I pause. "Even thinking what I'm thinking makes me wonder if I'm losing my mind." It feels good to say it out loud.

"Did I ever tell you about what happened when Svetlana Telets's *The Woman of the Rain* was gifted to the museum?" Cecil asks.

"I don't think so." I haven't heard this story, but I know the piece.

The Woman of the Rain is said to be cursed. It was painted by the artist Svetlana Telets in only five hours; a self-described fever-dream creation. The first few owners of the artwork described terrifying experiences: horrible nightmares once it was hung in their homes; things breaking, and a sense of being watched; and some even claimed to have seen the rain woman walking through rooms in the darkness of night.

"I worked on the conservation with a colleague, Julia Dreyer, who I believe you know?"

"Yes, Julia and I had some crossover at the AGO." Julia is now in Germany, heading up a conservation program there. We exchange messages once a year, at Christmas.

"I've never had this happen before, nor since, but there was something about that painting . . ." Cecil's voice trails away. "Julia and I both felt it. A malevolence we couldn't explain. I had perplexing insomnia the entire time we worked on it, which continued even after it went on display. Awful nightmares that would wake me in a cold sweat. It was the eyes, I think. There was something strange about her eyes."

I set a hand to my throat and swallow hard.

"In the years since I've often wondered if my mind created that experience of fearfulness. That me knowing the painting was rumored to be cursed then made it so in my reality."

"Hmm. A form of cognitive bias," I murmur.

"Precisely," Cecil says.

I consider this in the context of my own situation. No question something similar could be happening to me. I'm well aware of the rumors about Leclerc's methods, the strange lore that follows her. Perhaps I'm hallucinating my mother too. The anniversary of her death is only a couple of weeks away. Wouldn't be unheard of—our reaction to a painful loss isn't predictable, nor is its timeline. Add in the stress of the pregnancy, plus the hours of focused work on the conservation . . .

Yes, that could explain it.

"We get so close to the art, and to the artist," Cecil continues. "Sometimes it's as though you've become one entity, as you well know. There's nothing pathological about that, Tilly. It's part of the job."

By the time we hang up I feel better.

The tree is up, though currently bare. Clementine and I are sorting through the decorations—many handmade over her school years, some from when I was a child, some from Wyatt's Christmases before I joined the family. All Christmas trees are artificial now, thanks to tree-protecting environmental policies, and so made of recycled and sustainable materials. Occasionally I miss the scent of a freshly cut pine in the living room, though ours has a built-in scent diffuser. However, the smell isn't natural enough for me, and it's somewhat overpowering, so the diffuser remains off.

It's Sunday, a nonwork day, and while I'm with my family in body, my mind is elsewhere. The Leclerc monopolizes my focus and it's becoming increasingly difficult to stay out of my studio. Especially because I'm hyperaware of how quickly time is passing. As the weekly MotherWise e-zines (the plum is now a pomegranate) pile up in my inbox, so does my impatience to finish the conservation. I *have* to complete it before this baby arrives—there's no other option.

Wyatt's job is the lights, and he's twisting the branches to turn on the laser-powered, fiber-optic channels that stretch down each branch. Soon the tree illuminates, a soft and warm glow emanating from every needle.

"Cookies are cooling," Shelby says, settling on the couch to help me and Clem with the decorations. She holds up a palm-size Santa hat, red felt, with an oversize yarn pom-pom that is barely hanging on. *Wyatt, 7*, is stitched along the brim with black thread, the letters uneven.

"Remember this one, Wyatt? You were so proud." She turns to Clementine. "Your dad made this when he was your age."

Clementine takes the hat from her nana, inspects the stitching. "Pretty good, Daddy."

"Bless your heart, sweet girl," Wyatt says, laughing. He's ensuring all the branches are evenly lit but turns from the tree and task to smile at Clementine. "I think that was the first and last time I used a needle and thread."

"Well then, you should be proud of yourself, Daddy." Clementine sets the hat in a row of decorations on the coffee table. "Nana, can I have a cookie before we ice them?"

Shelby glances at me and I nod. The shortbreads are a family recipe and baked only during the holidays. Clementine loves them.

"The boss says yes! Lucky us!" Shelby stands, holding out a hand. "Let's go choose one each."

"Bring me one too, okay?" Wyatt says.

Clementine says she will as she scrambles to her feet, hand in hand with Shelby. In the kitchen she's debating which cookie to pick. ("I think the Christmas tree one is taller, but the sleigh is wider . . . which one do you want, Nana?")

"She has such a sweet tooth," I say, laughing.

"Takes after her dad." Wyatt steps back from the tree, checking his work.

"Great job with the lights, hon."

Wyatt comes behind me, wrapping his arms around my midsection. With his hands clasped across my stomach, it becomes clear how much I've popped recently.

"We have so much to look forward to this year." Wyatt rests his chin between my shoulder and neck, and I lean back into him.

"By next Christmas we'll be five, including Shelby," I murmur. A pulse of joy moves through me. "And Clementine will have a sibling."

"I know. I can't wait, babe."

"Me neither." I twist my head to kiss him. The moment lingers, a stirring beginning in my body. But it's soon dashed by Clementine, who returns with a cookie in each hand.

"Here you go, Daddy. I brought you a Christmas tree." She has a sleigh-shaped cookie in her other hand.

"Thanks, Clem. Good choice." He takes a big bite of the cookie and groans. "Mom, as delicious as ever."

Shelby smiles, looking pleased.

I'm basking in these happy moments with my family, so the tickle on my arm barely registers. At first. But soon the itching can't be ignored. I scratch lightly at the underside of my wrist.

Wyatt offers his last bite of cookie to Stanley, who has been waiting patiently at his feet for a morsel. "Good boy," he says, scratching Stanley under his white-whiskered chin.

Scratch, scratch, scratch. I itch my arm in time with Wyatt's scratches on Stanley's chin.

There's a slightly raised red circle around the tattoo, though the dots remain clear and glossy. Not darkened, like before. Maybe a reaction to the new laundry detergent I bought recently? Or dry skin? I used the last of my lotion yesterday, am waiting to buy more in case a bottle ends up in my stocking.

Either way, likely nothing to be alarmed by.

My arm—specifically the skin around my MotherWise tattoo—has been itching on and off for more than a week. Ever since we put the tree up. I've still not mentioned it to anyone but did a search on Edu-Net, which was largely unhelpful, most advice nonspecific and anecdotal. But aside from that and the occasional mild redness, there's nothing else to report. No pain, no ache. The tattoo itself is unchanged—the dots clear against my skin. Calling Dr. Rice or Mother-Wise so close to the holidays seems pointless, as offices are emptying out for the break.

It's Christmas Eve. Wyatt, Clementine, Shelby, who has Stanley—sporting a holiday-themed sweater—on a leash, and I attend our community's annual gathering. It's cool tonight, so I'm wearing a long-sleeved dress, which clings enough to show I'm pregnant. Every now and then I touch my necklace, safely hidden under the turtleneck of the dress.

Poppy's ring is on the chain tonight. It felt wrong to leave her behind in the drawer on this family-oriented, celebratory evening.

"Momma, there's Briar! Can I go say hi?"

I look to where Clementine points—Dawn; her husband, Robbie;

and their daughter, Briar, stand near someone in a red-and-white-striped candy cane costume who hands out holiday greeting cards and hot chocolate to passersby.

"Go ahead, Clem. But only one hot chocolate, please."

"Yes, Momma. Promise." She darts off, careful not to bump into anyone as she makes her way to her friend (and, as important, the hot chocolate). There's a hurried urgency to her pace, as though she's trying to win a race.

Wyatt laughs. "I miss that."

"Which part?" I ask. "Sugary hot chocolate, or being a kid at Christmastime?"

"Both," he says. I watch him watching Clementine. The corners of his eyes crinkle with his smile. This is what no one prepares you for when you become a parent. The sheer delight of observing your child participate in this thing called life. It's magical and mesmerizing. With a rush of happiness I realize we're about to get to do it all over again.

"I'm fixing to get a hot chocolate myself," Shelby says. "Let Stan have a walkabout, and say hello to a few people. Anyone else?"

She has a large social network, far more robust than mine or Wyatt's. There are friends she walks with, friends she volunteers with, friends she lunches with. Community-based programs are particularly geared toward those in their twenties and those over seventy, both groups that suffered most during the loneliness epidemic following MorA.

"We'll join you in a minute, Mom." I pick up a hint of exhaustion in Wyatt's tone. Probably left over from work, his projects behind schedule due to a flurry of people being out sick with the inevitable December germs.

I set one hand on my stomach, then reach for his and place it beside mine. "She's awake." I can refer to the baby's sex, confirmed during the visit to Dr. Rice, because Clementine isn't nearby. It's been hard to keep it from her, but I'm determined to honor the wish for a surprise.

Wyatt's hand stills, waiting for movement. It's likely too early to be felt, at least on the outside of me, but she's incredibly active tonight. I feel a soft nudge, and then Wyatt grins, eyes widening. *Good girl*, I think, happy to see him light up. "This never gets old," he says.

A moment later the carol singers begin, and the baby moves again. I grin. "She likes Christmas music."

Wyatt and I join in with the caroling. He can sing ("the voice of an angel," Shelby says), and thankfully his strong voice drowns out mine. I'm as terrible a singer as he is a good one, but I love carols.

I drop Wyatt's hand partway through "Silver Bells" to scratch at my arm, which goes unnoticed because Clementine and Shelby have returned with hot chocolates. Clementine talks a mile a minute, the high of the celebrations, and sugar, flooding her small body.

She's excitedly sharing school gossip ("Miss Lauren"—her teacher—"might bring her pet guinea pig, Chuckles, to our class!"), when Stanley starts growling. I look at him, curious about what's made him so upset. His body shivers under his red-and-black plaid sweater as he barks a few times. He's a social butterfly like Shelby, and loves the attention he commands in a crowd like tonight's.

"What's up, Stanley?" I ask the dog.

"Simmer down this minute." Shelby's tone is quiet but firm, and Stanley lets out a pitiful whine. He stops growling but continues to stare across the square. Over by an oak tree, whose trunk is wrapped in strings of twinkling white lights.

I see her then. My mother. Standing beside that tree, in the shadows of dusk and Spanish moss. Her head tilts farther to the right, sending shivers down my spine and a rolling nausea into my stomach. The twinkle lights illuminate one side of her face, the effect ghoulish.

This can't be happening . . . not now.

The itch on my arm crescendoes. I wish I could ask if anyone else sees the woman standing by the tree. We lock eyes then, and she smiles. There's a moment of comfort—*it's my mother's beautiful smile!*

But soon the smile warps. Her mouth opens impossibly wide, lips stretching thin, then twisting, pulling taut with the effort.

"There's only one way to make that stop, Mathilde." Though she's at some distance, and the crowd of holiday revelers is still singing, I have no trouble hearing her. Even through that terrifyingly freakish mouth.

She gestures to her own arm, and I understand she's referring to the itching of mine. Then she tells me how to get rid of it.

I whisper, "I can't do that."

"What did you say?" Wyatt asks. I shake my head, discombobulated.

"Nothing," I manage. He turns back to Clementine, who is pestering him for the rest of his hot chocolate.

I'm struggling to stay present, my mother's voice louder now in the space between us. Drowning out all the others. Even the music fades further into the background when she tells me again what I have to do. I don't reply this time, instead give a shake of my head. *No.*

My mother quiets, her lips remaining stretched in the disfigured grimace. A moment of stillness follows, until she sets her hands to her abdomen, as though she's about to be sick. A stream of moths suddenly pours from her mouth. Southern flannel moths. My body goes numb; everything shuts down.

She continues heaving in rhythmic waves, bringing up more and more of the moths. I register the main chorus of "Joy to the World," faintly. But it can't mask the gurgling, retching sounds coming from my mother's body. Soon, the pile of insects has grown to where it swallows her entirely.

"*STOP!*"

I snap back to myself with the same intensity of a rubber band stretched to its limit before being released. Everyone nearby turns to me, as my voice is louder than the holiday music.

While most faces appear curious at the outburst, Shelby, Wyatt, and Clementine look at me with alarm. Wyatt in particular.

"Tilly? You all right?" he asks.

Do I look all right? I'm still dazed. "I think so?"

"Here, Daddy." Clementine hands Wyatt back the cup of hot chocolate. Her eyes dart repeatedly to my face. "I promised Momma I'd only have one."

"It's fine, Clemmie. That wasn't about you or the hot chocolate." I sound as weak as I feel. I clutch at Wyatt's arm for support, woozy.

"Whoa." Wyatt grabs hold of my elbow with both hands, steadying me. "Tilly, if you're not feeling well, we should go home."

I see him in my peripheral vision, watching me. But I can't look his way. Not even to reassure him, because I'm afraid of what he'll see on my face.

"To be honest, I'm a bit tired," I say. "But let's wait to go until the carols are finished." Risking a quick glance to the oak with the twinkly lights, I see that my mother and the moths are gone.

"You sure?" Wyatt asks. He glances at Shelby. "Maybe we should head out now."

"No. I can rally until after the carols." I offer what I hope is a reassuring smile.

My mother, and the sick pile of moths, may be gone, but the itch in my forearm has intensified. The sensation more a burning pain now. Demanding my focus.

With hands clasped behind my back to avoid being seen, I rake fingernails over the itchy spot. There's a moment of relief, but it disappears seconds after I stop scratching.

"I can't get this open." Clementine's face scrunches up with annoyance. She's picking at a piece of sealing tape, which holds the flaps of the box together. It's Christmas morning, early, because when you have a seven-year-old the hoopla is over by the time the sun comes up.

Wyatt, Shelby, and I never go overboard on gifts for one another, though we do our best to ensure a tidy pile rests under the tree for Clementine. You only get so many Christmas mornings as a child. I distinctly remember the thrill of seeing so many wrapped gifts, covered in sparkly holiday paper with whimsical bows, waiting for me to tear into. My mother always spoiled me at Christmas.

The box in Clementine's hands contains a pair of sneakers she's been asking for. Self-lacing, with solar-powered multicolored lights and springs that pop out from the soles, allowing the wearer to bounce with each step. They're made of mushroom "leather," and the most expensive pair of shoes I've ever bought. I can't wait for her to see them—she's going to lose her mind.

But her progress is slowed by the box's sealing tape, which remains impenetrable to her picking and pulling. Clementine's impatience grows by the second, as she's guessed what's inside. However, she won't hand the box over for help.

"I want to do it myself," she says huffily.

"I'll get the scissors. That should make it easier." I shift the contents of my stocking to the couch cushion beside me and head to the kitchen.

Scratch, scratch, scratch. A moment of relief, before the itching begins again. It kept me up for hours last night, as did the anxiety about seeing my mother by the tree. *All those moths . . .*

I try to shake it off, focusing instead on getting the scissors for Clementine. Holiday music plays through built-in speakers, and homemade cinnamon buns—a Crewson family Christmas-morning tradition—bake in the oven. The kitchen smells incredible, and my stomach growls. I should eat something.

Scratch, scratch, scratch. I'm going to have to call MotherWise about this itching. It's becoming unbearable, relentless, my skin mottling red in a star pattern around the tattoo. Like a cluster of mosquito bites that won't heal. But the office is closed today, and Clementine's gift opening comes first. I'm reaching for the kitchen shears, resting in a sharp-safe sheath on the side of the refrigerator, when I hear her voice.

"That's it, my darling," she says. *"You can fix this."*

Whipping around, I look for my mother, but she's not in the kitchen. However, she continues repeating, *"fix this . . . fix this . . . fix this,"* until I'm frantic and crazed with the intrusion. I can't think. My arm itches so badly I'm delirious. I start to cry. Desperation fills me.

Then she says, *"You have to remove it, Mathilde. It's hurting you and the baby. You know it is."*

It's as though I'm under water, everything muted. My thoughts race on, jumbled and cluttered until suddenly something shifts into sharp focus. My mind is the clearest it has ever been. I look at the kitchen shears in my hand and slowly slide my fingers into the handle loops, opening and closing the blades a few times. I'm calm, my movements precise and controlled. My mother's voice returns, and I smile.

I feel silly not seeing the solution myself. *"Mother knows best,"* she says, then, *"Fix this . . . fix this . . . fix this . . ."*

I poke the sharp tip of one of the blades against my skin, adding pressure. The skin yields with a burst of pain, leaving a drop of blood when I remove the blade's tip.

"That's right, Mathilde. Fix this."

"Here are the scissors," I say brightly, walking back into the living room a few minutes later. "The cinnamon buns smell so good, Shelby."

Wyatt and Shelby have their backs to me, watching Clementine pick at a loose corner of the tape. She's barely made progress.

"Thought we lost you to the temptation of the buns." Wyatt laughs, then turns my way. His face drains of color when he sees me, or, more specifically, sees my arm.

Blood drips down my fingertips, falling in steady droplets to the floor below. I see the slow-moving rivers of blood against my bare skin, my sleeve pulled up to my elbow, yet I'm oddly detached. No pain whatsoever.

"What's wrong?" I don't understand the look on Wyatt's face. I fixed the itching! It was as simple as my mother said it would be. *Mother knows best.*

I have the kitchen shears in my other hand and hold them out to Clementine. "Here, sweets. To open the box."

"Tilly! What the hell did you do!" There's terror in Wyatt's voice.

It unnerves me, and I'm confused about why he sounds so scared. *What is going on?*

It's as though everyone is frozen in place—like a Christmas-morning tableau. The tree lights twinkle, the bars of "Jingle Bell Rock" play, there's wrapping paper scrunched in balls on the floor, festive-colored stockings draped over the back of the couch. My family stares at me, each with a similar wide-eyed and openmouthed expression. They're in shock—this registers, even though I remain perplexed as to why they aren't happier for me. I solved the problem.

"Goodness, why does everyone looks so worried?" I say. Drip, drip, drip. I glance at my arm, at the blood that isn't slowing. At the hole I've carved out, near my wrist. *Hmm . . . that might need a small bandage.* Later, though. Clementine's gift needs to be opened first. I can't wait to see her expression.

Again, I extend the scissors toward my daughter, smiling. But instead of taking them from me she drops the shoebox, slaps her hands over her ears, and starts screaming.

The woman's name is Ana Clairmont. Ana, she tells me, is short for Anaïs.

"First things first," she says, within moments of arriving at the house. "Would you prefer Mathilde or Tilly?" She pronounces my given name perfectly, and I tell her so.

"I lived with my French grandparents for a summer as a teenager. Learned to speak fluently."

Ana is dressed in lavender scrubs, the MotherWise emblem on the upper left-hand side of her top. Her wiry gray hair is tucked into a bun. She's polite yet efficient with her questions, no extraneous small talk. I get the sense those blue-gray eyes miss nothing, that she is the no-nonsense sort.

"Tilly or Mathilde, either is fine," I reply.

Ana regards me curiously. "You don't have a preference?"

I pause for a beat. "I prefer Mathilde."

Ana also used to prefer her French name, but "everyone butchered it, so I changed it and now it seems easier to stick with Ana."

"I understand exactly," I say.

"Well, Mathilde it is." She holds a small tablet in hand and types something into it. We're sitting at my kitchen table, cups of now lukewarm tea in front of us. It's the day after Christmas. The day after I cut out my MotherWise tattoo while the cinnamon buns baked, after my dead mother told me to.

"So, let me go over how this works," Ana says. Her eye contact is intense, and I wait for her to blink. She doesn't.

"I'm your 'personal health connector'—the term MotherWise uses—though I like 'nurse,' because everyone understands what that means. I'm here to make the rest of your pregnancy smooth and easy."

My lips are dry, my arm throbbing under the large bandage that covers a bio-printed skin graft. The wound, though shallow, was too large and ragged for stitches. I've been home from the hospital for a few hours, the graft surgery done late last night.

"For now it's only me," Ana says. "Morning and afternoon in person, and one evening video visit. Heads up, my avatar is from over ten years ago. I used to be a blonde, and things were . . . perkier." She gives a wry look. "Vanity is boring, but it's hard to let go of."

I nod and smile politely, unsure of how to behave in front of Ana—and by proxy, MotherWise.

"I'm pro-aging, in case you're wondering. But there's no harm in reminiscing from time to time," Ana adds, not looking at me as she taps something into the tablet. "So, I'm going to become a familiar addition to your household, at least during the daytime. If needed, there are night nurses as well."

"I'm sure that won't be necessary." I'm mortified to need one of these health connectors, let alone round-the-clock care. "This seems excessive, to be honest, Ana. My mother-in-law is here most of the day with me."

At this she pauses briefly. "Honey, if you take kitchen shears to your own arm, you get me, at a minimum. It's that simple."

I look down at my hands, clenched in my lap. I'm embarrassed by what happened, yes, but also terrified. Who wouldn't be? I went into the kitchen to get scissors to open Clementine's Christmas present and then sliced a two-inch-by-two-inch hole into my arm before returning to my family like nothing happened. Bleeding all over the floor, feeling no pain. Not the actions of a stable person.

"We'll keep an eye on those zinc levels," Ana adds. "And watch your pressure, too."

After Wyatt called the ambulance—something I repeatedly said was wholly unnecessary, even as my arm bled through the kitchen towel Shelby held in place—I was taken to the hospital's MotherWise unit.

"You're in shock," the paramedic said, when I explained it didn't hurt at all and *surely I don't need an ambulance*. Wyatt spoke over me, despite me being perfectly lucid by then. "She's pregnant. Almost twenty-one weeks." At least they left the sirens off.

A battery of tests pointed to a zinc overdose.

"I'm guessing the mixed nuts, plus the supplement from the vitamin and mineral pack," Dr. Rice explained. I felt awful that he had to come in on Christmas. He said it was fine, *young kids and early starts and all that*. "You have a sensitivity to the mineral, Tilly. In very rare cases it can cause auditory hallucinations."

I ended up telling Wyatt—and then Dr. Rice—the truth, or part of it, anyway. My tattoo was itching horribly and then I *heard* someone tell me to cut it out of my arm, after which I went into this trancelike state. I don't remember the actual cutting, something Dr. Rice says is "the best Christmas gift that doesn't come under a tree."

I leave out the part about who suggested it, as well as the fact that I was also seeing her somewhat regularly.

"What about a new tracker?" Wyatt asks Ana now. I almost forgot he was in the kitchen with us, leaning against the pantry door and so out of my sight line.

"Doc Rice thinks Mathilde had a reaction to the tattoo itself. Hence the itching," Ana says, addressing Wyatt. "Safer to leave it out of her body for now."

"Can I still work?" I ask. "My arm feels okay."

"Honestly, Tilly," Wyatt says with a heavy sigh. He looks pissed off, and wan. Neither one of us slept a wink at the hospital last night. "Please tell her that's not a good idea, Ana."

The nurse shrugs. "I don't see why she can't work, at least for a few hours a day."

Wyatt frowns, displeased.

"From what I understand, the work isn't overly taxing or stressful. Mostly desk work, it says here," Ana adds, reading off her tablet.

A harsh laugh explodes out of Wyatt. Yep, he's pissed off. "Who told you that?"

"Please, Wyatt." I turn from him, back to Ana. "It's an important project. *Critically important.* I can't afford to lose momentum."

Ana raises a brow. "*Critically important* sounds both taxing and stressful."

"Thank you!" Wyatt's quick to say, but Ana stays focused on me.

"Look, Mathilde. I think you can probably still work. *Some,*" she says. "This is a case of prove to me you're fine, or work is the first thing to go."

I glance at Wyatt, who stares up at the ceiling, blinking rapidly, his right hand clenched into a fist. Seeing Wyatt emotional isn't easy for me—he is typically so steady, and that makes me steady. I swallow hard around the knot in my throat, knowing what he holds in his fist.

See, I was wearing Poppy's ring on my necklace when I cut out my tattoo.

It was Christmas—of course I was wearing it.

But in the chaos and panic of the ambulance, I forgot to take it off before going to the hospital. Wyatt was shaken (shocked) to see Poppy's ring alongside Clementine's when he helped me change into a gown—*Where did you get this?* and then before I could explain, *Why in the hell are you wearing this?* We both know my ring for this baby won't arrive for weeks yet.

There was an outside chance we could be fined. "The last thing we need is another bill to pay, Tilly," Wyatt had angry-whispered at me, though I knew it was fear more than anything. However, I suspected Poppy's ring had deactivated years ago, which I whispered back to Wyatt.

What if they cancel our MotherWise contract? Wyatt worried next, which felt irrational to me, for how were the two connected? "What about the twenty-four seven medical care, then? What if something's really wrong with you?"

He quickly pocketed Poppy's ring before the intake nurse noticed, and I believe he's still holding it hours later. As though it's the only safe place for it to be. There's a difficult conversation coming, but not until after we've both slept, I hope.

"You'll need to wear your watch day and night," Ana says. "Otherwise we can't be sure of accuracy."

I touch the watch face. There's a new app installed, tracking a list of biometrics. All of which are being fed directly to Ana and MotherWise. Oh, and Wyatt.

"As long as you don't overdo it, keep your hydration levels up and your stress levels down, I think we'll be just fine."

For the first couple of weeks under Ana's watchful care, nothing happens.

Wyatt and I talk about Poppy's ring, and I tell him the truth about why it's important for me to keep. He understands (*I miss her too, Tilly*), and simply asks that I don't wear it outside the house. I tell him I won't, and I mean it.

I follow the rules. I work *some* (a couple of hours a day), I rest, I go to my MotherHelper meetups with Kat, where I learn about upcoming events, including a new meditation class specifically for the third trimester, and a baby-clothing exchange.

New Year's Eve is fun. Maeve and Jenn are in California visiting family for the holiday, so we have Kat, Nick, and the kids over to celebrate. We go to bed too late, after playing board games, sipping bubbly things, and enjoying the hopefulness and excitement that a new calendar year brings.

Everything is on track—no blips in the system. I've had no hallucinations, and no further sightings of my mother. Maybe it was all those nuts, and a simple zinc sensitivity, after all?

But then I lose time again.

It's midday, and I'm in my studio. Ana left an hour ago; my vitals and blood work are "spot on." Wyatt's at work and Clementine's back at school after the holiday break. Shelby's at the vet for Stanley's checkup. Suddenly, I come to on the stool in front of the painting. I'm woozy and dreamy, like I've awoken from a deep sleep. I'm holding something in my right hand—my nail clippers.

Then I notice the blood. There's a throbbing in my left-hand fingertips, as though I've caught them in a slamming drawer. At first I don't understand what's happened, even though it should be obvious.

Nail clippers. Throbbing fingertips. Dried blood in semicircles under what's left of my nails. I've cut them to the quick; I have no recollection of doing so.

Tiny crescents of nails form a small pile in my lap—translucent white against the black fabric of my dress. A jolt moves through me. I hold my hands in front of me, the fingernails on my right still intact. They are decently long, and I keep them filed into an oval shape. On my left, there's no white remaining at the tips. Instead, only the semicircles of dried blood at the top of the nail bed. The throbbing in that hand increases.

My eyes shift to the canvas under my still-outstretched hands, scanning its surface for . . . what, I'm unsure. Up close now—the slight smoky odor making its way through the mask—I squint and scan, landing on a speck of something that rests in a textured swirl of black paint. Something that wasn't there when I last worked on this area.

Is that . . . ?

I lean closer again.

A fingernail clipping?

I touch the tiny, nearly translucent crescent and it transfers to my fingertip. Inspecting it with my magnifier glasses I see that indeed it's the top of a fingernail—from a thumbnail, I guess, due to the shape and thickness. As I look at my thumb, it all falls into place. The nail clippers drop from my hand.

I get a "good behavior" pass, thanks to a run of excellent biometric readings.

"Don't call it that," Wyatt says, when I tell him Dr. Rice signed off on me having dinner with the girls, to celebrate Maeve's birthday. I'm leaving in an hour. "It makes it sound like you're in prison or something."

He's on edge. Someone was injured at work, and there's talk of a lawsuit against both the construction company and Wyatt's firm.

"Fine. I *get to* leave the house for dinner, at a restaurant, which is something I'm dying to do because I'm not allowed to go anywhere anymore, and I'm excited." I sound like a petulant teenager, but I can't help it. I'm on edge too, except I'm keeping the reasons why to myself.

Wyatt raises an eyebrow but doesn't bite. Nor does he remind me I'm in this position because I carved into my own arm on Christmas morning. But that was weeks ago, my arm has healed, and we've all in theory moved on. "Where y'all going for dinner?"

"The Olde Pink House."

"Nice. What are you going to get?" Wyatt asks. Shelby and her late husband were married at the restaurant, and Wyatt takes his mom to the Olde Pink House each year on her wedding anniversary.

"Do you even have to ask?" I mean to sound playful, as my order never changes, but it comes out tinged with irritation.

"Let me guess. This is a tricky one," Wyatt replies, tapping his fingers against the countertop, his face screwed up in deep concentration. I laugh, grateful to him for lightening the mood. My shoulders relax.

"Fried green tomatoes . . ." I nod. "She-crab soup . . ." Another nod, the crab, cream, and sherry bisque my favorite thing on the menu. My stomach rumbles. "Macaroni and cheese?"

"Nailed it," I reply. "You know me well."

"Sure do." Wyatt leans across the counter to kiss me on the lips. Then he notices my left hand. "What happened there?"

The bandage on my thumb covers what's left of that fingernail. This one was clipped the farthest down, and the slice in my nail bed keeps opening up and bleeding. I've trimmed the nails on my right hand to better match the left, and they're much shorter than I'm used to. My fingertips are supersensitive, the delicate skin no longer protected.

"Oh, a minor conservator accident," I say. "Nicked it with the scalpel when I was trying to sample paint."

"Ouchie," Wyatt replies. He shakes out his hand as though feeling pain in his own thumb.

"It's fine. The bandage is keeping it clean." I casually slide my hand from the countertop, out of view.

"Who knew art conservation was such a high-risk line of work?" There's a teasing smile on his face. "You should ask Raoul for a raise. *Danger pay.*"

I laugh, but it's hollow. Wyatt doesn't notice.

The colonial mansion on Abercorn Street is one of Savannah's remaining historic buildings, dating back to 1771. As most eighteenth-century mansions have been converted to residences, the Olde Pink

House is a unique reminder of the before times. Named as such because of its exterior, made of plaster turned pastel pink due to humidity-induced bleeding of the red clay bricks underneath, the restaurant has a menu that has remained essentially unchanged over the years. It's been a lovely evening so far. I've missed spending time with my friends and am grateful for conversation unrelated to my pregnancy or MotherWise. Happy that Maeve is the center of attention tonight.

I'm coming back to our table after using the restroom, excited about dessert. Pecan pie. It has a cinnamon-pecan crust and dark chocolate and is served warm with vanilla ice cream. The dark chocolate will give me a boost of caffeine, and I feel moderately rebellious for ordering it. Especially because pecans do contain zinc, but apparently (according to my EduNet search) not enough to trigger my sensitivity.

I see the pie's already arrived, then notice Maeve and Kat huddled close, side by side. It seems a serious conversation, based on body language and facial expressions—not a smile to be seen. I stop walking. Should I give them a few more moments? Maybe they're having a heart-to-heart, Kat confessing to Maeve that she was upset by her reaction to her pregnancy news. If so, I'm glad—it's awkward having unsaid things and hurt feelings between friends.

But then Kat glances up, notices me watching them. She abruptly stops talking. Maeve looks my way too, and smiles, but something's off. Kat fiddles with her silverware, looking at neither Maeve nor me. Something flits across Maeve's face, and I think . . . *I know that look.* I've seen that look.

Maeve is an excellent clinician, and an expert at maintaining neutrality when in therapist mode. However, she's an imperfect human like the rest of us and at times can't keep what she's thinking from clouding her expression.

Once, a couple of years ago, when Maeve and I were out for dinner after a breath work class while Kat was at a school fundraiser, I noticed how quiet she was. When I asked if she was okay, she said "not really" and then shared a story about a client interaction. She remained appropriately professional, giving no details about the woman, but did tell me one specific thing about their session.

This woman had asked Maeve if she had any children. When Maeve replied, *No, I don't*, the woman then asked if she wanted to be a mother. Maeve was vague in her response, explaining that they weren't there to discuss her personal life.

That means no, the woman said. *So, you don't want to be a mother?*

Not particularly, Maeve replied, trying to shift focus back to her client, who was desperate for a baby and had been trying to conceive for years.

The woman went off on Maeve. Accusing her of pretending to understand the agony of being childless, when how could she? *And you would get pregnant in a flash!* the client said. *It's always like that—the wrong people get the best luck. What a waste.*

This upset Maeve, even as she understood the venom came from a place of sadness (and wasn't about Maeve at all). She told me she felt guilty because part of what the woman said was true: Maeve *could* get pregnant.

It had happened in graduate school. Long before she started her infertility-focused practice, before she met Jenn. *Obviously there was no baby in the end*, Maeve added, and I didn't ask what that meant. I never knew if it was her choice or not. But I remember the look on her face as she said it.

It was the same look she had now.

"She feels guilty, Mathilde."

My breath hitches when I hear my mother's voice, to my left. The fried green tomatoes, she-crab soup, and macaroni and cheese threaten to come back up, right on the floor of this lovely restaurant.

"Be quiet," I whisper, not turning toward her voice. I don't want to see her.

"You know they're talking about you, honey. About what happened at Christmas. No one trusts your judgment. But they don't understand what you're trying to do, Mathilde! What you're trying to uncover."

Kat and Maeve look my way. The guilt on Maeve's face is gone (did I imagine it?). Kat smiles and points to her dessert, doing an in-the-chair dance with her shoulders and arms. She loves the Pink House's fresh fruit pie with custard.

"They're talking about you, and they're going to tell Wyatt they're worried. You know they will. And once they do, you know that—"

"Stop it," I say, with more volume this time. I set hands to my ears, pressing hard to block out the sound of my mother's voice.

Kat tilts her head, a frown coming to her face. "You okay?" she mouths. Maeve pushes her chair back to stand. If they weren't talking about me before, they will be now. I drop my hands from my ears, flushing with embarrassment.

Maeve comes toward me, urgency in her steps. Her giant glittery purple "It's my birthday!" button, which Kat gave her as a lark and Maeve proudly pinned to her shirt, glimmers in the dim light. She reaches for my arm, makes eye contact.

"You okay?" she asks, her tone hushed.

"Be careful, Mathilde," my mother says. *"You can't be kept from the painting. Not when you're this close."*

"The slightest of wobbles, but I'm fine. Maybe it was the she-crab soup? The sherry mostly cooks off, but I'm a lightweight now." I roll my eyes, smile for good measure.

Maeve nods but remains all business. No returned smile. "Maybe we should get the bill?"

"Yes, go home. Go home right now, Mathilde."

Shut up, I reply in my mind, but to Maeve I say, "Absolutely not. I have pecan pie waiting for me. You should never keep a pregnant woman from her dessert, Maeve. Look at Kat."

We both look Kat's way—she's dipping her fork tines into the pie's custard, then licking it off. Technically not starting without us. Maeve laughs. Slings an arm around me as we walk back to the table. I can't tell if it's simply friendly or because she's still concerned I'm not well.

I glance over my shoulder. With relief I see my mother isn't there.

I can't hear her either. A waitress comes up behind us, carrying the plate with Maeve's dessert. The flameless candle she'll "blow out" after we sing "Happy Birthday" is glowing bright.

Maeve sees the candle and groans, knowing what's next. "You know, the best birthday gift would be for you *not* to sing, Tilly."

"It's bad luck not to sing 'Happy Birthday,'" I say.

"That's not a thing," Maeve replies, laughing harder.

"Well, I won't risk it." I launch into "Happy Birthday" with Kat, the waitress, and a few fellow diners at other tables. Maeve makes a wish and blows out the candle.

My mother, who has appeared across the table from me, watches too, clapping along with the rest of us. Her head is severely tilted, her ear almost touching her shoulder now. It's awful to look at; I can't avert my gaze.

Please go away, I think.

"It's too late for that, Mathilde."

Without warning my mother's head suddenly tips, detaching from her neck. Her head lands on the table with a hard thud, rolls, and comes to a stop in front of my pecan pie.

"I thought I saw a rat. I'm so sorry for scaring everyone," I say, justifying my piercing scream upon seeing my mother's head roll across our dinner table.

But I can tell no one believes me. Rats are well controlled in the city, and a restaurant like the Olde Pink House does *not* have rodents running about. In retrospect, I should have said I saw a ghost (closer to the truth, anyway)—there are many rumored to reside in this restaurant. Laughed the moment off, blamed the sherry once again. Regardless, no one believes me about the rat, and everyone is "concerned."

As my mother predicted, Kat tells Nick what happened. Nick tells Wyatt. Needless to say, my "good behavior" pass is revoked.

My nails have grown long enough to cover the sensitive tips of my fingers, and the dinner fiasco has faded from collective memory (though I can't stop seeing my mother's head tumble onto the white linen tablecloth), when Clementine's nightmares begin.

The first night, after a scream that rips Wyatt and me from slumber, we find Clementine sitting up, catatonic in bed. Eyes wide open, hands outstretched as though warding something off, and jaw clenched so tightly I use my Luminara glasses later to make sure she hasn't cracked a tooth.

The routine becomes exhaustingly familiar after five straight nights of this, all of us wrung out by the nocturnal episodes that shatter our sleep. I'm left tossing and turning in Clementine's bed, where I've taken to spending the second half of the night, as she tries to sleep in my arms.

I get on EduNet to see what I can learn about the sudden appearance of catatonic nightmares in children. Strangely, she doesn't seem to remember the episodes, nor the moments of wakefulness that follow. There are a variety of things it could be, EduNet tells me, including suboptimal vitamin D levels. This can cause night terrors, particularly in children, the research suggests. We start giving her supplements, hoping it's as easy as that.

On the seventh night of this, I settle a weepy Clementine against my chest and stare up at the dark ceiling in her bedroom, my arms wrapped tightly around her. Soon, my body gets heavy and I close my eyes, hoping for at least a couple of hours. But then her body jerks violently, and I'm wide-awake again.

"Momma?" The faintest of whispers. There's fear in her tone.

"What is it, baby?" I cuddle her closer, her breath warm against my neck.

"Why is she here?"

I crane my neck to look down at her, to see if she's fully awake. In the near blackness I can't tell if her eyes are open. She clings to me.

"Who?" I ask softly.

"That woman. Over there."

She points to a corner of her room, near the window. My eyes, semi-adjusted to the low light, make out the elements in her room: her small desk and chair, a floor lamp, a bookshelf, a beanbag chair covered in fuzzy pink fabric. I don't see a woman, which I'm about to say when Clementine asks, "Why is her head like that?"

I can't breathe, my mind instantly in the Olde Pink House restaurant, my mother's head sitting in front of my uneaten pecan pie. I look around the room, focusing on the darkly shadowed areas. My heart thumps furiously in my chest. But I see nothing, which I tell her.

"She says she knows me," Clementine whispers. "But I don't know her, Momma."

I reach over quickly and turn on the night-light, which releases a soft red luminosity designed to preserve circadian rhythms. It adds an eerie glow to the room but illuminates the space somewhat.

"Look, baby. Look," I say, with an urgency I try to tamp down. "There's nothing there. It's just us."

Clementine raises her head slightly, her hair tousled. Her forehead is sweaty when I set my hand on it, checking if she's feverish. She's not. Her eyebrows knit together, and she looks back to the same corner of the room.

"Can't you see her? Over there, beside my desk?"

Bile rises in my throat as I force my gaze to Clementine's desk. I don't see what she's seeing, which terrifies me even more.

"No. I can't." My voice shakes, out of my control.

"That's okay, Momma," Clementine says, hearing my distress. She sighs and snuggles back into me. A moment later her breathing slows, and she's asleep.

I keep the red light on and remain alert. But the hypervigilance gets to me, my senses overtaxed. Now I hear an odd swishing, sweeping sound from my studio above (*what is that?*), and could convince myself there *is* someone standing in the corner near her desk. My watches buzzes, and I try a round of box breathing, but Clementine is heavy against my chest and it's difficult to fully inhale.

Blinking repeatedly, I will the looming shadow by the desk to shift. I pray it isn't who, or what, I think it is.

Eventually, I fall asleep. When I awake at dawn, the shadow is gone.

After a virtual visit and mobile blood work appointment, Clementine's pediatrician suggests further increasing her vitamin D intake. He agrees it's the most likely culprit. We add another two drops to her water glass at dinnertime, and within a few days her nightmares, and night visions, cease.

I'm grateful for such a simple fix and think it's all behind us. I've become adept at compartmentalizing, my ability to mentally "lock the door" on recent inexplicable and disturbing events robust. Until Clementine comes downstairs one morning before school, a photograph in hand.

I'm busy packing up her lunch, behind as per usual despite having been up for a couple of hours already. But I took advantage of my early wake-up and the quiet of the house to get back to the treatment. With Clementine's nightmares and my lack of sleep, I haven't trusted myself to work on the piece for the past couple of days—there's no room for a sloppy, exhaustion-driven mistake.

This morning I uncovered the subject's full chin and bottom lip. The hum of focus, the thrill of getting closer to completing the cleaning, flows through me. Only a handful more weeks until I'm finished, which is good, as the baby won't be far behind.

"Who's this?" Clementine asks, holding the photograph out to me.

"Hmm?" I ask, zipping up her lunch bag. I would love another cup of coffee. But with Ana visiting soon, I can't risk more caffeine in my bloodstream.

Clementine sets the photo down on the countertop in front of me so I can't avoid it.

She's irritable I'm not paying enough attention.

I look at the photo and take in a sharp breath. "Where did you get that?"

"It was inside this book," Clementine replies, and I see a Nancy Drew hardcover—from my collection—in her other hand. "I wanted to bring it to school for reading time, and this fell out when I took it off the shelf."

"You know you can't bring these books to school." I'm only getting little sips of air. My mind races.

"Since when?" she asks.

"Since I said so!"

Clementine's face falls, and I instantly regret my harsh tone.

"I'm sorry, baby. You know these books are precious to me. School isn't a great place to take them, okay?"

She nods, setting the book down beside the photograph. "But who is this person? Do you know her?"

"I do. That's my mother." Pause. *Catch your breath, Tilly.* "Your grandmother Margot. Don't you remember?"

Clementine goes pale.

"Are you feeling okay, sweets?"

She nods, but I'm not convinced. Worry crests inside me. Maybe this is something worse than low vitamin D. My watch buzzes, my heart rate elevated.

"I've seen her," she says.

"I know," I reply, taking in a deep breath and letting it out slowly. "I've shown you photos before."

"No, I mean, I've *seen* her. Not like this." She frowns, and her worried expression worries me further.

I hold one of her hands, squeezing her fingers so she looks at me. "What do you mean, Clem?"

She points at my mother in the photograph, dressed in the navy lab coat and fitted gray trousers she preferred to wear for work. She's seated in front of a series of painted canvases, stacked up against a white wall. Her hands cup her crossed knees, and she has an easy smile on her face. It was taken to accompany an article about her career as a conservator. I remember she was embarrassed by the fuss, but she did it hoping to educate people about conservation work. To drive more visitors to the museum, and to art appreciation in general.

"She was in my room the other night, Momma. Remember? You couldn't see her, though."

My throat constricts, and it's hard to swallow. "You must have been dreaming, Clem."

She purses her lips, considers this. "It didn't *feel* like a dream."

I'm filled with dread, and it bursts out in a snippy tone. "Well, I assure you that your grandmother was *not* in your bedroom. You were dreaming. That's the only explanation, Clementine."

I tuck the photograph into the pocket of my work apron. Out of sight, out of mind—hopefully for both of us. "Let's not worry about this anymore. You need to get ready for school."

My words are measured, my tone controlled and firm. However, my body buzzes with the panic of our exchange, and a moment later it revolts. Saliva pools in my mouth and I know I'm about to be sick. I turn from Clementine and lose my morning coffee into the sink.

"Are you okay, Momma?" Clementine asks. Her hand rests on my lower back, giving quick little pats. I've scared her. But before I can tell her I'm okay, I heave again. This time nothing comes up.

Pull yourself together. I take a couple of deep breaths. The nausea abates.

"I'm fine," I manage, turning on the water to rinse out the sink, and my mouth. "Sometimes the baby doesn't like early mornings. It's nothing to worry about, honey."

Wyatt walks into the kitchen then. From his expression I know he senses a shift in energy. Luckily he's arrived a few moments too late to know exactly what's transpired. He raises an eyebrow, looks between us. "Everyone good?"

Clementine glances at me, her eyes full of concern. I nod at her, then smile at Wyatt. "All good."

"Come here, kiddo," Wyatt says, and Clementine obliges. He hugs her, then kisses her atop the head. "We're leaving in ten minutes."

She says she's ready to go.

"Have you brushed your teeth?" He pours himself a coffee.

"Not yet." Clementine looks chastised.

"Well, guess that means you're not ready," Wyatt says. "Hop to it, bunny."

Clementine smiles at the pet name, then picks up the Nancy Drew book to take back upstairs.

"You know what, Clem?" I say. "You can take that book to school. I know you'll be careful."

"I will, I promise." She smiles wider, and I hold out my hand to slide the book into her school bag. She takes off up the stairs to brush her teeth, and Wyatt and I are left alone.

"You sure everything's okay?" he asks. "Seems I walked into something there."

He sips his coffee, staring at me over the lip of the mug.

"A small issue with the book. She wanted to take it to school for reading time, and I didn't think it was a good idea. But I changed my mind. So yes, everything is okay." I reach for my mug to refill it with coffee, out of habit.

"Haven't you already had one?" Wyatt asks, glancing at the coffee maker. The number on the display reads "6." Our machine makes eight cups every morning. He's had one and knows I'm a "the minute my eyes open" coffee drinker.

"No. I had an herbal tea. Your mom had a coffee, though." The lie is easy. Wyatt will be gone in ten minutes, and Shelby is in the shower getting ready for her day.

"Herbal tea, huh? That might explain the tension." Wyatt laughs easily. He pours coffee into my mug until its half-full. Like, *precisely* half-full. The machine's display switches to "5.5."

I take the mug, thanking him. Inwardly, though, I curse his controlling behavior.

He smiles, oblivious. "You're welcome, darlin'."

For a time, nothing unusual happens and the unsettling moments further lose their sharp edges.

My blood pressure, zinc levels, and stress hormones remain stable. I have gained the appropriate amount of weight, according to MotherWise. My watch spits out gold stars, and Dr. Rice and Ana, still on twice-daily visits, are pleased.

"Well done, Mathilde," Ana declares, after a full week of consistently excellent results. "Your body seems strong, and all systems are singing beautifully. How are you feeling?"

"Great," I say, and it's true. My arm has fully healed, the scar patch making it less noticeable every day. I'm also more clearheaded than I've been in weeks; productive too. No signs of apparitions, no hallucinations, no "bumps in the night" that steal my sleep.

I suspect I'm only a handful of sessions away from completing the cleaning. *So close*, which means I'll soon be able to finish the treatment and collect my fee. Not to mention, get a reprieve from the work. I long to be free of the painting, even as I'm increasingly drawn to it. *Soon, Tilly. We're almost there.*

I daydream about squeezing in a mini vacation before the baby comes. Ana said if things continue as they are, we can reduce her visits. A couple of times a week, maybe, with only daily virtual check-ins.

"What do you think about Disney World?" I ask Wyatt as we snuggle in bed. Clementine has visited the theme park in VR but not yet in person. "We could rent a car? It's only a few hours' drive. Shelby and Stanley can join us."

"Let's see how things shake out," Wyatt replies, with a gentle smile meant to placate me. My enthusiasm doused, I bristle at his tepid response. But it's late, and I don't want to fight before bed. "Sure," I say, to appease him.

I'm thirty-two weeks pregnant, and the window for out-of-state travel is closing. According to MotherWise rules, I can travel up until thirty-seven weeks. As long as both baby and I are healthy and I'm visiting a destination with an affiliated maternity center. That gives me about three weeks to finish the treatment.

At breakfast the next day I tell Clementine we're going to Disney World when I'm finished with the project.

She squeals in delight. "The actual place? Not in VR?"

"The actual place."

"This is all I've ever wanted!" She throws her arms around me as best she can, because of my bulging stomach. I smile and squeeze her tightly, imagining Clementine hugging her little sister. Barely able to contain my own excitement, for I'm close (*so close*) to getting exactly what I want too.

"What's all the commotion about?" Wyatt asks, coming to the kitchen to rinse his coffee mug. He has an off-site meeting this morning so is taking Clementine to school on his way.

"Momma said we're going to Disney World!" Clementine is bursting at the seams. There's nothing better than seeing your child happy.

Wyatt's eyes shift to mine. "Did she, now?"

His tone is mild but his expression anything but. “I thought we were going to wait to talk about that.”

I shrug, Clementine’s excitement overshadowing Wyatt’s displeasure. “Not everything needs to be a discussion,” I murmur. He says nothing in return.

I'm medically cleared to pop by the lab and have lunch with Dale, at the café inside the GIA building. I claim to need a few supplies and appreciate that Ana doesn't ask why they can't be delivered. She signs off on the request, and it's as though I've been released from a long grounding.

My colleagues ooh and aah over my protruding belly. *You look so healthy! So happy!* My hair is shiny and thick, thanks to the hormones, my skin clear and cheeks rosy.

You're all belly, Isla says. *You don't look like you've gained an ounce anywhere else.* I flush with the compliment, enjoying it more than I'll ever admit.

Over lunch, which we are late getting to (my watch alerting me I'm overdue for a nourish break), Dale fills me in on what's happening at GIA. The gossip, mostly.

"This may or may not surprise you, but Tony and Isla are the latest lab romance." He forks his salad but keeps his eyes on me to see my reaction.

"Really? Huh. I guess I'm not that surprised?" I chew a bite of pasta, a roasted cherry tomato popping in my mouth. The swirl of flavors—sweet basil, tart lemon, briny feta—mingles pleasantly on my tongue.

"Apparently it's been going on for a while," Dale adds. Then he glances around and leans closer. "Tony told me he's going to propose."

"They're so young!" I shout-whisper, matching his conspiratorial tone.

I'm happy for Isla, even as part of me thinks she has no clue what she's getting into. Marriage is a one-way ticket to motherhood, and career aspirations, of which I know Isla has many, often take a back seat.

As if reading my mind, Dale asks about my work, and I am appropriately, purposefully vague. We dance around it for a time, until dessert comes—poached pears, dressed up with vanilla sugar crystals—and then shift back to personal topics. Wyatt's work. Our trip to Disney World. Curtis's latest cookbook, which he recently signed a publishing contract for.

"He's been testing recipes for the past couple of months, and this is his best collection yet." Dale pats his stomach. "I married well. Though my pants aren't as pleased with the arrangement."

"I didn't notice," I say.

"You're a terrible liar," he says, before digging into his second poached pear. "But bless your heart."

When I arrive back home, well satiated from both the food and Dale's company, there's something waiting for me. A small box, delivered as promised by Nick and signed for by Shelby.

It's my gold ring, for the new baby.

When I received Clementine's ring she was almost a year old. I was happy about the discounts. Glad to participate, because it was as easy as clasping my necklace when I left the house.

I take the ring out of its package and hold it softly in my palm.

Identical to the others, it's the circumference of a large blueberry. It shines with its newness. I glance at the delivery envelope and see the date, and am hit with a sickening punch in my gut.

Today is the anniversary of the day we lost Poppy.

Last year I suffered alone, because Wyatt seemed to forget the devastating anniversary. Or at least he didn't mention it. Five years had passed by that point, and I was heartbroken when the sun set without us speaking her name out loud. But I let it go, because Maeve said we all moved on in different ways, on different timelines.

Not bringing it up doesn't erase her existence, or her story, Maeve added. I nodded, but I wasn't sure I agreed.

Now I'm the one who has forgotten. Enamored with this new pregnancy, and baby. Having my ego stroked by my coworkers. Gossiping over lunch with Dale. All the while . . . forgetting. I want to cry. Why couldn't Nick have waited one more day? They are typically delivered between weeks thirty-one and thirty-three of a pregnancy. Why did the ring have to arrive *today*?

The baby shifts, an elbow nudging me from the inside, reminding me to breathe even before my watch can. I take one ragged breath, then another. She's running out of space now, and her movements are less acrobatic these days. But I'm grateful for even the slightest nudge, because it means she's still alive. *Close the door. Lock it. Walk away, Tilly.*

"See you soon," I whisper, pressing the gold ring against my belly. "Je t'aime, ma belle fille."

I've treated halfway up the bridge of her nose. The face is distorted, one side of the chin longer than the other.

Her lips are full, her mouth closed and at rest. There is a slight pulling down at the corners, suggesting emotion hiding behind the serene expression. Charlotte Leclerc took great care with the neck and lower face, and I can't wait to uncover the eyes.

The woman appears more skin and bones now, as though she thins out the higher we go. A lithe frame covered in skin, shadowed and highlighted to reveal the sinew and bony protuberance of her clavicles, the sharpness of her jaw, the tight cords of tendons in her neck. My impression is that she's unwell—though the black hourglass at her center makes me think grief, rather than illness, made her this way. Not for the first time I wonder if this isn't a self-portrait.

"Slow down, there," my mother says. *"You don't want to miss anything."*

She's with me in the studio—has been every day this week.

I've stopped searching for a logical explanation, am waiting her—*it*—out. Clearly this has nothing to do with a zinc overdose, or sherry in bisque, or even extreme exhaustion. I've come to believe it's not actually my mother, nor a manifestation of her—ghostly or otherwise. I don't know what *it* is, or what it wants from me, and so decide to accept the most straightforward explanation: my brain has concocted the vision due to the emotional stress of both the pregnancy and the conservation.

This figment—both exactly like the mother I remember and also nothing like her—is meant to help me with my repressed grief, my mind attempting to heal itself before I become a mother again. I've longed many times to discuss my career with my mother. To share the challenges and satisfactions of the work. *Enjoy it*, I think now, for once the conservation is finished and the baby is here, I suspect the apparition—my mother—will disappear.

Somehow, I suppress the most terrifying moments—the moths on Christmas Eve; her insistence that I cut out my tattoo; her head falling off at Maeve's birthday dinner—and focus on the more serene ones. Like when she sat beside me a couple of days ago, guiding me as I cleaned the sweep of the neck. *"A second pair of eyes,"* she said, her voice whisper-quiet. *"Think of me as a second pair of eyes, my darling."* Inexplicably, her presence soothed me that day, calming my nerves and steadying my hand.

I've taken to tracking these visits in a paper notebook, so as to avoid notice. An uppercase *M* scrawled into the date box on the days she shows up. I'm also counting down the pregnancy in the same notebook, grateful for each day added to the baby's gestation. With everything that's happened recently, I'm haunted by the thought that this baby may be safer outside my body than in it.

"I know what I'm doing," I reply now to my mother's *"slow down"* comment. My tone is sharp, for today she's less helpful. More incessant with her interruptions, and I'm struggling to concentrate. "Please be quiet."

She ignores the request. *"Check the bow of the lip, Mathilde."*

I long to shut her out, but she's piqued my curiosity now. I zone in on the cupid's bow of the subject's mouth. There's an odd texture to the upper lip, overtop the paint. *A finely patterned mesh?* I put my glasses on, clicking the magnifier button on the arm.

"What is that?" I murmur. Under magnification I see a touch of sediment within the textured area, preventing me from getting a clear visual. I take a soft-bristled brush from my apron's pocket. With a steady hand I apply the bristles delicately, gently removing the silt. I'm cautious not to change the integrity of Leclerc's original vision but also want to remove anything that isn't original. Like a fire-blistered section of paint, or dust and grime from its years in storage.

Despite my caution, there's a slight crack when the whisper-soft bristles meet the lip. The sound of a small twig breaking in two. My heart flutters, and I let out a small "Oh!" Something has come free, and it's caught in the bristles. *Shit.*

"Oops. You should have been more careful, Mathilde," my mother says in a hollowed-out voice. I ignore her, upset I didn't take more time to observe the area before reaching for the brush. Far too anxious about the painting's integrity to pay attention to my dead mother's criticism.

I remove the quarter-inch piece of debris from the brush with my tweezers, holding it carefully in the pinpoint ends. There's a thin layer of paint on the backside of the section, and on the front, a series of connected thin lines, creating vesicles.

"Is this . . . an insect wing?" I murmur. It's impossible to tell what type of insect, though. Looking at the subject's lip and the area the wing piece came from, I see the mirror image left behind in the paint. Leclerc seemingly used the wing to create structure and add form to the lip. "Strange, but clever."

"Not strange at all. Charlotte's mother was a medical entomologist, studying the role insects have in human diseases," my mother says. *"She joined her on many field expeditions. It's where Charlotte developed her love of medicine, along with a working knowledge of insects."*

"I didn't know that," I reply. I'm focused on the piece of wing, placing it under the AI-connected microscope for analysis. The result is returned seconds later. It's from a *Rhyothemis semihyalina* dragonfly, from Madagascar.

"I told you all of this years ago, Mathilde."

I turn off the glasses, lost in thought. "I've found blood. Fingernails, hair, sand, and flower petals." I enumerate the items I've uncovered in *The Mother* on my fingers, saying them out loud as I do. "Plus, that nerve bundle. And now an insect wing . . . all natural, biological elements . . ."

I'm trying to put it all together, muttering softly. "But for what purpose? Is this more than symbolism?"

"You know, Mathilde."

"No, I don't." I look to my mother then, and wish I hadn't.

Her head is reattached, after the pecan pie incident, but it's facing the wrong way. I see the back of her hair, even as the front of her body faces me. She's like a decapitated doll put together in the dark by a child's hands.

Again: *"You know, Mathilde."*

I'm queasy and need to stop looking at her. Sourness gathers in the back of my throat, along with rage. "Why won't you just tell me?!"

My mother sighs audibly, and I recognize the tone of it. Patient, though with a touch of condescension and mild disappointment, because I didn't try hard enough to figure it out myself.

"She's painted a portal, my darling."

I frown, turn back to the painting. Try to see it with this new information, which honestly makes even less sense. "A portal for what?"

"For you, of course."

I've lost my mind.

I'm talking to my dead mother—or at least the back of her precariously balanced head—as though she's a colleague, as though she's alive. Worse than that, I'm asking my dead mother *for advice*. Any comfort I've found in my flimsy explanations disappears in an instant.

I should call Maeve. Tell her what's happening and get her professional advice. She did gently offer her services after her birthday dinner, "at the best-friend rate," which I know means free of charge.

But I don't call Maeve, because I don't know where to start.

I also don't call Kat, because she'll tell Nick (*why does she have to tell him everything?*), who will call Wyatt.

Something is seriously wrong with this painting. Possibly with Charlotte Leclerc herself, when she painted it. Circling the problem brings no clarity. I can't tease out answers to my fear-soaked questions, because there aren't any. This defies logic.

"A portal," my mother said.

A portal . . . for what?

"For you, of course."

What the hell does that mean?

"I need you to leave," I say, the next time my mother shows up in my studio.

I'm about to start on the section where I'm sure to find the subject's eyes, and I want complete silence. No further distractions. I can't focus with her here. More than that, I don't want to have to justify this apparition of my long-departed mother anymore.

"Mathilde, I'm only trying to help," she replies, in my mother's voice. It's so exact today, it's heartbreaking. I glance toward her, noting she's turned. Or at least her head has. I see her face, her slight frown. But I also see her back, her palms facing me. It's discombobulating and makes me feel ill. Still, I force myself to keep my eyes on her face.

"I don't know who you are, or why you're here—maybe I am sick, who knows." I mumble the last part, mostly to myself. Shake my head. "But you can't be here. I don't want you here. Leave, *please*."

She smiles, and it's my mother's smile. A sharp pain fills my chest.

"I shouldn't leave, Mathilde. We're too close," she says.

"Close to what?" I ask, impatient as I set my cotton-tipped swab down on my thigh. My heart rate beats steadily, but I know it's increasing the longer I look at her. Sure enough, my watch buzzes and I quickly glance down to hit the OK button, promising to do breath work.

"Close to what?" I ask again, looking up at her.

But she's not there. The corner of the studio is empty.

"Mom?" I call out quietly. Turning around on the stool, looking for her, I even check under the workbench, in case she's lying underneath it—where I found her yesterday, face down and body up.

My studio is silent, eerily so. "Mom, are you here?"

Again, no response. But I notice something else. The room feels . . . lighter. As though a refreshing early-spring breeze has come through the windows, clearing out the stale indoor air. I take a deep breath, then let it out.

She's gone.

A week later there's still no sign of my mother. I can't see her, I can't hear her, I can't feel her. I'm both thankful and heartsick.

I've also uncovered the subject's eyes, which are closed as though she's asleep. There are delicate purplish veins on the eyelids. Long, beautiful lashes that surprisingly contain feathery moth antennae. I announce this discovery out loud. "Mom, you won't believe what I found in the . . ." My voice trailing off when I remember I'm alone in the studio.

On the next garbage day I toss the journal tracking her visits. I'm steadier now, and the compulsion to count down the days of the pregnancy has left me. I try to destroy the pages first, wishing to tear them into illegible pieces, before recalling the paper is rip-proof. *That's a weird glitch*, I think, because water- and rip-proof paper is a long-ago innovation. An odd oversight on my part. *Baby brain*, I surmise.

"You're nesting," Shelby tells me, when I make tea with my mom's kettle, becoming emotional for reasons I choose not to share with my mother-in-law. "I went through the same thing, Tilly, around the same point in my pregnancies. I also made chicken and dumplings every day—it's all I ate for weeks! Insatiable craving for it."

She smiles then, dipping her tea bag in and out by the string. "I believe the past nurtures us when we're getting ready to welcome the future." It's a lovely sentiment, and I'm comforted by it.

After finishing my tea, I check in with Clementine.

"How was your sleep, honey?" I ask, as we're packing her bag for school.

"Good," she replies, tucking her hydration pack into the backpack. "Last night I had a dream I was a mermaid. In the ocean. It was fun to be able to breathe underwater, and my tail was *so sparkly*."

She hasn't mentioned my mother in weeks. I wonder if she remembers the nightmares. I don't bring them up for fear I'll spark a regression.

Everything seems fine, and soon enough I begin to trust it is.

Things are going well, so effortlessly well that I'm slow to become superstitious.

Then I get word Cecil has been injured in a fall—he broke his hip while visiting his family in Vancouver. Unfortunately it requires surgery and he'll be in a specialized rehabilitation unit for his recovery. I briefly worry about what this means for the conservation timeline, but he assures me he'll stay in touch.

"Only a phone call away, which is no different from before I decided to step on my grandson's hoverboard, to see what all the fuss was about."

The following night we wake at three in the morning to blaring sirens. By the time Wyatt and I get downstairs, paramedics are carrying a gurney into our neighbor's home. Panic seizes me—is it one of the kids? Has something happened to Becca or her husband, Chip?

"I'll go," Wyatt says, his face grim in the flashing lights coming through our front windows. He ties his bathrobe around his waist and slips on his house clogs. The door opens and the sirens increase. I'm glad when they recede again, though I perch on the arm of the chair by the front window, trying to see what's happening through the blinds' slats. Shelby wakes up and makes us tea—she's become fond of the kettle. Clementine stays soundly asleep.

The ambulance is for Becca. Wyatt later tells me when he got upstairs, ready to help Chip with the kids as needed, the paramedics were working to stabilize her. Apparently she woke up to nurse ten-week-old Chloe—her fifth child, and only girl—for her two a.m. feeding. Chip was later awoken by the baby's cries and found Becca flat on her back in the nursery, having a tonic-clonic seizure.

Becca survives, thank goodness, but remains in a drug-induced coma after the subarachnoid hemorrhage in her brain is repaired. When Wyatt and I take dinner over on the following Tuesday, our meal-train night, Chip tells us "that's it" for children. Becca's doctors conclude it's unsafe for her to become pregnant again.

Wyatt squeezes Chip's shoulder as he cries at the dinner table, a forkful of the chicken pasta we've brought over shaking in his hand as his body quakes with sobs. I'm uncomfortable. We are friendly with Chip and Becca, but we are not close.

So while Wyatt comforts Chip, I help the kids wash up after dinner and then feed Chloe a bottle. She rests against me as she drinks, soon falling asleep in my arms. When I place her gently in her crib, I don't stay long. I don't want to inadvertently wake her, and I also don't want to linger on the rainbow plush carpet where Becca seized days earlier.

The whole ordeal shakes me to my core, both knowing how close Becca came to dying and leaving her family behind, and how quickly life can change. It also unleashes a flood of memories. The same sirens and lights, the speed with which the paramedics packed me up to get me to the hospital, like with Becca. The devastation of realizing none of that chaotic urgency mattered, in the end.

"First Cecil, now Becca," I say once we get back to our place after dinner with Chip and his family. I can't calm the restless anxiety pooling inside my chest, the sense that there's more to come. "Bad things happen in threes."

"Says who?" Wyatt's tired and it shows both on his face and with his temperament. I pull out a premade vegetable curry from the freezer and set it in the reheater.

"Says the universe," I reply, sitting back down.

Wyatt sighs, coming over to the stool. He nudges my knees apart to get closer to me.

However, I'm too far along for a proper embrace in this position. The best Wyatt can do is rest his hands on my upper arms, rubbing up and down like he's warming me up. It does little to soothe me.

"Let's not do this, okay?" I know what he means—*Let's not make up stories that aren't real, let's not catastrophize, Tilly.*

"Do what?" I cross my arms now, forcing Wyatt's hands to drop.

"This isn't good for you, Tilly," he says with frustration. "Or the baby."

Don't tell me what's good for me, or this baby—you have no idea what it's like to be pregnant.

"I'm thinking roti with the curry. It's faster than rice," I say instead.

Wyatt pauses briefly. "I'll go get Clem to help."

I'm relieved when he leaves the kitchen.

I don't have to wait long for the third bad thing, proving me right. But I can't tell Wyatt about it, due to the nature of the bad thing.

Two days later, while I'm working, I lose time again.

When I regain consciousness, I see a blood-filled syringe from my conservation kit sticking out of the crook of my elbow. It's still embedded in my vein, while the painting is uncovered behind me.

"Oh, Tilly . . . my word!" Shelby stands in the open doorway of my studio, one hand pressed to her chest, the other gripping the side of the doorframe. Her knees quake inside her slacks, as evidenced by the fabric quivering, like the ground is vibrating under her feet.

I stare at Shelby, who stares at me and then my arm. I am unsure how to answer. The fogginess remains, and I'm momentarily paralyzed by the conflicting emergencies.

I remove the syringe. Drop it into the trash bin. It clangs against the bottom, and Shelby's eyes go to the bin. Then I stand, too quickly, and am dizzy. Pushing through it, I step in front of my workbench and the painting on it.

"Everything's fine." I try to infuse calm confidence into my tone. I'm panicky, though, my heart hammering inside my chest. I press my fingers into the spot in my elbow where a tiny pinprick of blood blossoms. I force a smile, cock my head with what I hope appears like mild, unconcerned curiosity. "How did you get in here, Shelby?"

The door requires a code to open it. A code only I know. Also, I'm sure I locked it behind me—I always do.

"I . . . someone was crying," Shelby says in a breathy tone. She's pale. I should offer her a chair but am hesitant to leave my position in front of the painting. "I called out your name but was worried something was the matter and you couldn't hear me."

She looks over my shoulder, toward the painting. I can't have that.

"How bizarre. Well, it wasn't me. The crying," I reply. Then, "Would you mind closing the door? The climate in here is finicky."

The moment it takes Shelby to turn and grasp the door's handle gives me enough time to retrieve the cover, which is on the floor near the workbench. I quickly set the top corners onto the canvas and then tug the sheet down to cover the rest. There, both emergencies managed. Now for damage control.

"Listen, Shelby, I can explain, but . . . why don't you take a seat?" I pull out the desk's chair. Then I sit on the stool across from her.

"Why were you crying?" she asks. Her hands twist in her lap. "Is everything all right?"

"I wasn't crying. I'm not sure what you heard."

"No, it was you, Tilly. And then I heard something else." She swallows reflexively. She's nervous. Now *I'm* nervous.

"What was it?" I ask. *Lub-dub, lub-dub, lub-dub,* I hear in the room. Is that my heartbeat, echoing beyond my chest?

"Your voice was raised, and it sounded like you were arguing with someone. You kept saying, 'No, *you can't have this, you can't have her*!'"

Something goes cold in my center. I have no memory of any of this.

"But when I got up here, the door was open and . . ." Shelby wraps tightly clasped hands around her crossed knees. The diamond wedding ring she still wears glimmers under the lights of the studio, her fingers whitening with her grip.

"*And* you saw me with the syringe." I keep my voice smooth, chuckling softly, and she looks at me in surprise. "I'm sorry if I scared you. I can only imagine how confusing this is. But I was drawing blood as part of the conservation."

I point to the small contraption on the desk—gleaming silver, with the GIA emblem on its side and an eyepiece on the top. The portable 3-D digital microscope, which I borrowed from the lab when I visited Dale. It looks similar, at least in size and shape, to an old-fashioned plastic kaleidoscope. "I need to do a biological sample comparison, with the microscope."

I need to do no such thing, but it's the first excuse I come up with.

"I can't give you any details about the painting, but I will tell you this," I continue. "The artist used unconventional materials in the art, blood being one of them."

"Oh!" Shelby exhales forcefully, her eyes wide. "How macabre."

I nod. *You have no idea.* "I'm sure it was distressing for you, coming up and finding me doing a blood draw," I say. "I'm so sorry, I thought the door was locked."

Why wasn't the damn door locked?

"Nothing is wrong, I promise you." I smile, pausing a moment before adding, "I was also listening to a true-crime podcast, which may be what you heard? It's a guilty pleasure when I'm working."

I hate true-crime podcasts and require total silence in my studio, but Shelby likely doesn't know either thing to be true or not.

"I don't know how all y'all listen to those shows." Shelby shakes her head. Her face has relaxed somewhat, her cheeks pinking up again. "I would have nightmares for weeks."

I laugh. "It's not the best at bedtime."

"Well, I'm glad you're all right," she says, standing. "I know you have a lot to do, with work, so I'll let you get back to it."

I open the studio's door. "Shelby?"

"Yes, honey?"

"I hope I have your discretion," I say. "I've, uh, signed a nondisclosure agreement saying I won't show the art to anyone. And obviously I messed up, with the door. I'm sorry to put you in this position, but I would appreciate it if you could keep this whole thing between us? Even Wyatt can't know. I wouldn't want to jeopardize my fee. Especially not with the baby almost here, and Clem's new school costs. I'm sure you understand?"

Shelby smiles warmly, though there's a hint of something in her eyes. Worry, I think. *Of course she's worried.* My mother-in-law found me drawing my own blood in my studio! Plus, I can't imagine how the Leclerc affected her, if she got a good look before I came to. It isn't exactly an uplifting piece of art—the grief in it is raw, visceral. The piece is disturbing both in ways you can put your finger on, and in others you can't.

But she doesn't mention any of that. "Our little secret" is all she says.

"Thanks, Shelby."

She glances at her watch. "Ah, looks like Wyatt and Clem are home. I'll go scrounge up a snack."

"I'll be right down," I say. I lock the door behind her, trying to control my ragged breathing. What just happened?

Eyes darting into the trash can beside me, I see the blood-filled syringe. My arm has stopped bleeding, though there's a tiny raised bruise around the pinprick mark.

"What the hell is going on?" I whisper, a swell of panic settling into my chest.

With quick fingers I grab the syringe and cap it, then swivel from one side of the room to the other, trying to figure out what to do with it. I can't just toss it—it's a biohazard. What if Clementine were to find it somehow? Besides, garbage collection isn't for another five days. I consider discarding the blood down the sink, hiding the syringe somewhere safe until garbage day. But it feels too risky with everyone home, the washroom sink a full flight of stairs below.

Opening the desk's top drawer I see the old plastic silverware tray I've repurposed to hold my tools. I tuck the capped syringe into the longest slot, at the back, which is three-quarters full of paintbrushes of varying sizes. You have to open the drawer all the way to reach it, and I know even the most curious in my house, Clementine, would be unlikely to find the syringe hidden under the brushes. Even if she were to breach my trust by opening my desk.

I open and close the drawer a few times, making sure it stays hidden, then decide to lock it for good measure. I'll get rid of the syringe when I put out the rest of the trash later in the week.

There. We're okay, I think, trying to center myself before I join Shelby downstairs. As I breathe deeply through my nose, out my mouth, it doesn't occur to me to question who else I'm referring to, with my use of "we're."

"Your pressure continues to be elevated." Ana is analyzing my biometric data. She looks up from her tablet with a frown. "How are you feeling?"

"Fine. Good," I reply, with enough confidence that I hope it rings true.

The bizarre syringe incident was two days ago, and I'm relieved Shelby seems to have stuck to her promise. Wyatt's none the wiser, nor is MotherWise. However, I won't relax until I get the syringe out of the house. I've been sleeping poorly again, having nightmares, and it all seems to be affecting my blood pressure.

"No complaints," I add. "Except for this beach ball I seem to have swallowed. I haven't seen my toes in about a week." I laugh, but it fades quickly when Ana doesn't join me.

"Hmm. Well, we need to see this trending in the other direction, pronto. Have you been doing your breath work? Three times a day?"

I nod. Again, a lie because I've maybe done it once a day, if that. And I skipped last night's breath work class with Maeve and Kat, citing mom homework-helper duties (another lie). I'm afraid to be alone with Maeve, if I'm being honest. She has always been able to read me and I'm holding a lot inside. One small push and it might spill out. Plus, Kat's a direct line to Wyatt these days and I can't risk further meddling, no matter how well-intentioned. Not at this stage. I have to get this conservation finished. I need to get this painting out of my house.

Ana waits for me to say more; I resist buckling under her gaze.

"I need you to log the sessions, Mathilde. It doesn't look like you've been doing that." She's pointing to the analysis—the breath work box showing "0." *Shit.*

"Yes, sorry. There have been a lot of distractions, and sometimes I forget that step."

"You and I both know you can log it with your watch." Ana raises a brow, and I nod sheepishly. I should have logged sessions, even if I didn't do them. But honestly, breath work has been the last thing on my mind. "Easy-peasy, Mathilde. So let's make sure we do that."

Yes, let's make sure we do that.

"I forgot about my watch," I reply, desperate to get off this topic. The more Ana digs in, the more likely it is I'll screw up. "I don't always wear it when I work."

Damn. Wrong answer. I am supposed to be wearing my watch twenty-four seven.

Ana sets her tablet down. "I can't help you if you don't follow the protocol. What's really going on?"

I shrug, trying to compose myself. Everything feels precarious. I need to tread more carefully or risk Ana further limiting my work hours. I read the amended MotherWise contract when I was put on home rest; I know how this works.

"It's been a tough week, that's all. Our neighbor had a seizure and is in the hospital. She'll be okay, but it was traumatic for everyone. We've been running a meal train, so extra cooking and shopping. And I've had a couple of, uh, challenging setbacks with my work project."

Ana sets clasped hands on the tabletop. Her face softens. "Listen, Mathilde, I know your work is important to you. I get it—I worked through all my pregnancies, and while raising my four kids. Now, times were different back then . . . better in some ways, worse in others."

She doesn't elaborate, and I try to imagine what it would be like to have four kids *and* a career. That's highly unusual.

"But my job is to make sure you're looking after yourself, and I'm good at my job."

"I know," I say. *Do I sound appropriately regretful?* "I'll do better this week. Thrice-daily breath work sessions, for starters. And I'll wear my—"

I pause, hearing something I can't place. Wait to hear it again. *Yes, there it is.* First, the *swoosh, swoosh, swoosh* sounds, but faint . . . and overtop of that, someone crying.

"Mathilde?"

"Do you hear that?" I ask Ana, glancing toward Shelby's room. I can't tell where the sounds are coming from. But then I remember Shelby isn't home. She and Stanley are at the park. No one else is in the house.

"I don't hear anything," Ana replies, after listening for a moment.

It's getting louder, the weeping. Distracting me, so I can't focus on anything else. I can tell it's a woman, the tone higher in pitch.

Maybe Clementine left her tablet on? But what could she have been watching that sounds like this? There are device controls to keep children from consuming upsetting content of any kind. Clem only watches *Clara the Cloud* and other similar shows deemed appropriate for her age.

The wails increase in intensity, soon filling the kitchen. I can't even pick out the *swish, swoosh* sound anymore.

"So, as I was saying, I think—"

"Shh!" I turn on Ana, setting a firm finger to my lips. My tone is rude, my actions aggressive. "You can't hear that?"

It's so loud now that there's a reverberation inside me, like how the bass at a live music concert vibrates through you. I use my fingers to plug my ears, which unfortunately does little to stem the noise.

As I squeeze my eyes shut, Ana's hand goes to my shoulder. She's shaking me. A moment later the wailing stops. I remove my fingers cautiously, afraid it will start up again. It's blissfully quiet.

Ana shakes me again, harder this time. She repeats my name when I don't respond. Her brows knit together in concern when I finally look her way.

"It's gone," I say. "That's a relief!"

I smile. Ana frowns.

I've earned a temporary leave from GIA and the Leclerc conservation.

"Two weeks." Ana turns her tablet around for my fingerprint signature. "Then we'll reevaluate."

"But I'll be almost thirty-six weeks pregnant by then." I'm panicking, doing the math.

These next two weeks are critical, I tell her. *I'm so close to completing the project.* I make no move to sign Ana's form.

She pushes the tablet closer to me. I still don't move. "What if I don't sign it?"

Ana gives me a look one would give a misbehaving toddler. "Mathilde, you are almost there! The most important thing is a healthy pregnancy and delivery. You can get back to work once you're through this and the mandatory postpartum period." MotherWise requires twelve weeks of complete focus on bonding with the infant.

"What if I have to dip into work during that bonding time?" I ask. "Like I said, this is such a critical—"

Ana gives a pointed look, interrupting me. "You'll void your contract. And all of this would have been for nothing, honey."

"Well, I can't take two weeks off, Ana." I'm up now, pacing the kitchen floor. My hands rub circles around my stomach. "I know it seems like art conservation isn't a time-sensitive line of work, but I assure you, that could not be further from the truth. Especially in this case. Because there are things about—"

"Mathilde, stop. *Stop.*"

I finally stop, and press my lips together. I'm close to tears.

"Fine, one week," Ana says. "Think of it as a vacation, except without a change in location. A staycation, I think they call it?"

More mental calculations on my part. "One week . . . like, five business days, or seven days total, including the weekend?"

"The second one. Seven total." Ana holds out her tablet, conversation over. "No more wiggle room, Mathilde. This is the best I can do."

I press my finger to the box and sign the form.

Wyatt tells me Disney World can wait. "Clem will understand. She's more excited about a new sibling than she is about seeing Mickey Mouse, babe."

Clementine does seem unbothered, particularly when she learns the trip isn't canceled—only postponed. "Then we can take the baby with us!" she exclaims.

"See?" Wyatt says over Clementine's head. He tousles her hair, which she has recently come to dislike as it messes up her French braids, her new favorite hairstyle. She ducks, says, "Daddy!" in a disgruntled tone.

The sound of weeping starts again, the *swoosh, swish, swoosh* coming in softly underneath it.

This time I endure it, saying nothing. I smile at Clementine and Wyatt, as though my ears aren't suffering this assault. The baby elbows me, and I inhale sharply. I wonder if she can hear it too. If maybe the crying is coming from inside me.

Clementine chases Wyatt around the kitchen island, a tea towel in hand, trying to snap it at him. She giggles, misses, chases him more. No one notices my strained look, my distraction.

The loneliness lands on me then, heavy and sickening. A sense of loss blindsides me; I know that soon enough (*god willing*) two little girls will be chasing Wyatt, giggling and snapping tea towels. I also know that there should have been three.

I'm struggling with my necklace when I hear Wyatt's footsteps on the stairs.

"Shoot," I mumble, the arm of the petite spring-clasp slipping from my fingernail yet again. The bathroom door is closed, and Wyatt stops outside it.

"You almost ready?"

"I'll be out in a sec." My hands are at the back of my neck, fumbling with the spring mechanism. The skin on my ever-expanding belly pulls tight, and I round my upper back to take some of the strain off. Finally, the clasp opens and I remove the necklace.

"Do you want me to send Clem and Mom on ahead? I can wait for you."

It's the third Saturday of the month, which means it's the neighborhood Rise and Dine day. This once-monthly community event, a potluck breakfast, started about a year ago. This month the Crewson clan is on granola duty, and we've been making nightly batches for the past few days. Clementine especially loves Rise and Dine because of Eunice Beer, our across-the-street neighbor who is in her eighties and bakes mini muffins with sugar sprinkles. She calls them "pixie puffs," and they are the first things to go.

"You go ahead," I reply. "I'll be right behind you."

I slide the new ring off the chain and place it back in its silicone pouch, the MotherWise logo emblazoned in a shiny golden font. My watch alerts me to the front door's opening and then closing, and I know my family has left.

Finally alone, I briefly consider going to my studio, even though I'm supposed to be off work at the moment. I could call Wyatt, saying I've decided to laze about this morning instead. But that will lead to too many questions. I reclasp the necklace with Clementine's ring only.

As promised, I don't step foot in my studio for the rest of the week. My blood pressure stabilizes enough that everyone is happy—MotherWise, Dr. Rice, Ana, and Wyatt.

But the painting is restless—it is *not* happy with the break. How do I know?

The heartbeat. The fucking relentless beating heart.

It's dinnertime, Sunday night. We've had a busy day preparing for the upcoming week: laundry; homework; meal planning; a playdate with Briar for Clementine. When the heartbeat starts, I'm chopping a cucumber and some fresh parsley from our garden. The parsley's peppery-green fragrance is strong, and my nose tickles.

At first, I think it's my own heart beating. Maybe my watch switched accidentally to speaker mode, my rate now being broadcast. But my watch is on silent when I check. It's not my heartbeat.

Shelby's making a marinade for the steaks, Clementine sets the table, and Wyatt's still not back from his FatherWise meetup, which is meant to bolster dads' confidence and offer support during the pregnancy and beyond. He's plenty confident about parenting—perhaps even more so than I am—but he's enjoying meeting with neighborhood dads and finding new pickleball partners. Plus, Wyatt and Nick attend the meetups together, with Kat and me on the same schedule.

"Can you hear that?" I ask Shelby. She's beside me in the kitchen whisking the marinade.

She pauses, tilts her head as she listens. "I don't think so," she replies, back to whisking. "What is it?"

"I'm not sure." I look at Clementine. "Clem, did you leave your tablet on?"

"No, Momma." She's focused on folding a linen napkin into a sharp-peaked triangle, the tip of her tongue sticking out with the concentration.

"Can you still hear it?" Shelby casts me a sideways glance. I know what she's thinking—that I'm having another auditory hallucination. Which might be true? But my forced rest week is up tomorrow morning, and I need to get back to work.

Lub-dub, lub-dub, lub-dub, lub-dub . . .

"No, it's gone now. Maybe it was the wind." We're having blustery weather this evening, and I hope Wyatt gets home before the rain starts. "Or maybe it's Stanley. Where is he, by the way?"

I know where he is, but I need to distract Shelby so she stops looking at me like that. Stanley is asleep on Shelby's bed. I saw him there when I set her freshly laundered towels in her bathroom about a half hour ago.

"Hmm. Good question." She wipes her hands, calls for the dog. A moment later there's a light thud from Shelby's room, and Stanley comes trotting out. He stretches—downward, then upward—yawning. "Stan, were you sleeping? Sorry, honey. Didn't mean to wake you."

Stanley, realizing it's not yet dinnertime, gives a grunt and jumps up on the couch, curling into a ball.

Lub-dub, lub-dub, lub-dub, lub-dub . . .

"I'm going to run to the washroom before dinner." I scrape the chopped cucumber and parsley into the salad bowl, rinsing both the knife and cutting board before setting them in the above-sink drying rack.

"Feel free to use mine," Shelby says.

"That's okay. I need to take my vitamins anyway."

I pass my bedroom door and head up the next flight of stairs, moving slowly to avoid heavy footfalls.

Lub-dub, lub-dub, lub-dub, lub-dub . . .

It's louder up here. Undeniably a beating heart.

Pausing outside my studio door, I wait for my own heart rate to decelerate. It's high, in part from climbing the stairs at eight months pregnant. I check my watch. Good, it's coming down. Pressing an ear to my studio door, I listen.

Lub-dub, lub-dub, lub-dub, lub-dub . . .

I pull back quickly. It's coming from inside the studio. My mind races. The studio has been locked for a week. No one, and nothing, has gone in or out.

I glance over my shoulder to make sure no one's followed me upstairs, my heart rate picking up again. So much faster than the slow and steady beat coming from inside the studio.

With shaking fingers, I press the code on the keypad. Three beeps followed by a click as the lock disengages. I'm not supposed to go in until tomorrow morning. But the heartbeat sound is agitating, and I have to know what it is. The compulsion to make it stop trumps my good sense.

I step inside, swiftly closing the door behind me.

My studio is dark, and I blink a few times to allow my eyes to adjust. I don't want to turn on a light for fear Wyatt is coming up the street at precisely this moment and will see it, asking questions I'm not prepared to answer.

I tap my watch screen so it illuminates, then step closer to the canvas. The heartbeat sound speeds up, matching my own. As I near the painting, which remains under its cover, the beating intensifies. The sound echoes through my tissues and bones. It's not exactly painful, but almost.

There's movement in the center of the cover. A sort of pulsing outward—a bubble forming in the material, then disappearing, then bulging out again.

It takes only a moment to see the in-and-out movement is timed to the heartbeat. The rhythm matches.

Every instinct tells me to get out of there. But I don't, even as the sound threatens to overtake me. It's now so loud I can barely keep myself from screaming, *Shut up!*

A *snap!* sound echoes in the small room, as one of the corners of the cover comes off the painting. The other three corners follow suit, as though invisible hands are releasing the cover. I gasp, then grab onto the desk, my legs unwilling to hold me.

There's an odd tug through my middle, a fuzzy static in my head. My heartbeat is erratic, each thud vibrating through my bones a match to the *lub-dub, lub-dub* inside the studio. My fingers caress the desk's keypad, then . . . *beep, beep, beep, beep.* I've entered the code as though by rote. The drawer unlocks, and the fingers I don't recognize as mine slowly slide it out until I can reach the back of the tray.

I don't want to look at the syringe; I can't take my eyes off of it.

My fingers are steady as they retrieve the syringe, slowly pulling it out of the drawer. A haze blankets my mind, the rational part of me screaming from somewhere far away. Straightening, I grip the syringe like it's an extension of my hand and slowly walk over to the workbench.

The canvas pulses, the heartbeat louder, as though acknowledging my presence. My hand moves mechanically, like I'm a puppet being manipulated. I'm not in control, but I don't resist it either. The syringe in my hand hovers over the painting, and the crimson liquid within gleams in my watch's low light. The blood should be clotted after all this time, but the syringe is warm to the touch, as though I drew it moments ago.

"Beautiful," I murmur, mesmerized by the scene, peculiarly fearless. Something within the painting catches my eye—the faintest of undulations—then, a *riiiiiip* sound like Velcro being pulled apart, ever so slowly.

I watch the subject's mouth open, tentative. Her lips part, a hollow black slit forming between them. There's a sigh, then a breath out, and the chill of it hits me in the face.

I know what she's waiting for.

She wants to be fed, Tilly.

Without hesitation I lean over the painting and press the syringe's plunger, releasing the thin stream of my blood between the subject's lips. It disappears, sucked into the blackness, and the now-empty syringe drops from my hand.

"Thank you, Mathilde."

The heart in the subject's hand begins beating. Visibly, audibly beating.

Lub-dub, lub-dub, lub-dub . . .

At first that's all I focus on. The small pink heart, the size of a large apple, glistens as it contracts in her hand. Over and over. But then I see another flicker above it—near the top of the canvas—and my gaze shifts.

At first I don't understand what's different, even though I know without a doubt that something is. It takes a second longer, and then I see it.

Her eyes are open.

I try to take in this impossibility—rejecting and then accepting it over and over so quickly I'm woozy from my seesawing thoughts.

Two unavoidable things percolate to the surface, speeding through my mind: one, the eyes *were* closed (I'm sure of it, because I remember the care I took with the eyelids, as though dealing with the thin skin on an actual human face); and two, these eyes are identical to my own—green, with a thick ring of gold around the pupil.

Did I do this?

Suddenly, I'm overwhelmed by the idea that I restored the subject's eyes to match my own. Maybe I came up here earlier in the week, had an episode where I lost time, and somehow painted open eyes on top of the closed lids.

In a frenzy I swing my arm around the room, using my watch light to see if there are supplies left out to offer a clue. My own heart flutters; I'm sweating and shaking like I'm ill. But everything is where I left it the last time I was in here, a week ago. No used brushes or paints, no sign I've been in the studio. The only thing different is the empty syringe, now on the floor beside me.

I look back at the painting. I haven't imagined it—the subject's eyes are open, they are the same as my own, and there is no evidence I had anything to do with this.

Which means . . . *which means* . . .

A blink. Once, twice. A smile forms on the woman's lips, the delicate paint-laden dragonfly wing I glued back on holding its shape.

I can't pull air into my lungs. I can't move.

The subject's hand—the one with the elongated, grotesque fingers that rest on her chest, above the black hourglass hole—twitches. I watch as she pries the hand from her chest with a crackling sound, before extending it slowly toward me. The hand flips over so her palm faces up. Her bony pointer finger beckons me.

"Come here, Mathilde. Come closer."

The baby shifts sharply inside me. "Oh!" I press a hand against my swollen, clenched abdomen.

There's a drawing-in sensation, as though some invisible string is being tugged from my belly button. Then an overwhelming pressure outward. My breathing is as rapid as my heartbeat.

I take an involuntary step toward the painting, countering my strong desire to move farther away. The subject's finger continues beckoning, and the wrenching in my core becomes unbearable. I have no control over my body. The baby inside me strains toward the subject, to the point of excruciating pain from the pull of it. I can't breathe.

"Momma?" Three tentative but rapid knocks on the studio door. "Are you in there?"

Clementine.

At the sound of Clementine's voice it's as though the invisible string has been cut—a sudden release fills me, and to my great relief, the pain evaporates. I don't waste a moment. Two quick steps and I open the studio door, slamming it behind me.

Leaning against the door's exterior, palms and forehead pressed into its surface, I try to catch my breath.

"Are you okay?" Clementine asks.

I take another couple of breaths, then turn when I know I can't delay any longer. "Yes, honey, I'm okay."

"You look sick. Like you're fevery." Clementine frowns. I'm sure I look awful.

A trickle of sweat drips down the side of my face, and there's dampness under my armpits. "It's hot in the studio." I hear the flutter in my voice and hope Clementine doesn't.

I can't even think about what just happened. What I saw.

My daughter doesn't look convinced by my explanation.

"It's hard work lugging another person around inside you." I smile at her, and she gives me a hesitant smile back. "Imagine carrying Stanley in a backpack, but on your front."

She giggles, shakes her head. "Stanley is heavier than the baby, Momma."

"That's true," I reply, taking her hand and leading her to the stairs.

I have to get us away from the studio. She holds the railing with her other hand—I don't have to remind her.

"Maybe not Stanley, then . . . Imagine a cabbage instead?" I say. "A cabbage in a backpack."

More giggling. We're halfway down the second set of stairs now. I hear Wyatt and Shelby talking, the sounds of dinner about to be served.

As we walk into the kitchen we're discussing what Clementine might name her cabbage baby in her backpack ("Cleopatra"—her class is studying ancient Egypt at school this quarter), and I force my shoulders down. I have no clue how I'm going to have a meal with my family and pretend like nothing happened.

I'm inside the painting. No, I *am* the painting. My limbs confined by thick swaths of oil paint, dried into a fortress for my body. But my belly sticks out beyond the canvas, and when I look down at it (my eyes the only part of me I can move), I watch it ripple. The knuckles of the baby's hands trace against me from the inside, creating an arc across my skin. My belly is painted a color I recognize as lampblack—and the paint film cracks with the movement. Suddenly, there's a blinding pain near my navel and my vision swims.

Beyond the haze I see the reason for the pain. A tiny fist has broken through the paint, through my skin. It's covered in glistening fluids. Bright red blood, and something else that is milky white, which begins to splash out of the fist-size hole and pool on the floor. Now another little hand, fingers with tiny but long translucent nails grabbing at the torn edges, stretching the canvas, and my skin with it. No sound leaves me, but I'm screaming nonetheless. As the baby's hands rip at my body, seeking escape, her fingernails begin to pop off, one at a time, gathering in the fluid pool below.

I hear soft humming—the singing of a lullaby, maybe? One I can't name, but it's familiar. I've heard it before. But where?

The humming builds, and I look to where it's coming from. The open doorway of the studio. A woman sits on a metal stool, the gauzy fabric of a paint-spattered, long layered bohemian skirt gathered between her knees. It's Charlotte Leclerc.

In her hand is a paintbrush, and she's applying strokes in the air, as though working on an invisible canvas in front of her. There's a tickle in my center and another, along the side of my belly. My skin stretches more, seemingly in accordance with where the paintbrush goes. I feel the brushstrokes on my skin, but we're six feet or more apart.

There are deep scratches on the woman's forearm, angry and red. Her head is turned to the right, sharply, so I can only view her profile. Then she turns toward me, and I see she's smiling as she hums. Her eyes meet mine, and something electric moves through me. With fresh horror I remember another nightmare—with the grotesque hand, and my unnerving reflection in the cracked mirror.

The humming woman isn't Charlotte Leclerc, she's . . . *me.*

It's the eyes. Green with a gold ring around the pupil. *It's almost time,* I hear her say—hear myself say—through tightly closed lips. The smile grows as though she knows a delicious secret she's about to share.

There's a sucking sound, a rip, and then a wonderful release as the canvas finally gives way. The baby tumbles from the hole in my center and starts to slither across the ground toward the woman on the stool. She sets her paintbrush in her lap and claps her hands delightedly, the way a mother does when her baby smiles or takes her first step or says "Mama."

No! She's mine! I think, but there's no sound and the baby continues inching toward the woman, slithering slowly across the floor like a snail on a sidewalk, leaving a trail of thick mucus behind. The umbilical cord grows taut, pulsing purple as it strains. I'm tipping over—the canvas teeters on the easel.

The woman reaches for the baby, who is mere inches from her, and with all the strength I can muster I rip a hand from the paint prison of the canvas. With this freed hand I grasp the cord with desperate fingers, trying to hold tight to the slippery, bulbous rope of pulsating tissue.

The baby wails, so close to the woman, who now frowns when she realizes what's happened, what I'm doing. She clucks her tongue, at me, it seems, then in a soothing hum says, *"I'm sorry, my darling. Mommy's here. Mommy's here."* She croons as she holds her arms wide, ready to embrace the newborn.

I scream and pull the cord with everything I have left.

Jerked awake, I'm sweating profusely and my stomach is clenched with what I assume are Braxton-Hicks, because the cramping isn't consistent. Wyatt wakes too, asks if I'm okay.

"Go back to sleep," I whisper, not answering the question. Around four a.m. I finally get out of bed and go downstairs, the heartbeat only I can hear still echoing in the quiet house.

The storm arrives fast and furious around six that morning, with barely enough warning to get the necessary measures in place, even with our sophisticated weather-warning systems.

Wyatt and I latch the storm shutters, closing us in from the outside. We switch our indoor lights to a warmer ambient color, to better represent sunlight. Obviously with the rainstorm there is no natural light, and our circadian rhythms rely on it for optimal functioning. The rain teems furiously, but it's the wind that cranks up my unease.

I watch the oak outside our town house on the front-door camera, swaying with the wind, the Spanish moss being tossed about. Tornados and tropical storms have become increasingly common, and the current warnings chirping on our tablets and watches suggest we're in for a doozy.

School is canceled, as is Shelby's cognitive therapy session due to internet instability. My MotherHelper meetup cancellation comes moments later. *Stay safe, Mommas! We'll make up the session once the storm passes* is the message that comes across my tablet at six thirty in the morning. GIA also sends out a notification that we're on a work-from-home mandate for at least the next twenty-four hours.

I sent a note to Raoul during last night's insomnia, after the nightmare, asking him to receive the Leclerc today and move it into Room D. I provided the excuse that I needed the facility's resources to finish the conservation properly. But I have no intention of ever touching the painting again.

However, Raoul has been dispatched to one of GIA's storage vaults, where original works are housed underground in climate-controlled pods. The facility southwest of Atlanta was originally built in 1969 by the Army Corps of Engineers and has since been repurposed as a safe haven for government initiatives. Dispatching a conservator to the bunkers is standard GIA protocol during storms, which I would have remembered if I was thinking clearly. Raoul replies that the lab is closed but he'll accept the delivery when he returns in a couple of days.

I don't have a couple of days, I think. But all I write back is Thank you—stay safe!

While I'm worried about our community facing a direct storm hit, the painting—which I can't get out of the house now—occupies much of my focus. The heartbeat won't relent, as though calling me back upstairs. It's almost a compulsion, to obey. I fight it with all I have.

I consider telling Wyatt everything, but before I can sort out where to start, his foreman calls. One of the developments is at risk of collapse. It's at a critical stage in the construction cycle, and they're concerned about structural integrity if the winds pick up more than they already have. Wyatt needs to provide his expertise, and time is of the essence.

"Can't you do that from here?" I'm panicked at the idea of him going out into the storm. Panicked at the thought of being alone with only Clementine, Shelby, and the painting. I don't trust myself, as I'm barely holding things together.

Lub-dub, lub-dub, lub-dub . . .

"If I could, I would," he says, with a smile meant to relax me. "I'll be careful," he adds. "And quick—back before you know it, darlin'." I burst into tears, blaming my hormones, the stress of the storm. He wipes my tears, kisses each cheek, then quietly tells me everything is going to be fine. "I wouldn't say it if I didn't know it for sure. You take good care of our girls, okay?"

I nod, trying to stem a fresh wave of tears.

Lub-dub, lub-dub, lub-dub . . .

Another kiss for me, and one for my belly, then he rustles Clementine's hair lovingly while she is preoccupied with the latest *Clara the Cloud* episode on her tablet and hugs Shelby. "Okay, family, stay warm and dry," he says. "Hot cocoa when I get home, Clem."

Don't go . . . I long to plead, as he presses the button to roll up the front door's storm shield.

Please stay! I wish I could cry out, when his hand reaches for the door's handle.

But I say nothing, do nothing, and a moment later he's out the door, with a final "Don't forget to reengage the storm shield once I'm gone" over his shoulder to me as he leaves.

As the storm rages outside, a different storm brews inside me.

Mentally I'm wrecked, my nightmare of the baby—*my baby*—slithering across the floor toward the malevolent mother plays on a loop in my mind. Physically I'm not doing much better, as the Braxton-Hicks continue, squeezing me from the inside out. But thankfully I'm able to hide both, as my family is preoccupied with other things. Clem's happy as a clam to have unlimited time with her tablet, Shelby's catching up on her correspondence in her room, and Wyatt's at the jobsite.

I'm restless and distracted, both from the discomfort of the preparatory contractions, and with the understanding that the painting can no longer exist. Not only in my studio, but period. Transferring it back to GIA is not the only option, I've realized. I don't know how I'll explain it to Raoul, Cecil, or the collector, and I can't even think about the money (nor the professional misconduct of obliterating a rare work of art), but *this painting can no longer exist*.

It has to be destroyed.

I sit on the stairs outside the studio, a pen and notepad in hand. I don't want any trace of what I'm preparing to do. Nothing to create an alert, as could happen if I search EduNet for solutions that could obliterate the painting.

I'm reaching back to my days in organic chemistry, writing down the list of what materials and solvents I have on hand. But there's nothing I can think of that won't be impossible to explain as an accident. While the conservation process is a delicate one, and things can and do go wrong, entire paintings aren't ever destroyed—even with significant errors. Plus, nearly every error can be rectified with the appropriate skills, which I possess.

As the gales of wind batter our town house, the baby begins flutter kicking inside me. With one hand on my stomach, rubbing where the kicks land, I glance at the window behind me. It's blocked by the storm shield, which accentuates the sounds of the rain tapping against it. A furious staccato beat. I hope the shield holds; we've had to replace windows in the past from less dramatic storms. I'm about to go back to my list when the idea hits.

This work is as much about being creative with your vision as it is about your problem-solving—often the simplest, most obvious solution is the best one, Cecil used to tell me when I trained under him.

I turn on the studio's desk lamp. My watch alerts that the storm has been upgraded to a tornado warning, and my blood pressure shifts closer to redline status (Time for a rest, Tilly? my watch reads). I hit OK on both notifications, even though I have no intention of resting.

My health data is constantly being fed to MotherWise, and Ana will soon be in touch about my blood pressure. Wyatt will come home, and then we'll all gather in the kitchen for hot chocolate and to wait out the storm. I have to finish this before any of that happens. I reach for the control panel to the side of my desk.

For a moment I hesitate. Once I do this, there's no going back. I think about Clementine's face when I told her about Disney World. I think about Cecil and imagine how disappointed he would be at my decision. I think about my mother, whom I long to talk to again—even the backward-head version of her, for within that horrifying apparition were parts of the mother I loved. Then I put them all out of my mind. I'll find another way to make the trip happen. I'll forgive myself for destroying a valuable piece of art. I'll choose to believe this is precisely what my mother would have done, if in the same position.

Pressing the top button, which has a symbol of a window in a circle with a line cutting through it, I hold it until the storm screen unlatches. Then the screen rolls up into itself, slowly. The wind and rain pummel the glass, and a chunk of debris smacks the window with a loud bang. I lurch back, the screen only three quarters of the way up, and then quickly step forward and press the button again.

I imagine Wyatt receiving my biometric notifications (*he needs to focus on staying safe, Tilly*), and I try to quiet my anxiety. But my heart rate won't settle. So I continue with my plan, wheeling the workbench as close to the window as possible.

As I remove the cover, I keep my eyes down, so as not to look at the subject. My heart races, my palms sweat, and I'm sick to my stomach. A wiggle of doubt moves through me. What if I'm wrong? What if *I'm* the problem, not the painting?

Then a familiar voice reaches me. Not a ghost, nor an apparition. It's my mother.

"C'est le seul moyen, Mathilde."

It's the only way.

Once the painting is uncovered and in position, I touch another button: window. My fingertip tingles with the pressure. There's a grinding noise, the frame holding against the wind. *What if this doesn't work?* But a moment later the window flies open, wind gusting into the studio and causing papers on my desk to lift and blow to the floor. It's now raining inside the room. The painting, so near the now-open window, takes a direct hit.

Soon, the canvas begins contracting. *Good.* Banging against the workbench with the wind, as it strains for release from the latches. The pounding rain soaks the painting, and the winds shriek. I move to the far corner of the studio, trembling as I watch the destruction in real time.

I'm unsure if I've done enough but am relieved when I see the canvas contractions have turned to more severe buckling. There are also large sections where the paint has smeared, the subject becoming unrecognizable. Walking quickly to my desk, I touch the window button again, hoping the storm hasn't damaged the mechanism. It closes quickly.

I consider adding a solvent to speed up the breakdown of the paint. When I glance over at the canvas, I can't at first understand what's happening. Openmouthed, I stare at the left side of the painting, which suffered the most damage due to its proximity to the open window.

It's . . . *healing.*

I'm aware as I think it that "healing" is not the right word to use for a two-dimensional static piece of artwork. At the same time, it's the first word that comes to mind.

While I watch, the buckles smooth out. The smears begin to sharpen, returning the art—and its subject—to the original textures and colors. The soggy canvas starts to dry in spots, and I know I don't have long. Without hesitation, I attack the canvas, scratching my nails up and down its length with as much force as I can.

The subject's features become contorted, grotesque, my nails ripping sections, creating slices through the canvas. My fingers burn and ache when I finally stop. The painting is barely recognizable, the damage awful.

Breathing hard, my abdomen tight from the Braxton-Hicks, I sit heavily on the floor and lean against my solvents cabinet. I'm facing the workbench and the destroyed painting.

I close my eyes, willing my body to stop shaking, when I hear what sounds like a zipper being done up. First it's a singular sound. *Ziiiiiiiiiip.* But soon there's another zip, then another . . . one more. My eyes snap open and I'm on my feet, a second later hovering over the painting. Watching as the rips and tears disappear, like they were never there. It takes less than a minute for the painting to restore itself. Flawlessly repaired.

Kat calls, but I let it go to voicemail. Then Ana calls moments later, as expected. This one I have to answer. I pick up on my watch, my goal to keep our conversation brief and hopefully sufficiently reassuring to avoid further questions.

She's at the hospital, in the MotherWise unit. A client has gone into preterm labor and Ana's supervising the care.

Wyatt had to go out in this too . . . Thanks, I'm sure he'll be fine as well . . . Yes, I'm okay. I'm resting—the blood pressure went up with my anxiety about the storm . . . feeling a lot of activity today—she's kicking right now! . . . Strong legs—getting ready to come out, but not today, okay, little one?

Ana makes a joke about one delivery a day being her rule. We laugh, though it's feigned on my side of the call. *Stay safe, Ana—I'll see you tomorrow.*

Suddenly, the subject's dragonfly-wing lip twitches. Seeing this steals my breath.

A slow smile spreads across the Mother's face.

It's close-lipped and subtle, but it's undeniable.

Fire.

It's an elegant, considering how the painting arrived to me, though challenging solution. Lighters are a thing of the past. As are matches, or any other type of fire starter. Combustibles are now highly regulated and controlled, due to forest-fire risk. No one smokes anymore (the health taxation program, colloquially named Up in Smoke, has seen to that), though you can still find vaping devices and cartridges for sale in dark corners online. So, burning the canvas won't be easy. But I have to try.

The black crystalline salt is stored in an airtight box, in a yellow-painted metal safety cabinet. Not dissimilar to a miniature school locker. POTASSIUM PERMANGANATE, the label reads when I pull it out. It's an inorganic compound, and a powerful oxidant that was once used to disinfect water systems and clean wounds. It has to be handled carefully, as it can cause inhalation and skin burns.

Though shelf-stable, when mixed with certain compounds potassium permanganate becomes combustible, which is why it's not in my solvents cupboard. I tighten my mask and slow my breathing, needing absolute focus.

I have used potassium permanganate only once, as it isn't a typical compound employed in art conservation. A film crew, working in Savannah a few years ago, wanted to "instant age" artwork to have that sepia-brown, vintage patina. They called GIA for consultation on the project, and I volunteered to help because it sounded like a fun change of pace. The compound worked beautifully, and the remainder of the oxidant has been sealed up in my studio cabinet ever since.

With a pipette I draw a few drops of glycerin from its glass bottle, then carefully deposit the clear, viscous fluid into the well I've created in a small pile of potassium permanganate. I'm using a glass beaker to mix the compounds and have tied a linen ribbon to one of my brushes, creating a small knot in the end of it.

I can't even think about how irresponsible this is—creating fire inside my studio, inside my *home*, with Clementine and Shelby two floors below. It's dangerous, but it's also illegal and I would face charges if I were to get caught.

It takes only a minute or so for the glycerin and potassium permanganate to ignite, a narrow but powerful flame leaping upward in the beaker. I touch the linen knot to the flame, and it soon catches, creating a mini torch. It's been a long time since I handled fire, and I'm nervous. I wrap my other hand around the trembling one, keeping it steady, and step carefully toward the painting.

One quick breath in and out, then I press the burning linen knot into the face of the Mother. Holding it there, I watch carefully so I can inflict enough damage but not create a fire I can't control. A small hole forms between the subject's eyes, which begin to droop due to the heat and flame's effects on the paint and canvas. Next, the mouth. The insect wing catches fire in a little poof of flame. Another hole forms in the canvas, the subject's face a mangled mask.

The ventilation system comes on, clearing the smoke with rapid efficiency. I'm about to set the flaming linen to her left eye when I notice smoke billowing from the hole between the eyes. It's subtle at first, and I surmise it's merely the canvas smoldering from the burn.

Soon, however, the smoke intensifies. It transforms into a thick band of fog that obscures the burned-through hole. I'm mesmerized, until the torch suddenly extinguishes in my hands, like a blown-out birthday cake candle. I watch the foggy smoke part like a curtain.

The hole I've burned between her eyes has disappeared. The paint is intact, no longer blistered and blackened. A moment later the fog patch drifts to the mouth, where I've made a second burn hole, and I watch the process repeat itself. When the smoke dissipates, the damage is once again fixed. There's no evidence whatsoever that I stuck a burning torch into the painting.

"It's too late, for I'm nearly whole again," a voice whispers. *"Save your precious energy. Save it for our baby, Mathilde."*

"No, no, no," I moan, wrapping my hands around my stomach.

The Mother's lip twitches once more, her smile deepening. I hold my breath as the twitch transforms into a Cheshire cat–like smile, revealing a row of teeth, sharp-looking and pearly white, and *not* there before.

I'm so distressed by the teeth that the sound of fluttering wings doesn't immediately capture my attention. But soon it's impossible to miss, and I'm reminded (with fresh terror) of the moths that took over Clementine's room. Whipping around, I search for the flying insects, but there are none to be found. Because the sound isn't from something in the room . . . it's coming from inside *The Mother.*

The paint quakes violently against the canvas, like something is trying to break free.

She's trying to get out.

I'm outside my studio, back against the landing's wall, staring at the painting through the open door. Still shocked by my workbench tilting up, without me being near the control panels. The painting is upright now, and the subject faces me directly. So, it's more accurate to say I'm staring at her . . . and she's staring back at me, still smiling.

I've put as much distance between myself and *The Mother* as I can, while still being able to watch the painting. I refuse to take my eyes off her.

It continues raining. Hard. The house creaks and groans with the shifting winds.

I think again of Wyatt working in this, hopefully safe.

I think, oddly, of Ana's client, fervently wishing both baby and mom are okay.

I take in gulps of air, my lungs refusing to fully inflate.

I imagine my baby, tucked up inside the safety of my body.

I remember that today would have been my mom's sixty-seventh birthday.

I'm shaking, tears streaming down my face.

Finally, I think about Charlotte Leclerc and the woman in the painting.

WHAT DO YOU WANT FROM ME?

The subject's eyes—exactly like my own—are wide open, watching me watch her. Every now and then I catch a flutter of her moth-antennae eyelashes. I stare with so much effort that my eyes twitch.

Eventually, I have to blink.

After a split second of darkness, my eyes open and everything has changed.

She's no longer smiling, those sharp white teeth hidden behind closed lips. Her eyes are now closed. The pink heart in her hand is motionless, the *lub-dub* sound gone.

There is no movement whatsoever in the artwork. It's still, once again.

I scramble to my feet, with some difficulty due to my belly and the aftereffects of my panic.

Was any of this real? I stand in the doorway, scanning the painting for any signs of life.

Wait . . . was that . . . ? Something's happening. A slight wheeze of breath reaches my ears.

Inhalations and exhalations. Steady and rhythmic, like the sounds of someone sleeping deeply beside you in the dark. I focus on the black hourglass in the subject's chest.

There's a faint pulsing around the hourglass's edge, then a rising of the chest until it hits the constraints of the canvas. Stretching out toward me; going flat again.

Then, a moment of quiet between the breaths.

My water breaks in the doorway as I'm trying to process that the subject is *breathing.*

It happens with such suddenness I'm initially confused about where the liquid has come from. *Is there a leak in the roof? Did I lose control of my bladder?* I reach between my legs, touch the expanding wetness, then sniff my hand. Not urine.

I'm almost thirty-five weeks, so it's too soon for labor. But my body has other plans. The pain in my middle is poker hot, searing me from the inside out. It's alarming, the pain. I don't remember it being this intense with Clementine. Nor with Poppy, at least not until things became horrific.

I shriek in agony before collapsing to my hands and knees on the landing, the puddle of fluid I land in seeping between my fingers, soaking my leggings.

Clementine comes running up the stairs, from one floor below, having heard me scream from her bedroom. "Mommy! What's wrong?"

I can't speak. My breath is gone, my lungs constricted by the blinding pain across my abdomen. I retch, but nothing comes up.

Clementine stands in front of me, her back to the still-open studio door. I can only see her feet, unable to raise my head. Her white socks grow damp from my waters. She picks up one foot, twists to look at her sock. "Why is my sock wet? Did you spill something, Momma?"

"Baby . . . get . . . away . . . from . . ." I need to get Clementine away from the doorway. Away from the painting.

But she can't understand what I want, because I can't communicate. I'm gasping for air. Clementine crouches, ducking her head to try to see my face. "Why are you on the floor? Are you okay, Mommy?"

I shake my head, stopping when the dizziness threatens to overtake me. The clenching agony comes in unrelenting waves. I gather energy and focus on my words. *Shut the door, baby. Don't look inside.* But I can't get them out. My head swims and I'm moments away from losing consciousness.

Suddenly, Clementine stands, then turns toward my studio. "Pardon me?" she asks, using her most polite voice. This tells me whoever she's speaking to is a grown-up.

For a moment I'm relieved, thinking Shelby's come upstairs to see what we're up to. Clementine is simply confused about where her nana's voice is coming from, which is why she's turned toward the studio and not the staircase. But then she steps over the threshold, and I realize she's about to walk into the studio.

I reach out to grab her. But I'm too weak, too late, and Clementine is inside the room, facing the painting. Over Clementine's head I see the subject's eyes, open again, trained on my daughter. The woman's lips are moving, whispering something I can't hear over my own roaring heartbeat and the ringing in my ears.

Clementine takes a step closer to the painting. "That's a pretty name," she says, seemingly unfazed that a painting has become animated and is speaking to her. But that's typical of this generation—they've grown up with such technology as a regular part of life. Inanimate objects are regularly animated, for entertainment, as well as for educational and practical reasons.

"Don't talk to her, Clementine. Please, baby, listen to me," I plead, my voice raspy. But Clementine doesn't appear to hear me, doesn't turn around.

"I still hope it's a boy. I like the name Virgil—'Gill' for short," Clementine says. There's a pause. I strain to hear what's being said, but there's nothing beyond the gale outside and my own body's alarm systems. My heart beats dangerously fast. I still can't move from my hands and knees.

"Clementine, please . . ." A deep cramp clutches me and I groan.

"Your eyes look like my momma's eyes," Clementine's voice rings out.

"No . . . Clementine," I try again, but the unrelenting contractions hold me in a vise grip, stealing my breath. The baby is coming; it's too soon.

"Turn . . . around . . . Don't look at her . . . no, don't talk to her. Please, Clem, *turn around*."

She finally seems to hear me and turns toward me. Her eyes are unfocused, her mouth hanging open. I need to get her out of there. I need to protect her from whatever this malignant spell is.

But before I can do anything, in an awe-filled voice, Clementine says, "Momma, did you see the painted lady's eyes? They're exactly the same—"

The door slams shut, cutting me off from my daughter, who is now alone inside the studio with the painting.

I drag myself to the studio door, which is only a foot away but seems at least a hundred times farther. Glancing behind me, I see I'm bleeding. Heavily. The pain continues its assault, tuning out nearly every other sense. But I'm single-minded on getting Clementine out of there and away from that goddamn painting. From *her.*

Back on my hands and knees I try to take a few deep breaths, but they're shallow and do little to clear the light-headedness. *Keep going, Tilly. She needs you.*

I reach up and grasp the door handle. It's locked. *Your watch. Use your watch, Tilly.* I sit back on my heels, scream with a fresh wave of pain, but at least in this position I can access my watch. Sweat drips down my face, and I hastily wipe at it with the back of my hand to clear my vision. "Unlock studio door," I say, holding the watch close to my mouth.

"*I'm sorry, I didn't catch that,*" the robotic voice says. "*Please try again, Tilly.*"

I rattle the door's handle with every bit of strength I have. "Open the door, honey! Open the door!"

There's no response.

"Unlock. Studio. Door," I say again, clenching my teeth to keep the chattering from muddying my words. There's too much noise in the hallway; the rain slams into the window's steel coverings; the wind howls through the oaks and between cracks in the home's brick and stone.

"*I'm sorry, I didn't catch that,*" the voice says. "*Please try again, Tilly.*"

I set both hands on the door handle and pull myself to standing. I cry out as I do, because it's as though I'm being split in two. The alarm pad on the door swims in and out of focus.

"Do not pass out, Tilly. *You cannot pass out.*"

Still clutching the handle, I lean heavily against the door and type in my code. But I've fumbled the numbers and the red *X* appears on the screen. I know I only have one more chance before I'll have to reset the password. On my work tablet, which is downstairs on the kitchen island. I'll never make it.

The keypad is old, and I wish I'd replaced it with one of the newer fingerprint or retinal scanner ones. But I try again, slower this time to ensure I hit each key only once: 0-4-1-9.

My mother's birthday—April 19—and again, today's date.

"I'm coming, Clem. Momma's coming!"

The keypad screen flashes green and the lock disengages. Relief fills me. I press down on the handle and the door flies open, my body's weight heavy against it.

I can't comprehend what I see when I stumble inside.

Clementine stands directly in front of the painting, rigid. The subject's hands are on her face, cupping her cheeks. The subject smiles, sharp teeth startlingly white against the blackness of the painting's background. Her eyes are locked on my daughter.

I don't hesitate. Closing the gap between us, one arm cradling my belly, I reach the other toward Clementine.

Almost there . . . almost there . . .

I close my hand around Clementine's, which is hanging by her side, readying to pull her toward me and out of the studio. But before I can, the subject's right hand leaves Clementine's cheek and wraps around my wrist. Her grip is ice-cold, vise-like and possessing superhuman strength.

Clementine stumbles backward with the push and pull, and I position myself between her and the painting. The subject tightens her grip on my wrist. There's a pop, a sharp pain, and I know it's broken. I scream but hold my position.

"Get out of here!" I yell at Clementine. She's fallen to the floor on her back and isn't moving. Her eyes have rolled back in her head, only the whites showing. I shout her name again, trying to rouse her. A moment later her limbs jerk, and she whimpers.

"Get up, Clem. Please, honey, get up." I'm moaning in agony, every part of me consumed by fiery pain.

She sits up, slightly hunched, and looks at me in confusion. "Momma? What happened?"

There's no time. "Run, Clementine. Go get Nana. *Run!*"

The subject's eyes—*my eyes*—remain on Clementine as she runs from the studio, before turning on me. We're locked in an unblinking stare. A second later a contraction consumes me, and I slam my free hand against the canvas. Trying to balance myself, to stay upright.

There's sudden movement under my hand. Like water ripples in a slow-moving creek tickling my palm, the oil paint becoming fluid. Running down the canvas, coating my fingers, then my entire forearm with warm, blackish paint.

"What do you want?" I whisper, staring into her eyes. I'm desperately trying not to succumb to the pain. Oh, what a relief it would be.

The subject tilts her head to the side, purses her lips. Then she blinks, and the moth antennae Charlotte Leclerc used for eyelashes shimmer like beating wings. *"I want what you have, Mathilde."*

The voice is like wind chimes in a lazy breeze.

"Why? Why me?" I'm crying now, for there is no escape. My fate sealed the moment I signed for that delivery, all those months ago. Oh, how foolish I was, so quick to agree to the work. To not question the wicked serendipity of the project, nor the perilous implications of our shared history.

An overwhelming scent of something floral fills my nose, though it's not fresh. It's the odor of decay and I cough, retching violently. I can barely see the woman through my tears.

"Your mother, Mathilde."

"My mother? What about her?" I can't understand anything. Black halos close in around my vision. I'm drowning, the decaying flowers clogging my throat.

"I lost my little girl, Marigold. My sweet Mari." The eyelashes shimmer rapidly. Something drips from the inside corners of her eyes. *She's crying,* I think. *"Do you know how she died, Mathilde?"*

pleasestoppleasestoppleasestoppleasestoppleasestoppleasestopplease . . .

"She choked," I manage to say. "When she was five."

"Yes, my perfect girl choked to death, on a piece of bubblegum. Pink bubblegum, Mathilde, of all things!"

Pink bubblegum. Nothing I've read about Charlotte Leclerc contained this small yet significant detail. My mind goes to the painting of *The Child.* To the pink-gum bubble the little girl blew as she skipped. I hear it now, the *swish, swish, swish* sound that first came to me the night my mother took me to the museum.

Then a vision fills my mind and I know the Mother put it there. It's of the Child, Marigold, and she's come to life. She's under a bluebird sky, skipping, laughing, the rhythmic sweep of the rope timed exactly to the swishing sounds in my head.

Charlotte Leclerc has been haunting me—haunting my mother—from the very beginning.

A searing pain slashes across my chest before settling on the left in a fireball. It's heartbreak—*her heartbreak*—visceral, palpable, and it's consuming me.

"Being Mari's mother is the most important thing I've ever done. Can you imagine what it's like, Mathilde, to be a doctor and still be unable to save your child? To lose her in such a pointless way? That's not grief you can live with."

"I know what it's like . . . to be unable to save your own child." The words leave me like they're being pulled out of me.

"Yes, I suppose you do." The woman pauses, the corners of her mouth dropping. The insect wing in her top lip cracks, a drop of deep red filling in the spot. *"Your mother felt my pain as she worked, and eventually it consumed her too."*

"My . . . mother . . . is dead." There's no oxygen left in the room. I'm gasping tiny breaths, but I'm fading.

"I know. I was there."

Staring at the figure in front of me, the one I've painstakingly—most regretfully—conserved, I suddenly understand.

You made her fall. My lips move soundlessly. We're communicating on a different plane now. I hear her like she's inside me.

"She was fulfilling a long-ago-made promise," the woman says.

The painting has come fully alive now. The parts of the insects used to create the woman's eyelashes, eyebrows, and lips try to reassemble into their whole beings. But tacky inside the paint, the wings and things strain to move, the delicate structures breaking with the effort. The sound of their struggle sickens me.

"I lost my daughter, Mathilde, and Margot wanted to help. So she offered me hers. It's time to collect on that promise."

You're lying . . . she would never have . . ., I say, again in my mind.

"You know that black feeling you have right now?" the woman asks. *"That devastation? That fear, the raw agony? Your mother couldn't take it, and she begged for an end. She pleaded for peace."*

My mother was strong. She wouldn't have let this happen.

"Oh, she tried, Mathilde. She did. But I am stronger. You'll see . . ."

I have a sense of falling backward, over a wide expanse of nothingness—right into the black hourglass-shaped hole in the woman's chest. It's wider now, like a never-ending cavern. Soon it devours the studio and everything in it. Me included.

The last thing I'm aware of is a poignantly familiar voice, tender and soothing as it says, *"I promise that I tried. I promise you, I tried . . .*

"I'm sorry, my darling."

It's early. I'm already out walking, hoping to beat the sticky July heat that will blanket Savannah by midmorning. Pushing the pink-canopied stroller—a baby gift from Kat, Nick, Maeve, and Jenn—I keep a leisurely pace, sticking to the shaded sidewalks. The extensive cover of oaks and moss provides a much-needed sunshade on a day like today. Thankfully, my broken wrist has healed well, and the cast was removed two weeks ago. It hasn't been easy caring for a newborn with a cast, even if I've had plenty of help.

A small bag of groceries nests in the basket under the bassinet—a few treats to supplement this week's NourishBox, including a jar of preserved cherries for Clementine. They were on sale, and I'm looking forward to surprising her. She's been a wonderful big sister so far, despite a brief moment of disappointment upon realizing she had a baby sister and not a brother. We discussed the name Gillian, so Clementine could still use "Gill" as a nickname. But Clem had another name in mind, and Wyatt and I agreed to let her name the baby, after everything that happened.

I glance at the name Shelby embroidered in purple thread onto the baby's muslin blanket, conflicting emotions racing through me. The name suits her beautifully, and yet, something about it continues to trouble me. A lingering sense the name didn't come to Clementine in a dream, like she says it did.

While the stroller has a music feature (the baby prefers classical, especially to fall asleep to), it's turned off this morning. Instead, we're enjoying the cacophony of birdsongs, the slight hiss and rumble of the trains as they leave the neighborhood station. The sounds of small children humming Clara the Cloud songs, scuffing their soles on the sidewalks as they skip, holding on to their parents' hands. A gentle breeze rustles through the leaves overhead.

Holding tightly to the stroller, I pause at the crosswalk. The lights and crossbars that provide safe passage engage, timed to my arrival. Another woman pushes a stroller from the other direction, though she's not holding the handle like I do. Her stroller is in self-driving mode, a useful feature as she holds two other children's hands—one of theirs in each of hers. We smile, say "good morning" as we pass each other at the midpoint of the crosswalk.

My stroller also has self-driving mode. But I haven't gone hands-off yet. Evelyn, from my MotherHelper group, tearfully recounted last week how her stroller malfunctioned, nearly tipping over when it came too close to the sidewalk's curb. Wyatt reassured me that our stroller, a brand-new model, has no such issues—Evelyn's was first-generation technology.

"This is three iterations past that, Tilly," he said, showing me the robust safety data. Still, it's not worth the risk and so I keep my hands firmly on the handlebar. I'm nostalgic for my first stroller, Clementine's, which had none of these newfangled technologies.

I'm beginning to sweat, beads dotting the back of my neck, under my arms. Thank goodness I chose my white linen tank top this morning, my current favorite because it has a lower-cut neckline that showcases the necklace. The two gold rings really stand out against the white fabric.

I'm about to turn right when I hear a woman's voice from my left. "Tilly! Hi!"

It's Yasmeen Taff, who is new to the neighborhood, as well as to our postpartum MotherHelper group. Kat is Yasmeen's mentor and has taken her under her wing. Yasmeen has even joined us at a couple of breath work classes and dinners and fits in well. I suspect our threesome may soon become a foursome friend group.

"Hey, Yasmeen," I reply. "How are you?"

Yasmeen and her family moved from London, England, two months ago. Her husband—a bioengineer—took a position at a medical 3-D printing company, which has a satellite lab in town.

Yasmeen's eldest is Clementine's age (a boy named Idris), and rounding out her family is a five-year-old daughter named Mariam and a four-month-old baby boy, Anwar, whom she has on her front in a wrap-style carrier.

We stand to the side to avoid cluttering the sidewalk. Yasmeen sets a hand against Anwar's back, leaning slightly forward to peek under my stroller's canopy.

"Oh my goodness, look at your perfect girl." Yasmeen smiles. "Such a great sleeper already, and at only three months! Ani here remains stubborn about sleep, as you can see."

She laughs and twists slightly so I can see her baby's face. He gives a gummy grin when I coo at him. His blinks lengthen, telling me he's actively fighting slumber.

"It's the only way he'll nap. On my front, while I walk. At least it's good for my step count." She pats Anwar's back, bouncing slightly in that unconscious way moms do when holding a baby.

Just then a cicada drops from the tree, landing in the stroller. It buzzes loudly, its bulbous body with the green-metallic sheen bright against the soft-pink blanket.

"Oh my goodness! Shoo!" Yasmeen says, waving a hand over the top of the stroller. "I loathe these things. They're *everywhere*."

I reach for the cicada with gentle fingers. I hold it in my palm, noting the bright red eyes. "They're actually quite fascinating. Most of their life is spent underground, but they can live up to seventeen years."

Crouching, I place the bug on a patch of grass, out of the way of pedestrians and bicycle wheels. "The nymphs feed on fluid that flows through underground roots, and each spring—during the growing season—there's an uptick in the fluid. The nymphs count the years based on these fluctuations and then crawl out of the ground when it is precisely sixty-four degrees outside. It's remarkable, really."

Yasmeen stares at me, nodding slowly. "Yes, that is interesting . . . if you like bugs."

I laugh. "I'm not sure 'like' is the right word, but I don't mind bugs."

"I mind them, *a lot*." She shudders, glancing at the cicada in the grass. "Anyway, are you headed to the meeting later?"

I nod. "You?"

"I am, though I may be a few minutes late because Ani has a checkup right before. Would you mind telling Kat and Margie? It will save me a note."

"Happy to," I say.

We talk for a minute or so about the weather, about Idris and Clementine's teacher for the upcoming year, who we both agree is wonderful. Yasmeen asks about a good place to get fenugreek supplements, to boost milk supply. As an expat, she didn't qualify for the NourishBox program, so I promise to send her the milk-making muffin recipe. She wants to invite me, Kat, and Maeve over for a post–breath work dinner, which I say sounds fantastic.

"I have to tell you, Tilly," Yasmeen continues. "I don't know what you're doing, but I don't think I've ever seen a mom to a three-month-old baby who looks so rested and relaxed."

I smile sympathetically, for Yasmeen does *not* look rested, with darkish circles under her eyes giving away that baby Anwar isn't sleeping well at night either. She also has stress blemishes across her cheeks that look like raised red freckles.

"I'm taking it as easy as I can, not pushing it," I say. "Besides, you have three kids and two dogs and zero help at home. I have Clementine, but she's so independent these days, and my mother-in-law is a savior."

"Well, keep doing whatever you're doing—you look amazing. Especially considering what you went through with your delivery. You're a superwoman in my eyes."

"Oh, I am no superwoman!" I reply, but I thank her for the compliment. "Honestly, I wouldn't be here to do any of this without Clem and those paramedics."

After running from my studio, Clementine found Shelby, who called 911. But the ambulance was already en route. My watch alerted Ana, and MotherWise, of my health crisis when I became tachycardic, my heart rate reaching dangerous levels.

Shelby told me they found me on the floor outside my studio door, which was locked. Clementine has no memory of being inside the studio, or of the woman in the painting.

Within a minute of the paramedics arriving, my heart stopped due to blood loss. Luckily, they were able to get it restarted after two minutes of resuscitation. The baby was delivered at the hospital, via emergency C-section, thirty-five minutes later. Wyatt arrived in time to see her born. She was healthy, albeit early so slightly underweight, with no signs the trauma affected her. She also shares a birthday with the grandmother she'll never get to meet.

"I'm very lucky, very grateful to be alive," I say to Yasmeen.

"We're all grateful, Tilly," she replies, setting a hand on my arm. "It's a blessing you don't remember it, if you ask me."

The cicada buzzes in the grass, drawing our eyes down.

Its six legs tuck tightly against its body, and it goes perfectly still.

"Is it dead?" Yasmeen sounds hopeful.

I shake my head. "It's *playing* dead. Probably a defensive carryover from the nymph stage. Watch."

With a gentle finger I touch the bug's back, and it comes to life again—buzzing wildly in the grass.

"How did you know that?" Yasmeen asks.

I shrug, sourness filling my throat. "Oh, I read an article about it recently."

I have no idea how I know this.

There's a fresh coat of paint on my studio's walls, a cheerful orange-pink color called "Peach Cobbler." I did it myself, the only paint I've worked with in months. These days I keep the door open and the lock disengaged, the studio now a playroom for both Clementine and the baby. We've decided for now the baby will sleep in our room, our renovation plans on hold.

I've managed to reframe the space, both physically and in my mind. With each passing day some of the dread about what happened here gets replaced with new memories, happy memories. The Leclerc fee also waits in our bank account, ready for the Disney trip we'll take over the holidays. Clem's been counting down the days.

"Only one hundred and forty-one days to go!" she announced over breakfast this morning. The baby, who is almost four months now, cooed and giggled when her big sister kissed her atop the head, telling her all about Mickey Mouse.

The baby rests on her play mat beside me. I'm still on postpartum leave from work, but I've been talking to Wyatt about maybe leaving GIA for good. To focus on our family, on what might be next for me personally. I've been given a second chance and I have no intention of wasting one moment of it.

Wyatt is thrilled by the idea of me staying home. I see it on his face, even if he's more tempered with his words. *Whatever you want to do, Tilly. I'll support you.*

Sure, it will put a pinch in our finances, but not for long. He was promoted last month, and it came with a healthy bump in salary. "We'll be fine," he says, as we lounge in bed early in the morning, the baby gurgling happily in her bassinet cradle beside us.

Clementine loves her baby sister, though she's admitted to being jealous of the infant's bright blue eyes—so much like Wyatt's. Clem's are a muted green, speckled with tiny gold flecks.

"I gave you those eyes," I tell her. "Green is the rarest of colors, you know."

"Actually, Mom, gray is the rarest." Since the baby's birth she no longer calls me Momma, or Mommy, and I miss it. She's also grown taller, her limbs less clumsy in their movements, her face losing some of its roundness.

"She's growing up so fast," I say to Wyatt one morning, after Shelby and Clementine have left for school. We need to go shopping for pants, again, as she continues to stretch upward in height.

"It's only because we have a little one for comparison," Wyatt replies, kissing my cheek. "She's the big kid now."

I want nothing more than for her to grow up, the way all children are supposed to. But still, some days I miss the little girl she used to be.

Sipping my vitamin-infused water (sweet-cherry flavored, and it tastes nearly identical to a handful of ripe, dark cherries), I open the desk drawer with my other hand. The baby's practicing tummy time on her mat. She's drooling, grunting with frustration, as she pushes herself up on her arms.

"Good girl!" I crow at her. "Look at how strong you are, my sweet baby."

I get down on the floor, facing my youngest daughter. She grins at me, adorably toothless, and I smile in return. Mirroring is an important part of her development, MotherWise reminds us weekly.

"Aren't you a happy little girl? Aren't you?" I murmur, cooing at her.

"Knock, knock!" Shelby stands in the open doorway, Stanley in her arms.

"Hi, Nana," I reply, coming up on one elbow. "Look at how strong our big girl is."

Shelby smiles, eyes only for the baby. She's a wonderful grandmother. So involved, ready anytime to change a diaper, read a story, fuss over the baby in a hundred other ways. Like she did—does—with Clementine. "Looks like y'all are having oodles of fun in here."

I laugh, because tummy time is not the baby's favorite, and she's usually a moment away from pitching a fit.

"Stanley and I are headed out for a walk. Do you need me to pick anything up?"

She steps into the studio, and Stanley lets out a low growl from her arms.

"Stanley Charles Crewson, that is enough." Shelby sighs. "I'm sorry, Tilly. The trainer is coming again later today. I told her there's been some improvement, but then he goes ahead and proves me wrong."

Stanley continues to growl my way, showing his teeth now, despite Shelby's shushing. "It's okay," I reply. "He's being protective of her. That's not the worst thing."

This is what the dog trainer, who specializes in "postnatal reintegration," a fancy term for introducing your dog to your newborn, has told us. Stanley seems especially bothered when I'm close to the baby, something this trainer calls *guarding behavior*, which she assures us is fairly common and fixable.

"Well, I don't care for it and we are going to get rid of that pesky instinct, aren't we, young man?" Shelby kisses Stanley on the snout, and he stops growling.

"Enjoy your walk," I say. "I can't think of anything we need, but thank you."

After Shelby and Stanley leave, my watch buzzes.

Time for your NourishSmoothie, Mom!

I get up from the ground, opening the door of the small refrigerator on my desk. The glass bottle is layered with different colored liquids, which blend together when I hit the button on its lid. MotherWise recommends one smoothie per day, to help with milk production and vitamin levels. It tastes like fresh-cut grass, with a hint of strawberry sweetness. Initially I had to plug my nose to drink it, but I'm getting used to the flavor after a few months.

I'm about to close the fridge door when a small box, the size of a bar of soap, beside it catches my eye. *How did that get there?* I frown, picking up the box. It's supposed to be in the drawer. Maybe Clementine found it, was curious about what's inside. The studio isn't locked, the solvent cupboards removed, so nothing's off-limits anymore.

However, the box makes me antsy. I should have sent it back.

The collection of *Rhyothemis semihyalina* dragonfly wings arrived last week. I have no memory of ordering them, two months ago from an entomologist in Texas according to the packing slip. First I think it's a delivery error. Until I call the entomologist, who assures me she spoke to me directly about the order. This detail is hard to explain, but I write it off as sleep deprivation. "Mommy brain," I declare to the confused entomologist, who laughs and commiserates, having a one-year-old at home herself.

I decide to return the shipment, but curious, I first take a peek inside. The wings are so delicate, so beautiful—thin as tissue paper, with fine webbed veins and patterns weaving through the translucence. *Surely Clementine can use them in a craft or art project*, I think. *No point in paying to ship them back.*

Now I open the box and remove a wing to show the baby with my soft-close tweezers.

"This is how you know what type of dragonfly this wing belonged to," I tell the baby. I use a finger to gently touch a part of the wing, and the metallic purple-black patch there. "It's so distinctive. So beautiful, don't you think?"

The wing slips from the tweezers, fluttering down to the baby's pudgy hand. "Oops! Need to be careful with this. They're incredibly delicate."

I retrieve the wing, being cautious not to pinch the baby's skin, and then lean down and kiss her fuzz-covered head. I close my eyes and breathe in her delicious new-baby scent, a combination best described as soft as felt and sweet like milk. Setting the wing back into the box, I close it up and put it back on the desk.

Tummy time complete, I settle the baby into my front-body sling and turn on the vintage record player I found at a neighborhood swap a couple of weeks earlier. I only have two records but hope to grow my collection. Ever since the baby was born I've been fiercely nostalgic. Longing to re-create experiences from my own childhood, like listening to records with my mom. I set the needle down on one of the black vinyl discs, and there's a slight scratching sound before the music begins.

I hum, swaying my hips to the melody, lightly singing a few bars here and there. Clementine and I plan to take singing lessons together—I've been cognizant of making time for my eldest, and this was her request. I suspect I'll be hopeless, but Clementine seems to have inherited her dad's vocal talents.

Reaching for one of the baby's hands, I dip my head so I don't have to stretch her arm too far. I use my teeth to nibble at her fingernails—experienced parents know this is the easiest and safest way to trim a baby's nails. They've grown a touch long, and I don't want her to scratch her face.

She's relaxed, used to this, and after I finish her first hand I do the other. Then I push the small slivers of fingernail to the tip of my tongue and spit them onto my palm. I gather them into a pile, carefully setting them on top of the dragonfly-wing box.

I'm sipping my smoothie, trying to get to the last dregs of the bottle, when a drop escapes my lips and lands squarely on the baby's nose. She starts, jerking slightly.

"Oh, I'm sorry, my love." I feel badly for startling her, especially because she was nearly asleep.

Her face reddens and she begins to cry, big, fat tears falling from her scrunched-up eyes, my cotton T-shirt drinking them in. Setting the smoothie bottle down, I reach for a muslin cloth and dab her tiny button nose. Her heart beats like hummingbird wings against my chest as she wails, and I encircle her with my arms and rock gently.

"Shh, shh, shh, shh," I say, pacing the small studio in circles. The record continues playing, and I hum along. Soon the baby softens against me, and though she continues whimpering, she's losing steam.

I bounce her gently while I look out the window, at the large oak in front of our home. It looks different now, the sudden disappearance of the Spanish moss a curious mystery that Wyatt is determined to solve. An arborist is coming by later today. Clementine misses the moss and thinks the tree misses it too.

"The tree doesn't need it, Clem," I say to her at breakfast, when she brings it up again. "Nature knows what it's doing. We shouldn't interfere." This mollifies her, at least for the time being.

The cicadas are loud today, their song piercing the studio's window, which is closed to keep the cool air inside. In another week or so the insects will go silent, their mass death happening seemingly all at once. For a short time our sidewalks will be blanketed with exoskeletons, before city workers arrive to clean up the mess.

"You'll be a teenager the next time this brood appears," I whisper. Her little body becomes still against mine. I smile into her soft wisps of hair, which tickle my lips.

"Sleep well, my darling. Momma's got you, Marisol. Momma's got you."

I haven't been truthful about everything.

For one thing, I remember what happened in the studio that day, during the storm. Before the painting took me and everything went dark. Though I can't explain how I was found outside the locked studio door, so I leave that one be.

However, I tell Ana, Wyatt, and Dr. Rice at the hospital, after I regain consciousness from surgery, that I have no recollection of what happened. "The last thing I remember is going upstairs, wanting to double-check the storm windows on the third floor," I say.

Like Yasmeen, they are grateful the memory of my water breaking, of the collapse, is lost to the trauma.

"All that matters is that you're still here. That you're both safe," Wyatt replies, through unrelenting tears, holding our brand-new swaddled baby in his arms.

I also can't explain the shape the painting is in, when I finally get home and unlock my studio door. Not only is it undamaged; it's completely conserved. Flat on my workbench, the inflated cover tightly wrapped against the corners. When I uncover it, holding my breath, I see the subject's eyes are closed. The heart in her hand still, no evidence it ever beat wildly in three dimensions. Insect wings and antennae intact, mouth closed in its original semi-frown. I arrange for immediate, same-day shipping. Raoul arrives to pack the piece for me, bringing blueberry and lemon muffins, a baby rattle ideal for teething, and an art kit for Clementine. Two hours later a drone carries the crated painting out of my house and off to the collector many states away.

While my ordeal left me with no physical reminders—minus the broken wrist—there have been mental fractures. Moments when I find myself drifting, not quite tethered to the present. Strange bits of knowledge I can't remember learning land in my mind, like with the cicadas. Or like the delivery of the dragonfly wings. Sometimes, odd sounds and smells reach me, like the flutter of insect wings, but without the insects. Or the sickly-sweet tang of old-fashioned pink bubblegum, which you haven't been able to buy for years because of governmental food additive restrictions.

Sometimes I wonder if it truly all happened the way I remember. It would be easy to doubt my experiences. To believe the stress of the pregnancy caused a mental breakdown, this bizarre separation with reality. I do try that on, to see how it feels. But I'm left with too many hanging threads. Far too many moments that don't fit neatly into that box.

These days, I think often about what my mother wrote in her presentation. The one she never delivered, because she fell down the stairs at our home and broke her neck before she could.

When we restore art—breathing new life into the brushstrokes, colors, shapes, and textures—a conservator must ask: have we also brought the artist herself back from the dead?

It's a good, relevant question that I don't know the answer to.

Or maybe I don't want to know the answer.

AFTER

When I install *The Mother* in the collector's home some months later, in the Leclerc Room, I suggest a change to the display.

"*The Mother* should hang on the opposing wall to *The Child*," I say. Claude, the collector—an elderly but spry man, with impeccably combed-over salt-and-pepper hair, green eyes, and a bespoke black paisley suit—raises an eyebrow but gives me his full attention.

"I believe it's how Charlotte Leclerc would have displayed them," I add. "With *The Mother* watching over *The Child*."

"Mathilde, you are the expert," he replies, his thick French accent making my name sound beautiful. I introduced myself as Tilly, but he scrunched his nose at that, asked if I minded if he called me Mathilde instead. I didn't, so he did.

We stand side by side in the large, windowless room, its eggshell-white walls stretching high to meet plaster crown moldings. The moldings are painted gold to complement the heavy gold frames encasing each of the four pieces. We're directly in front of *The Mother*, and the protective film has been removed.

I've felt much trepidation about this moment. I've been dreading it, in fact. What if my mind plays tricks on me? What if I lose time, here in the collector's home? But it has been months, and I know from personal experience that even the most traumatic memories lose power over time. Yet, I wasn't sure how I'd react, being in her presence.

Raoul offered to install the painting, which I seriously considered. But when I discussed it with Maeve, whom I've also kept certain details from, she suggested seeing it through.

"Facing that painting again—now that Marisol is here, and you're healthy and strong—may help process the trauma of her birth experience," she said. Her words sent a mini shock of realization through me, and I knew she was right. So I decided to finish what I started. To prove I'm stronger than the demons that painting brought forth in me.

I expect the installation to be smooth and simple, and it is. Nothing out of the ordinary, which bolsters my confidence that this was the right choice. I did experience a jolt of adrenaline and a rise of emotion when I first walked into the room, taking in *The Healer*, *The Dreamer*, *The Child*, already on the walls. Noting *The Mother*, still covered, on the installation robot called ARTIS (Automated Robotic Technology for Installation and Sculpture). Charlotte Leclerc's final piece; the last memento of her strange and mysterious legacy.

Time to close this door, Tilly. Don't forget to lock it and throw away the key.

After I enter instructions for the ARTIS installation, *The Healer* is taken down and reinstalled so *The Mother* can be displayed across from *The Child*. It all takes no more than an hour, and then Claude asks me to sit with him for a moment.

My flight home to Savannah isn't for a few hours, so I nod and sit on the cushy velvet bench. I'm suddenly exhausted, the stress of this trip catching up to me, and am glad to get off my feet. We sit next to each other, facing *The Child*, which Claude has told me remains his favorite of the four.

Marisol, who handled her first flight like a champ, sleeping most of the way, is in her umbrella stroller beside me. She's gumming a frozen teething ring with gusto. Her second tooth is about to pop through her inflamed, swollen gums, and this toy that came in last week's NourishBox has proven a lifesaver for her fussiness.

"C'est magnifique," Claude says, in a hushed tone, eyes on *The Child*. "You were right, Mathilde. I like this spot for her. Parfait."

"Hmm. I'm glad. And I agree," I say, keeping my voice low as well. I let my gaze drift around the room, and the gold moldings catch my eye again. "Those moldings are beautiful."

"Merci. But they require much maintenance. We have so many earthquakes here," he says with a deep sigh. "Ils sont toujours petits, but even the small ones cause cracks. C'est dommage."

I nod and smile, remaining politely detached, as Cecil told me Claude is an intensely private man and not one for many questions.

Yet, I have so many questions. Like, why is he a Leclerc collector? What is it about her art that has made him build this room specifically for these paintings? *Does he feel it too, the disconcerting chill in this room?*

"You've done beautiful work. And have come a long way today, so thank you, Mathilde," Claude says.

"Marisol and I were happy to get a few days away. A mini adventure, right, sweet pea?"

The baby gives me a gummy smile as I tickle the tip of her nose. I'm glad for the pack of cotton bibs Margie gifted me—each with a day of the week embroidered on it—for she's drooling a lot. I would hate for some of it to land on the spotless parquet wood floor under our feet.

I notice Claude observing Marisol. Truly, that's the best word for it. *Observing.* Taking in her face, her pudgy hands holding the teething ring, but with little expression except maybe mild curiosity. *Perhaps he's not a fan of children*, I think. Looking around at his home, which is straight out of the architectural digest e-zines Wyatt subscribes to, it certainly seems that way. Far too much white for messy little fingers, far too serene for the inevitable wails of a hungry or tired baby.

"Is there anything . . . you would like to ask? About the art, perhaps?" Claude says, turning his attention back to me.

"Actually, there is," I start. "How did you first learn about Charlotte Leclerc? She's somewhat obscure, even in the art world."

"Well, Mathilde, in order to explain that, I do have to confess something to you," he says, eyes back on *The Child*.

"Oh?" I keep my tone mild, watching his profile. There's a twitch in his jaw that makes me wonder exactly what this confession is about.

"Margot was a dear friend of mine, long ago," he replies. "Before you were born."

Claude pauses for a beat, begins to say something, then seems to change his mind.

"I didn't realize that," I say, my voice steady even as my heart rate goes up, and up, and up. There's a buzz against my wrist. My watch wants me to relax. Time for breath work, Tilly? But I can ignore it now that I'm not pregnant, the most limiting MotherWise restrictions lifted.

"I learned about Charlotte Leclerc from your mother. We stayed in touch over the years, and I remember how . . . *taken* Margot was by her conservation of *The Child*."

Now I look to the painting my mother restored. The pink gum bubble is vibrant against the black background, the child so obviously joyful. Another shiver moves through me, seeing the bubblegum. *"You shouldn't have come here, Mathilde."*

It's my mother's voice. It's *my* voice.

"Margot told me Leclerc's art isn't like other paintings. 'The pieces aren't meant to be alone,' she said." Claude pauses again, a thoughtful look coming across his face. "But how did she put it, exactly? It was odd, her wording . . . 'They don't like to be apart, Bernie,' I think she said . . . Oui, c'était ça."

Bernie? I'm finding it hard to take a full breath.

"After her tragic passing, I wanted to own a piece your mother worked on. Something tangible to remember her by. I learned *The Child* was in a private collection at that point. The owner was happy—almost relieved—to sell it to me. Money problems, perhaps," Claude says with a shrug.

He knew my mother. Well enough that he was compelled to build this room and fill it with Leclerc's macabre art after my mother died. *A collector reached out . . . asked for you by name*, Cecil said.

"I bought the other two Leclerc paintings not long after, from other galleries, wanting the complete set," Claude continues. "I know it would have made Margot happy, to see the pieces together like this."

They don't like to be apart.

There's a strange sense of déjà vu, as though I already know this story. I'm about to ask him if we ever met—when I came to France with my mother, maybe—but the door suddenly opens, Claude's house manager appearing.

"Monsieur Bernard, vous avez un appel," he says.

My throat gets tight. A wisp of something tucked away long ago drifts to the surface.

"Ça peut attendre?" Claude asks the house manager, who shakes his head.

"Excuse me, Mathilde. I must take this, but I won't be long." Claude glances at Marisol in her stroller, who has begun reaching for me. She's likely hungry. "Are you both all right to remain here?"

"We're fine," I reply, managing to keep the shake out of my voice. What I want to say is, *Please don't leave, I have so many questions.* And then, another thought: *Please don't leave me alone with . . . them.*

Claude nods, smiles at Marisol, and says to me, "I'll only be a few minutes. Enjoy the gallery, Mathilde."

He's gone a moment later, the door closing behind him.

My heart races. *Claude "Bernie" Bernard.* A *C. Bernard* sent me a condolence card from Paris after my mother's death. Claude knew my mother, well enough that he's procured art she worked on, built a room for it, hired me specifically to handle the conservation of the final piece, the installation . . .

Marisol begins to cry, snapping me back to the present. "What is it, sweet pea? You hungry?" As I ask it, my milk drops and there's a dull heaviness in my breasts.

"Hang on, baby girl," I say, unbuckling her from her stroller. She's soft and warm, and I snuggle her close for a moment, but she's impatient and resists me. With deft fingers I unbutton my blouse, the strap of my nursing bra. I'm still shivering, stunned with the revelation of who I believe this collector to be. But the baby's needs outweigh mine.

Normally she's an excellent nurser, but today she's having none of it. Tossing her head back as she cries, using her hands to push me away. It's strange behavior for her, and I start to worry she's coming down with something. Terrible timing, if so.

"Okay, you're not hungry," I say, staying calm despite the increasing tempo of her crying. The room is even chillier now, probably because I'm half-undressed. I quickly resnap the bra, button up my shirt. Then I hold Marisol in front of me and bounce her on my legs.

"This is the way the horses ride, the horses ride, the horses ride . . ." My voice has improved with the singing lessons, but it's still far from good. Normally Marisol doesn't mind her favorite song being off-key. But she's inconsolable. I'm getting worried.

"What is it, Marisol? What's going on?"

I set her in my lap, facing me, and hold my watch a couple of inches from her forehead. The thermometer setting engaged, it beeps when finished. Normal, it reads. Frowning, I use the back of my hand to double-check. She's sweaty and sticky from crying but doesn't feel warm. If anything, she's cool.

Maybe it's the room's temperature. I'm full-on trembling now and decide we'll wait for Claude outside. It's cloudy, but at least it's warmer.

"Fresh air will be good for both of us," I say. I'm about to stand when Marisol suddenly stops crying. I watch as her eyes widen, drifting to something behind me. She tilts her head to the side, trying to see past my head. Then she starts to laugh and squeal, standing on my thighs, her little hands waving excitedly as she pumps her legs the way babies do when getting ready to try to walk.

"Well, that's nice to see!" Relief floods me. But it doesn't last long, because a moment later I realize what she's so enamored with.

The Mother.

Marisol is staring at the painting.

No, no. There has to be something else that caught her attention. *But what else could it be?* There is literally nothing else on that wall except *that* painting. A ribbon of dread fills me, even as I continue searching for another reason for my baby's sudden delight.

Her eyes stay locked on *The Mother* as she continues squealing in delight, stopping occasionally as though she's listening to something... to someone. I do everything I can to distract her. Including turning her so she can no longer see the painting.

But my efforts only agitate her, and she twists her little body, grunting in frustration.

"Okay, Marisol. It's time to go." My voice is firm, but I can hear the panic in it. I want to get the hell out of this room and as far away from *The Mother* as I can. I'm reaching for the stroller's handle when I hear it, and everything slows down.

A rhythmic *swish, swish, swish*. Frighteningly familiar—the same strange sound I heard at the museum that long-ago night with my mother. Exactly like the *swish-sweep* I heard more recently in my studio.

Now a soft *thud* joins the melody, coming in after each swish. I turn slowly toward the sounds, breathless. At first, nothing seems amiss. Until the *swish-thud-swish-thud* becomes louder, as though someone has turned up the volume. Then I see it. The Child is skipping, inside the painting.

The *swish* is the rope brushing the ground under her Mary Jane–clad feet.

The *thud*, the sound of her feet landing once they've cleared the rope.

Something fractures inside me. My eyes stay on *The Child* for a few more seconds, enough time to see her blow a glistening pink bubble as she skips. Then her eyes move, locking onto mine. She smiles, and the bubble pops. I'm overcome by the scent of sweet bubblegum, which somehow fills the cavernous room.

I shout for help before remembering the room has been designed for a fully immersive experience. No sound can get in or out. But the door is only fifteen feet away. I can make it.

Marisol lets out another happy giggle, still staring at *The Mother.* I don't want to look, but I can't stop myself. *Something's changed*, I think when I turn my head. There's a flutter of the feathered insect antennae, her long eyelashes batting.

The Mother's eyes open, landing on Marisol first. The baby laughs, reaching away from me, straining to get closer to the painting. I hold her tightly, and she thrashes about and wails in my arms.

"No . . . you can't have her," I whisper. Shaking as I walk backward, toward the door and away from the painting. I'm afraid to look at her; more afraid to take my eyes off of her.

A shocking coldness spreads through my limbs. I can't feel my fingers, and I'm terrified I'll lose my grip on Marisol. My legs won't move faster, even as I'm willing them to *run*. My watch buzzes continuously on my wrist, my heartbeat pounding in my ears.

"Come out, come out, wherever you are . . ." the Mother says in a singsong voice, smiling as she turns her attention back to the baby. Marisol beams a gummy, nearly toothless grin at the painting, at the woman.

Adrenaline courses through me, and suddenly the feeling comes back to my hands. The electric tingles are painful but reassuring, because I have control over my body again. Clutching the baby against my chest, I shield her as I race to the door.

A sickeningly loud beep, then a *click* reverberates just as my hand reaches the handle, which won't turn. I'm locked in, stabbing at the keypad though I don't know the code. With one hand, the other holding Marisol tightly to me, I pound on the door and scream for help, but it's useless. No one can hear me.

Marisol starts crying, reaching over my shoulder toward *The Mother.* The skipping sound escalates, the Child's footfalls louder now. Then, above the baby's cries, the relentless skipping, and my own ragged breaths, I hear what sounds like cracking ice. A second later, a suctioning sound, as though something is being pulled out of thick mud. The baby shrieks with excitement, hands waving. I refuse to turn around, but my body defies my mind's order and a moment later I'm facing *The Mother.*

Wrapping Marisol in my arms, I have one goal: to protect my child from whatever is now slowly stepping *out* of the painting. The figure—the Mother—lumbers toward us, leaving tacky black footprints on the beautiful parquet wood floors. She extends the now-beating heart out, like it's a gift. Never taking her eyes off Marisol.

The Mother envelops me like a soupy fog. I can no longer draw breath, my vision fading quickly. I'm in excruciating pain. My skin stretches and rips from the inside out. My bones snap like tree branches in a violent storm. Blood vessels burst with hundreds of tiny explosions. I want to fight, but there isn't enough of me left to do so.

I'm dying, I think, before hearing a voice as clear as my own.

"No, Mathilde. We are reborn."

The baby laughs, and then the wind-chime voice: *"Found you, my darling! Here I come . . . here I come . . ."*

ACKNOWLEDGMENTS

Each time I imagine writing acknowledgments for a book, I intend to keep them short—ideally a paragraph. Elegantly brief. Gratitude resonant. Prose slim.

And yet, here we are again. It turns out that writing a novel—at least for me—is too complex and all-consuming a process for this final tribute to be skeletal.

If you're wondering how, after six novels, I ended up writing a horror debut . . . here you go: Horror is my first love. Proof: My current "comfort" bedtime reads are *The Stepford Wives*, *Rosemary's Baby*, and *The Shining*—on rotation. For me, horror is what romance is for others: escapist, cathartic, and an emotionally safe way to explore fear. That kind of release feels especially vital in a world that increasingly resembles the setup to a horror novel itself.

On that note, this book is both utopian and dystopian. I wrote it that way deliberately—to reflect both what I long to see and what I fear most. Some fictional elements now feel eerily close to reality. There's a strange terror in that. And yet, I hold onto hope. That storytelling can help us see more clearly, and that art—like the best horror—can illuminate even the darkest corners.

Now, the gratitude. In abundance.

To Christina McLean-Alsaidi, assistant conservator, paintings, at the Art Gallery of Ontario (AGO): Thank you, thank you, thank you. When I reached out to the AGO years ago, hoping to connect with someone in paintings conservation, I had tempered expectations. But Christina responded immediately—and with generosity. She offered her time, wisdom, and expertise without hesitation. *Mother Is Watching* simply wouldn't exist in its current form without her.

Christina gave me a behind-the-scenes look at the daily life of an art conservator, answered countless emails, hopped on phone calls, indulged my questions over many coffees, and read an early draft of the manuscript—offering invaluable feedback on its technical elements. She inspired Tilly and brought her to life for me. Any mistakes on the conservation front are mine alone. Thank you, Christina—for your insight and patience and for deepening my appreciation of both art and your extraordinary work.

Thanks also to Rachel Stark, assistant conservator, contemporary art at the AGO, who welcomed me behind the scenes and answered wonderfully macabre questions—like "How would one integrate human blood into art?"—with thoughtful enthusiasm.

The AGO is a treasure. I've always loved wandering its halls, discovering new artists, and revisiting beloved pieces. Now I do so with a deeper appreciation for the work—and the people—behind the art.

To Carolyn Forde and the stellar team at Transatlantic Literary Agency: Thank you. I'm an author who bristles at the idea of "branding"—I follow my curiosity, even when it leads into unfamiliar territory. Carolyn, you've been my agent for over a decade, and I deeply value our partnership. No matter what story I bring you, you always respond with a spirited "Yes!!!" (always with at least three exclamation points).

To Maya Ziv and Brittany Lavery: You have read more drafts of this novel than I can count, and with every pass, your care, insight, and unwavering belief in the story—and in me—made it shine brighter. Your editorial brilliance, patience, and passion shaped *Mother Is Watching* into what it is, and I will never forget the generosity of that labor. I feel so lucky to collaborate with you. Thank you for championing this book with such heart.

To the extraordinary publishing teams at Dutton and Simon & Schuster Canada: from copyediting to production to cover design to marketing and publicity, your creativity, care, and expertise lifted this book at every stage. It takes a village—and I truly lucked out with mine.

To Addison Duffy at UTA for her brilliant observations about the novel and for championing it for the possible screen. Your belief in this story and its future beyond the page means more than I can say.

To Colleen Oakley—thank you for braving haunted restaurants, cemeteries, and a ghost tour of Savannah (at night!) despite not doing "scary." That is true friendship.

To Stephen King, who showed me how delicious darkness can be: Thank you. I've been a devoted fan since reading *Cujo* at the age of ten—a questionable choice, perhaps, but a formative one. It opened a door I never wanted to close.

To the writers who read drafts, brainstormed, and weren't afraid of the dark: Julie Clark, Amy Reichert, Mary Kubica, Ashley Audrain, Ashley Tate, Nicole Blades, Jennifer Robson, Taylor Reid, and Hannah Mary McKinnon—thank you. Your feedback, encouragement, and friendship mean the world.

To my family—the founding members of the Karma Brown Fan Club, and who have promised to read this book even if they need to do so in broad daylight—I love you. And I'm sorry it's scary.

To Adam—you ground me, care for me, and make the world feel safer just by being in it with me. To Addie, my daughter and fellow horror fan: The apple doesn't fall far. You are my greatest joy. I hope the world becomes a kinder place, especially for our fellow women.

And finally, to you—the reader. If you don't like scary stories but have made it this far, thank you. If horror is your happy place, thank you too.

To everyone who picks up a book—mine or otherwise—and gives it a slice of your time or presses it into someone else's hands: I'm endlessly grateful.

ABOUT THE AUTHOR

Karma Brown is the author of six novels: the #1 international bestseller *Recipe for a Perfect Wife*, *Come Away with Me* (a *Globe and Mail* Best Book of 2015), *Globe and Mail* and *Toronto Star* bestsellers *The Choices We Make*, *In This Moment*, *The Life Lucy Knew,* and, most recently, *What Wild Women Do*. She is also the author of the bestseller *The 4% Fix: How One Hour Can Change Your Life*. An award-winning journalist, Karma has been published in *SELF*, *Redbook*, and *Today's Parent*, among others. She lives just outside Toronto with her husband, daughter, and a Labradoodle named Fred.